GW00738178

The Luxury of Exile

Louis Buss was born in 1963. He studied politics at Durham University and until recently, worked as a teacher. *The Luxury of Exile* is his first novel and has already won a 1996 Betty Trask Award.

THESE ARE UNCORRECTED BOUND PROOFS.

Please check any quotations or attributions against the bound copy of the book. We urge this for the sake of editorial accuracy as well as for your legal protection and ours

Louis Buss

The Luxury of Exile

Jonathan Cape
London

First published 1997

1 3 5 7 9 10 8 6 4 2

© Louis Buss 1997

Louis Buss has asserted his right
under the Copyright, Designs and Patents Act 1988
to be identified as the author of this work

First published in the United Kingdom in 1997 by Jonathan Cape,
Random House, 20 Vauxhall Bridge Road, London SW1V 2SA

Random House Australia (Pty) Limited
20 Alfred Street, Milsons Point, Sydney,
New South Wales 2061, Australia

Random House New Zealand Limited
18 Poland Road, Glenfield,
Auckland 10, New Zealand

Random House South Africa (Pty) Limited
Box 2263, Rosebank 2121, South Africa

Random House UK Limited Reg. No. 954009

A CIP catalogue record for this book is available from the British Library

Papers used by Random House UK Limited are natural,
recyclable products made from wood grown in sustainable forests.
The manufacturing processes conform to the environmental
regulations of the country of origin.

ISBN 0–224–04317–X

Typeset by Palimpsest Book Production Limited,
Polmont, Stirlingshire
Printed and bound in Great Britain
by Mackays of Chatham PLC

In the first place – I am not aware by what right – the Writer assumes this work which is anonymous to be my production – He will answer that there is internal evidence – that is to say – that there are passages which appear to be written in my name or in my manner – but might not this have been done on purpose by another?

Lord Byron, Some Observations (1820)

One morning the giant was lying awake in bed when he heard some lovely music . . . Then the Hail stopped dancing over his head, and the North Wind ceased roaring, and a delicious perfume came to him through the open casement . . .

Through a little hole in the wall the children had crept in and they were sitting in the branches of the trees.

Oscar Wilde, The Selfish Giant (1888)

Oh! there is an organ playing in the street – a waltz, too! I must leave off to listen. They are playing a waltz which I have heard ten thousand times at the balls in London, between 1812 and 1815.

Music is a strange thing.

Byron's journal, Ravenna, 1821

PART ONE

I

TAKE MY WORD for it, the box arrived on a Wednesday. Even now, skimming the long list of my days, I still find that one picked out in fluorescent ink. At the time, it seemed a marvellous present, the crowing prize of my career; only later did I come to see things differently. In any case, I shall never forget the day of its arrival. Even now, across all the distance between Italy and England – a distance proved by the chant of the cicadas and the speed of that hydrofoil out there, skiing sparks off the bay – still comes the feeling of London and Wednesday.

When I got back to the shop that afternoon, I found Freddie lowering his filthy head towards the bin outside, soiled hair swinging. He seemed drawn to that bin, a green plastic drum just like all the rest, as though if he rummaged in it long enough he would eventually uncover a fiver. He spent so much time there that I often suspected him of being in the employ of Blackwall's, my rivals across the road.

As I approached him, I pulled a bit of a face. The weather was warm and, like a cheese or a corpse, a tramp ripens in the heat. This one, in response to the first day of spring, had sadistically put on a couple of extra cardigans under his overcoat, with the result that people were now crossing the road to avoid him. Steeling myself, I tapped him on the shoulder.

'On your way, now, Freddie.'

He shuffled round and stared blankly at my silk tie.

Years of rummaging had altered his posture, pushing him gradually down towards an invisible bin. Now, as he inched around London, he was as slow and stooped as a man who'd lost a contact lens.

'You're bad for trade,' I explained bluntly, and not for the first time. 'The United Nations could use you to enforce sanctions.'

He stared at my tie a little more closely, possibly trying to work out how much it might have cost. The breeze touched the leaves of a nearby tree. The light swayed sleepily, falling as a gold fuzz on Freddie's filthy shoulders.

'Sod off, Fred,' I said, waving my arm up the road towards the British Museum. This won a few disapproving looks from the good people of London on the other side of the road, but no reaction from Freddie. There was only one language he understood. 'Here's a quid. Now clear off till tomorrow.'

At last Freddie responded. From what one could tell through his matted beard, he smiled.

'Ta very much, Mr W. God bless.'

'No, look,' I said suddenly, reaching for my wallet. 'I've got a better idea. It's called caring capitalism. Here's a fiver. See that bin over there, the one outside Blackwall's? Right, go and have a bloody good look in it. Long as you like.'

Freddie snatched the fiver, which disappeared into one of his many layers of clothing. You wouldn't have thought such a broken old thing could move so fast. He began to shamble off in the direction of my competitors, grumbling at the sunny day, bent like a detective looking for a tiny clue.

With a smile which some might have considered malicious, I went inside.

Perhaps you know the shop I used to own. Everyone did. It was one of those antiquarian bookshops that huddle around the British Museum. Being as much a lover of books as I was an entrepreneur, I'd frequented it for about thirty years before I'd taken it over. At that time it had been dark, cluttered and altogether uninviting, having remained virtually unchanged since the 1920s. The original owner, whom I could only dimly remember, had been old Mr Dewson. On his death, the shop passed to his son, Vernon, whose eccentric business practices gradually ran it into the ground. Hearing that he was in danger of going under, I stepped in and made an offer. Though the price was a little on the lean side, Vernon was by that time in no position to refuse.

When I walked in that afternoon, still smiling, Vernon was dealing with a customer. Hearing me open the door, he shot me a look, and I knew that he'd been watching through the window when I moved Freddie on. If Vernon had had his way, Freddie would probably have been ensconced at the back of the shop, enjoying a cup of cocoa and a bun.

The look he now gave me was carefully purged of any open disapproval. Having dispatched it, he returned his gaze to the ceiling, which he tended to address when talking books. Quietly, I moved a little closer: Vernon was marvellous to listen to once he got going.

'We have them in from time to time, sir,' he creaked, swaying like a vicar. 'The first edition – which was in 1752, as you probably know – was rather a large one, about 5,000 if I remember rightly. This means that they're not terribly expensive, when you consider that it's Fielding. I sold a wormed copy last year for £150, so you should obviously be prepared to pay more for a fine example . . . say £250? Anyway, you're almost certain to find one if you hunt around the area. In fact, I have a feeling that Blackwall's, across the way . . .'

He trailed off, no doubt remembering my presence. If I'd told him once, I'd told him a thousand times. Vernon knew his books inside out, just as I knew my antiques.

Unlike me, however, he didn't have the knack of turning expertise into cash.

The customer, who looked as if he had money to burn, thanked him and left, a sight which caused me almost physical pain.

As I went towards him, Vernon took in my new Savile Row suit without a flicker, which is what he would have done if I'd been wearing a party hat and a necklace of shrunken skulls. For his own part, he liked to disguise himself as one of the more genteel characters in Dickens: half-moon glasses, tweed jackets and carefully-pressed waistcoats. His skin was scrubbed, but dry and flaky, as though he'd just arisen from the page.

'Vernon, Vernon,' I said sadly.

'I do apologise.' Only his pale eyes were moist, threatening rheumy tears. 'It just slipped out. Force of habit, I suppose.'

I could believe that. He'd been recommending people to Blackwall's all his life, like his father before him.

'But it costs us money, don't you see?' If he'd been a normal employee, I'd have given him a proper dressing-down. A certain respect was due, however, to his special position and his age. At that time he was asking people to believe, rather optimistically, that he was sixty-three. Respect was due also to his intellect. I'd seen him finish *The Times* crossword in under three minutes, filling the answers in without needing to pause, as though from memory.

I went on quietly, so that Caroline, who was sitting at the back of the shop, wouldn't hear me telling him off.

'If we don't have what they want, try and flog them something else. Failing that, tell them we'll have one in next week. Always tell them to come back. Never, under any circumstances, encourage them to scour all the other bookshops in the area.'

Vernon raised his hand to muffle a soft rustling in his throat.

'Yes, Mr Wooldridge.' For the merest instant, I thought I saw his damp eyes burn. 'I do understand.'

These last words, like so many things about him, were a discreet code: he understood. Literature was all that mattered. Business, and consequently yours truly, was strictly secondary. In other words, Vernon had failed to see behind my wealthy exterior. Being so good at crosswords, he should have understood that people can also give simple or cryptic clues.

'Look, Vernon,' I said, irritated. 'I know you like to think that books are somehow above the grubby world of commerce, but the fact is that a book is just a product, and a product has to be shifted. For all that I'm no expert, I could have sold that chap any book in the shop. You know that, don't you?'

Vernon knew it. He'd seen me in action a couple of times, doubling his day's turnover in an hour.

'I can't deny,' he said smoothly, 'that you are a quite remarkable salesman.'

'Vernon, you – ' When I saw the completely blank look on his face, I decided not to bother. 'Oh Christ, I give up on you. Just do it your own sweet way.'

Vernon gave a dignified little bow.

'Very kind of you, Mr Wooldridge.'

The old man walked off cautiously. He made a point of moving around the shop like that, as though still picking his way through the vanished clutter, to remind me of my crimes. When he reached the window, he planted his feet on the expensive carpet and stared out in a manner calculated to scare people away. Then he gave a sigh, long and gentle. It was like a draught from deep within him, where sadness shook its paper wings.

When I heard that sound, a little pity joined my annoyance. The shop had been his entire life, but there'd been no way to save it without making radical changes. The secret of retailing is very simple: make it almost impossible to see the shop from the street without wanting to go in, then make it almost impossible to go out again without buying something. To do this with Dewson's I'd had to move out half the old shelves, redecorate, recarpet, install larger windows. Then I'd moved in a few carefully chosen items from the more exclusive of my two antique shops – the Regency dresser which now displayed the most expensive volumes, the Georgian chairs around the walls, the table at the back – all of which Vernon had accepted without showing any sign of horror. He had watched in silence as I destroyed his world.

The silence had somehow become more intense when I'd moved in a marble bust of Byron, and I'd known that this was the acquisition of which he most disapproved. For him, the beautiful face with its abundant ringlets was a symbol of all my own shallowness. Vernon knew as well as I did that the milord had slept with his hair in papers, that the haughty expression had been assumed solely to impress posterity. Vernon saw him less as poet than poseur. But to me Byron had been a real artist, one not afraid to get out and grab life by the balls.

Now, a couple of months after my takeover, the bookshop was transformed. Only two things had survived intact. One was the legend 'Dewson's Fine Books', which I'd allowed to remain above the door, although I'd insisted on having it done in gold-leaf. The other was Vernon himself, more dry and still than ever in his new environment, a moth surprised by dawn.

The set of his back as he stared out of the window suddenly infuriated me again. The ungrateful old bugger was lucky to have a job at all. If I'd taken the shop over in my twenties, I'd have sacked him on the spot and hired someone who knew how to sell. Fortunately for him, I was by now less hungry, greedy for distraction as much as profit. I had also been wise enough to see the advantages of not alienating his client base. Vernon had kept his job. Perhaps it was presumptuous of me to expect gratitude.

At that moment, he had one of his little turns, which were beginning to worry me slightly.

This one was brought on by a motorcycle courier roaring down the street outside: a roll of thunder which sped towards us, materialised as one window-rattling flash of chrome, then hurtled out of earshot. When silence returned, I heard Vernon sigh again at the window.

'Odysseus or Agamemnon,' the old man murmured, 'would have taken that young vandal for a god. A god . . .' Vernon's glasses glinted as he shook his head, himself surprised, and his voice fell to a whisper: 'Some god of lightning and storms.'

Then he softly folded his hands over his modest belly, causing a wave of sadness to sweep down the shop. My anger vanished. Vernon might be a batty old bookworm, but we had more in common than he would ever understand. I was fifty-two myself and beginning to feel like him, tired by the pace of time.

At the back of the shop, I found Caroline reading behind the desk. This was by no means unusual. A tense, jerky girl, Caroline had just finished her English degree and she consumed books with unhealthy greed, holding them right up close to her face as though literature could shield physically as well as in other ways. I'd taken her on to help Vernon in his infirmity, and he thoroughly approved of her.

As I approached the desk, Byron stared at me out of his milky eyes. Then Caroline lowered her book enough to stare at me through thick glasses and lank tails of hair.

'Good morning, Mr Wooldridge.'

At that moment, my stomach-ache bit and I rubbed it absently through my shirt, more convinced than ever that it could only be an ulcer. It was like having a gas-ring suddenly turned up in my midriff. As the fire died, my eye lighted on the box: a shallow cardboard pallet, crammed with books, sitting under the desk at her feet.

'What's this?'

'That's a box, Mr Wooldridge,' said Caroline, who tended to be rather literal-minded.

'Good Lord, is it? Next you'll be telling me that those things in it are lobsters.'

'A shabby little man left it. With a beard.'

'He left a *beard*? Ugh! Where is it?' I looked wildly round the shop, while Caroline shifted in embarrassment, still not quite sure what to make of her new boss and his feeble jokes. 'Never mind. This fellow looked like a tramp, did he?'

'A little bit, yes.'

'Dubious Dave!' I groaned. 'It had to happen!'

Dave was a Cockney 'entrepreneur' who followed me around London in a beaten-up old van, trying to sell me antiques of very mixed quality. Now he had obviously got wind of my move into books.

'Is he a friend of yours, Mr Wooldridge?'

'One of life's losers, Caroline, who I do business with out of sheer kind-heartedness.'

A rustle from the front of the shop showed that Vernon was listening. Since the box had been brought by one of my own connections from the shady world of antiques, Vernon hadn't condescended to look through it. This, as it turned out, was more than a little ironic.

'Right. I'll take this upstairs and have a butcher's.' I lowered my voice and leaned across the desk. 'If old Vern tries anything on, sound the fire alarm.'

Caroline spluttered.

'Mr Wool dridge!'

I crouched to lift the box and, as my fingers touched the cardboard, I glanced under the desk. What I saw disgusted me slightly. In response to the warm weather,

Caroline had daringly put on a short skirt. Not being used to wearing them, she hadn't closed her mottled legs, so that I found myself staring right up at her knickers.

Only Caroline would have sat like that while a man crouched in front of her. The girl was innocent of herself. She was surely a virgin and would no doubt remain one all her life. She would always work in bookshops, becoming more literary and less alive, until she was as withered and barmy as Vernon himself. Every time she heard the brass bell above the door, her head would jerk up as though she expected to see Heathcliff or Darcy there, in riding-boots and high collar, come to carry her away.

When I stood up, the box sagging in my arms, Caroline was already masked by her book. I staggered towards the stairs, glancing at her hunched shoulders with all the sorrow such women make us feel.

There were times when being in the shop with those two gave me the absolute creeps.

Since taking Dewson's over, I'd been using the stock-room upstairs as a cross between an office and a den. Only on first walking into it had I begun to appreciate the full eccentricity of old Mr Dewson and his son.

The room was as long as the shop downstairs, but bare, carpeted only in dust. The roar of traffic was muffled by the thick air, which smelled of paper and age. In overflowing shelves around the walls, in piles on the desk and floor, were thousands of books which Vernon, and his father before him, had decided for their own obscure reasons to put into storage. Lurking in the darker corners of the room, near the bottom of some of the piles, were volumes which hadn't seen the light of day for over half a century. The piles formed a stunted forest, so thick in places that it was impossible to pass between them, making this without doubt the most chaotic stock-room in London. It only functioned at all because Vernon seemed to know the name and exact location of every book.

Not all of the stock was ancient. The room also housed my own collection of recent first editions, which I was buying as an investment. Vernon's refusal to dirty his hands with the twentieth century had been one of the reasons for his failure with the shop. When I'd told him that, like all our competitors, we should start dealing in collectable modern books, he had almost sneered. A week later he'd seen me take five hundred pounds for a copy of Brighton Rock (fine, in dust-wrapper). Even the imperturbable Vernon had been hard-pushed to conceal his fury, and I couldn't help feeling that, if he'd been alone in the shop that day, he'd have hidden the book rather than sell it.

In one corner of the office, at the end of a little pathway through the piled volumes, was a strong-box, which now functioned only as a red herring. It had been unused since another of my dodgy antique-dealing friends, as the result of a drunken bet, had proved to me that he could deflower it in under a minute. The revelation had been well worth the fifty quid I'd lost. Since then, following his advice, I'd kept any valuables under a loose floorboard. Above the strong-box I'd hung a print showing the cremation of Shelley, Byron looking self-consciously noble and windswept beside the flames.

Sometimes, when I'd been sitting up there for a while, it seemed to me that the strange silence of the room emanated mainly from that frozen image of the poet with his chin lifted and his hand resting on his cane. At others, the stillness seemed to come from the endless piles of books, some of which teetered towards waist-level. Then the place would take on the air of an elephants' graveyard: books retreated there from a world which no longer really cared, to find peace and solitude, to die in the understanding dust.

My desk was under the window at the far end of the room. Having cleared a space amongst the papers, postcards, pens, drawing-pins and other rubbish, I lifted the box up and placed it in the hot parallelogram of sunshine. Then I examined the books one by one, because, even with Dubious Dave, you never knew.

Of course, it was a waste of time. Though the selection was slightly more classy than one might have expected from Dave – there were a few Victorian volumes mixed in with the tattered fifties hardbacks – they were all obviously worthless, even to my untrained eye. Vernon himself wouldn't have given them a second glance.

For some time I sat there, wondering how I could tactfully discourage Dubious from trying to set himself up as a supplier of antiquarian books: Vernon was an old man, and the sight of Dave, swaggering into his shop with boxes of paperbacks, might prove too much for him. The thirty years of our acquaintance had been trying enough for me. Dave was part of the twilight world between small business and petty crime which so thrives in south London. Where he got his antiques from was a mystery into which I had never probed too deeply. Truth, after all, is the first casualty of commerce.

Staring at the tatty, disparate spread of books on my desk, I began, as usual, to wonder where the hell they could have come from. Then, also as usual, I began to feel sorry for poor old Dubious. My eye lighted on an early nineteenth-century bible, and I wondered whether I couldn't give him twenty quid for that, at least. When I examined it, however, I found that it was in terrible condition. The flyleaf was torn, the binding worn and frayed. The sad truth was that no collector would be interested.

With a sigh, I put it back down on the sunny desk.

The front board didn't even lie quite flat. It stayed in mid-air, a couple of millimetres above the flyleaf. I picked the book up and shook it to see if there was anything inside, but it was empty. The only possible explanation was that the binding had somehow contracted, causing the cover to rise.

As I sat there, wondering how the leather could possibly have shrunk, I fiddled with my wedding-ring, turning it around my finger. This was a habit of mine whenever I was thinking deeply. I am a man whose hands, like the rest of me, must always be busy. If I'd ever managed to get the ring off, I'd probably have found it had worn a groove into my flesh: I'd been twisting it for twenty-five faithful years.

A few moments later, I had completely forgotten about the book. My mind wandered off into nothing, as it had recently taken to doing: the mind of a man who'd made it, whose kids had grown up, who wasn't driven any more.

My stomach brought me back to earth. It wasn't the full fire, as I had felt in the shop, but merely an echo, almost a caress. The gas had been turned down to a circle of little blue blobs, pulsing softly. Perhaps all I needed was a bite to eat.

I got up and walked to the window, squinting down in time to see Freddie being moved on from Blackwall's across the way. In the spring sunshine, the room felt as hot as an incubator.

Deciding to go out and feed myself, I turned and left the office. The old stairs creaked beneath my feet. At the bottom I stopped and looked into the shop. There were no customers. Vernon had gone out, probably to chat with his cronies in one of the other bookshops nearby. Caroline was reading, too engrossed to have heard me.

For a moment I stood there, swaying, seeing nothing. Then I turned and began to climb rapidly back up to my office: I had remembered the bible and understood, as though my subconscious had been gnawing at the question all along, why the cover wasn't flat.

2

THE ELEPHANTS' GRAVEYARD upstairs seemed even more
still than when I had left it a moment previously. Perhaps
it was the stillness of expectation. The abandoned books
stood motionless. Byron stared into the wind exactly as
before, one hand frozen on his cane, shamelessly posing
at the cremation of his friend. A few sparks idled in the
broad buttress of light which leaned between my desk and
the grimy window. There in the warmth the bible waited,
cover still raised, leather gleaming.

As I walked into the room, my pace, which had been
rapid up the stairs, suddenly slowed. The stillness was such
that, for the first time since taking over the shop, I really
felt like an intruder and a wrecker. Vernon's father had
begun some of those piles of books long before I'd been
born. They were meant to be left in peace. They breathed
silence: the drone of traffic was deep but impossibly distant,
like a Tibetan horn heard at the foot of the mountains, a
call to contemplation or prayer.

Unable to shake off the feeling of desecration, I sat down
gingerly. Then I opened the bible as far as it would go, so
that the spine lifted, and held it up to the brilliant window.
To my joy, I saw that I'd guessed correctly: the apparent
stretching had been caused by an object carefully hidden
in the spine. It was a moment of perfect excitement and
delight such as you experience only once or twice in a
career like mine.

After that, I entirely forgot where I was. Unable to

remove my eyes from the book, I groped for a pencil. After a couple of firm pushes, the obstruction dropped on to the desk – a bundle of faded writing-paper bound with a blue ribbon. The sheets were so fine that I could see the writing through them even before, very softly, I undid the bow. When I did, the bundle loosened a little and released a faint musk, which vanished like a chill in the sunshine, so that I was left thinking that it might have been no more than my imagination. Yet my nose and antique dealer's instinct told me: it had been the smell of sealed age. In undoing the bow, I had broken into a tiny time-capsule.

They were letters, and there were more of them than I had originally imagined. They were the handiwork of some Regency fellow called, of all things, Gilbert, who had been on the Continent back in 1817. When I realised this, I felt another tremor of excitement – Byron had been in Europe at that time. Telling myself not to get too worked up, since the chances of the two men having met were impossibly remote, I began to read.

The handwriting gave me my first clue to Gilbert's character. It was perfectly precise and legible, yet thrown down on to the page with a violence which at times had almost sliced the paper. The cross on some of the 't's, for example, recalled the neat slash of a razor. Even if the letters had been typewritten, though, the first paragraph would have been enough to reveal the man. Paris was 'the dullest Thing in Christendom'. Travelling by carriage was 'dusty and beastly uncomfortable'. The conversation of Gilbert's companions was unbearably mundane. As far as he was concerned, they could 'go to the Deuce'.

Perhaps a personality can invest itself directly in paper and print and remain there for hundreds of years. Perhaps even a shopping list could send a shiver down your spine if it had been written by a murderer. All I know is that after a couple of pages, I was somehow so overwhelmed by the sheer power of the writer's personality that I had to stop reading for a moment.

As soon as I did, I found that a picture of him had been forming in my mind: a nobleman, no doubt of it, with the aristocrat's aquiline nose, lazy eyes and petrified sneer. Sitting there in my office, I pictured him climbing from his carriage into the courtyard of a Parisian hotel. His movements had the same precise violence as his handwriting. Upstairs, he sat stiffly by the window and began to scratch, dip, and scratch, attacking the page, patrician face unruffled. Outside, the foam-flecked harnesses were being lifted and the horses led away, snorting and tossing their heads, clattering over the cobbles.

Gilbert was jaded almost to the point of exhaustion. He would have relished an execution or a duel simply out of *ennui*. The letters were addressed to 'My Dear Amelia', presumably his sweetheart or wife, yet there was not one word to indicate affection, let alone love.

For some time I sat there, staring at the tea-coloured paper without really seeing it, wondering that a man so unpleasantly alive through his words could at the same time be dead. In the end, overcoming my repugnance, I began again to read.

The third page of the letter saw Gilbert complaining about French servants and the standard of his hotel. He described in some detail how he had gone to bed the night before, right down to blowing out his candle and seeing the stars over Montmartre through his window. Then he shocked me.

The remainder of the page was covered in meaningless symbols. There were arrows pointing in all directions, triangles, circles, squares, wriggling worms, falling waves and black stars of ink. At the bottom were the words 'Yrs, Gilbert' and that was it. The next letter of the series was written in normal English.

After I had stared at the page for a few minutes, I got up and walked to the window, too agitated to sit still. Even the hope of finding that one name was temporarily buried in a blizzard of implications and possibilities. The encoded information could have been amorous, criminal, or even political. Whatever it was, a lot of trouble had been taken to keep it secret.

Abruptly, I turned from the window, went back to my desk and, breathing deeply, bent down towards the letter, suddenly feeling that the message would be as unpleasant as the writer himself. Gilbert's normal handwriting had given an impression of violence which was nasty enough, but the symbols were distinctly sinister. There was a whiff of the occult about them.

Reading more quickly now, I followed Gilbert over the Alps. These, of course, were 'far too highly considered by All', including the other members of his party, whose romantic raptures filled him with scorn. Every two pages or so, there would be a section in code. In about the fifth letter, Gilbert announced that he was off to Venice for the carnival, and my pulse started racing.

I skipped through the next couple of pages, both of which sneered at the marvels of Venice, almost without noticing, searching madly for that name. Then, to my amazement and delight, I saw it.

'*My dear Amelia, it has happened just as I knew it would. I have met* Him. *You know to whom I refer, of course. The infamous author of Childe Harold himself, the Exile, Lord Byron.*

'*It was at the Opera last night. Our box faced his above the chattering crowd. The meeting of our eyes was indeed a moment of Destiny. I can confirm, Amelia, that there is real Greatness in Lord Byron's face. Everything we have heard about his beauty is true – a sublime mixture of Intelligence, Strength and Sensitivity is to be read in his countenance. He has that power which can mesmerise the ordinary man. All eyes were on him. In his own eyes were* Tears *as he listened to the music, the tears of Genius.*

'*We must have gazed at each other a full five seconds, during which an understanding passed between us.*' Here there was a long paragraph in code. '*In short, we are invited to dine with him tomorrow evening.*'

The writing was florid by Gilbert's standards, and there was no doubt that he'd found a companion worthy of him at last. Whatever pleasure or excitement he might have felt, however, was nothing to mine, as I sat there with the London traffic droning outside my office window and read those paragraphs.

For a few minutes I was too astounded even to read on. Most Byron scholars and admirers of the great man would have given their eye teeth to be in my shoes at that moment.

First of all, I counted the pages remaining, knowing they would all concern Byron at the most splendid stage of his career. There were five in all. Then I forced myself to wait, savouring the moment. History was in the making. Through Gilbert, I was about to witness an episode from Byron's life which no one in our age had ever seen. I felt almost unworthy.

When I could stand it no longer, I began to read the first remaining page. As I had hoped, it contained a description of the dinner party. Gilbert, who had sneered at the Alps, who had yawned and sighed his way through the great cities of Europe, could not hide the fact that he was impressed by the poet's household. He was staggered by the wild vulgarity of the servants, amazed at the exotic menagerie – peacocks, horses, chimpanzees – which wandered freely on the ground floor, horrified by the grubby bastard children he found crawling over the billiard table. The man himself Gilbert found almost overwhelming. In those days, after all, Byron overwhelmed the world. To them he was like a god.

Reading that letter was perhaps the highlight of my career. For me, it was like being allowed to travel to nineteenth-century Venice and visit Byron's residence in person. As I read, I realised what I had always felt for the poet, particularly during that period of his life: a mixture of pity, repulsion and awe. There is by definition something disturbingly alien about all exiles, something ogrish.

Byron's exile, played out with such fairy-tale grandeur against a background of incest and infamy, made him seem more of an ogre than most. There was doubtless a magic charm about the dandy alone in his dilapidated *palazzo*, blessed with talent, beauty and wealth. Yet none of it could quite dispel the taint of his past. All the time, Gilbert's host, the giant of his age, was struggling with the deformity which had separated him from the rest, the twist in his club-foot soul.

After speaking at length about the household, the letter went on to the dinner itself.

'Lord B' (Gilbert, as you see, already felt that he could be familiar) *'was ill-tempered this evening. Despite this, he was quite, quite charming, treating us with all the courtesy of his rank in that chaotic place. It is strange – however petty he may be, he cannot ever be anything but* Great. *The reason for his ill humour was a low Neapolitan woman with whom he had a three-day liaison. I have good reason to remember her name – Maria Apuglia – because he cursed it all evening, and said he should have known better than to associate himself with a name so ugly and vulgar.*

'After some time had elapsed, however, the Great Poet became more sanguine. Having indulged himself in vast quantities of claret and soda water – he drinks a prodigious amount, Amelia, quite as much as I – he explained mysteriously that he had been angry for a friend as much as for himself. This gentleman is called Shelley, and is also a Poet of whom we may one day hear. B described him as by far the most beautiful human being he had ever met. All ill humour forgotten, we passed a pleasant evening, mesmerised by the Great Man's talk.

'*The meal over, Byron desired to converse with me alone.*'

There followed two full pages of code.

The excitement took twenty years off me. Without pausing to think, I rushed to the door and charged down the stairs into the shop.

'Vernon!' I bellowed. 'Vernon!'

Caroline looked up and stared at me as though I were insane. Vernon, just coming in from the street, pointedly finished wiping his shoes before lifting his bald head in my direction. This was a comment on the plush red carpet I'd had put down the month before.

'Yes?'

'Come upstairs. I've found something which may interest you.'

Although I hadn't invited him up to the office since I'd taken it over, Vernon showed no sign of surprise.

'Very good, Mr Wooldridge.'

It seemed to me that he walked down the shop with deliberate slowness. If this was meant to make me suffer, it worked: by the time he reached the foot of the stairs, I was almost jumping up and down on the spot. As I held the door open for him, he climbed the first stair, gave a low groan, and stopped.

'What's the matter?'

'I'm afraid I suffer from arthritis. It's tolerable when I'm standing or walking, but stairs can be a problem. Would you mind taking my arm?'

Getting him up the stairs took a full minute, and this time there was no question of his doing it deliberately. At each step he winced, and I could actually hear the creaking of his ruined knees. When we reached the office, he stood still and sighed, looking around him approvingly at the clutter.

'You haven't changed much up here, at least. I hope you won't mind my saying so, but this is what I've always felt the shop itself should be like. It's so much more interesting for the customers to . . .'

'Never mind about all that now.' I walked quickly into the room, picked up the spare chair and tilted it to tip the rubbish off. 'Come and sit down,' I said, placing the chair in front of the desk.

By the time Vernon had crossed the room and lowered himself down, I had opened my strong-box, from which

I produced a bottle of Glenfiddich and two glasses. Going back to the desk, I poured him a generous measure.

'Drink this. You're going to need it.'

'Well, at this time of day I don't usually . . .'

'Just drink it, for God's sake,' I said, 'and stop being such a bloody stuffed shirt.'

He stared at me for a moment. Then he gave a soft cough, a fall of dust in his throat.

'I think I'd better leave.'

I took a deep breath.

'Vernon, Vernon, I'm sorry. Just wait till you see what I've found and you'll understand why I'm so worked up. Forgive me.'

To my relief, the old boy picked up his glass and took a cautious sip.

'Now,' I said, handing him the first page of the first letter. 'Read this and tell me what you think.'

Vernon pushed his glasses up his nose.

'Paris – journey most dull – da-da, da-da – servants insolent – de-dum, de-dum.' At the point where most people would just have been finishing the first paragraph, he placed the page on the table and looked up at me. 'Letter written by an early nineteenth-century tourist, arrogance suggesting minor aristocracy, possibly a young man doing the Grand Tour. Interesting curio, virtually worthless.'

'Yes, even I know that. Genuine, though, I assume?'

Leaning forward, Vernon removed his spectacles and held them like a magnifying-glass above the page.

'Convincing flecking on the paper. Ink faded. Style and content consistent with the time. Yes,' he said, leaning back again, 'I don't see why it shouldn't be. Why does it interest you so much?'

'When he left Paris, Gilbert crossed the Alps and went on to Venice. There . . .'

'Don't tell me,' said Vernon, raising a tired hand. 'There he met the sulky exile himself, Lord Byron.'

This deflated me somewhat.

'Very bloody clever.'

'What else could have caused you such excitement?' Vernon carefully replaced his glasses. 'You obviously worship the man, after all. Why else erect a bust of him in my shop?'

Though I'd never have admitted it to Vernon, the fact was that I had worshipped Byron in my time. I'd once paid the best part of a thousand pounds for a lock of his hair.

To cover my embarrassment, I topped up Vernon's glass. Then, in a more subdued voice, I summarised the letters for him: the opera, the invitation to dinner, the detailed description of the household. Vernon didn't even raise an eyebrow.

'Come on,' I said when I'd finished. 'You've got to admit that it's a find.'

Vernon said nothing, and suddenly it was as though his mask had slipped – the old man was jealous. He'd been running that shop all his life, probably longing for a find like the one I'd just made. Instead, he'd made nothing but a loss and had been forced to sell. I'd turned up, having amassed a small fortune in the sordid world of antiques, taken his business over, and almost immediately made the discovery which had eluded him.

'What do you think these letters are worth, then? Give me your expert opinion.'

'It's difficult to say.' Vernon smoothed his hands down his waistcoat, considering. 'I always find it so hard to estimate the folly of the buying public when it comes to Byron. It would probably run into thousands, but you'd know that better than me.'

For a moment we stared at each other. I knew that he was testing me, like a naughty child, finding out how far he could go before I lost my cool.

'There have been times, Vernon,' I said softly, 'when I've been tempted to give you the sack . . .'

He sipped his whisky. In the bright sunlight of the office, his face looked even drier and more seamed, a sheet of paper which had been screwed up in fury then smoothed out again in a fit of ineffectual remorse.

'You own the business now, Mr Wooldridge. You may employ precisely whom you wish.'

'The reason I haven't sacked you, though,' I continued, 'is that I'd rather we were friends. I respect your expertise, Vernon, your learning . . .'

There was silence. The sun was getting lower. As Vernon lifted his head to stare at the ceiling the light glinted from his glasses as though in warning.

'Look,' I said, 'I know what you think of me. You think I'm just a businessman and nothing more, a sort of soulless calculator. Well, that's not true, Vernon, and I wish you'd . . .'

Since there was absolutely no response from him, I gave up. After a moment, he lowered his head, the light dying in his glasses.

'You and I will never see eye to eye, Mr Wooldridge. We come from different worlds. The best we can do is find a way of co-existing.'

With that, the pompous fool knocked back his whisky and started to lever himself out of his chair. Fury filled me. This time he had gone too far. Before I told him he was fired, I decided to make him suffer a little.

'Vernon, there is just one other thing I haven't told you about those letters.'

'Indeed? And what might that be?'

Without saying anything, I handed him the third page with its mass of symbols. Vernon sat back down and looked at it for a moment. This time he did raise, not just one, but both eyebrows, causing tiny corrugations up his forehead. A small smile set on his parched lips, which seemed to remain motionless when he spoke.

'My God. Now, this . . .' He left the sentence hanging in mid-air. Just as I'd decided that he wasn't going to finish it and was about to speak myself, he took it up again. 'Is interesting . . .'

He trailed off and sat staring at the page of symbols in complete stillness. Watching him, I suddenly remembered the speed with which he did *The Times* crossword, and decided to keep quiet. For about ten minutes the room was silent except for the thoughtful hiss of Vernon's breathing and the drone of traffic outside. At one point, I did take the risk of refilling his glass. After a vague nod in my direction, he sipped steadily as he examined the letter. The sun had lost its strength. There were no sparks any more, only weightless molecules of gold. The piles of books stood watchfully, seeming now to exhale not only silence, but premature gloom.

As time went on, I began to expect that at any moment Vernon would look up and announce that he'd cracked the code. I didn't dare move for fear of distracting him.

'It looks quite sophisticated,' he muttered at last. As though speaking had called him back into himself, he shifted stiffly and stretched his fingers. 'Original, too . . . inspired, almost. Are there coded sections in the Byron letters?'

'Yes. Much longer than that one, in fact.'

'Fascinating.' He looked up at me. 'Look . . . ah, Claude . . . I feel I ought to thank you.'

'Whatever for?'

'Showing this to me. A lot of people would have kept it to themselves.'

'It's nothing.'

'As long as you understand. This shop's been my entire life. Being forced to . . .'

'Forget all that. The important thing is, how can we crack the bloody code?'

'Oh, I can do that . . . but it may take time. Give me a few of the letters and I'll have a go at it tonight.' As he spoke, his watery eyes were drawn back to the page as though they couldn't bear to be away from it. 'That was my job in the war,' he said vaguely. 'Code-breaking.'

At that moment, it struck me that I might have made

as many glib assumptions about him as he'd made about me.

'Tell me about yourself, Vernon,' I said, topping up his glass.

'How do you mean?'

'Well, are you married, for example?'

Vernon gently placed the letter on the table and reverted to his sad, old self.

'If you don't mind, Claude, I'd rather not . . .'

'Mr Wooldridge?'

We both looked round. Caroline had appeared in the doorway.

'Yes?'

'Do you think I could go home now? It *is* twenty to six.'

'Jesus, is it? No, of course, you run along.'

Instead of running along, though, she stood on tiptoe and peered down the twilit office, obviously dying to know what we were up to.

'If you're good, Caroline,' I said, 'we may tell you about it in the morning. Now run along.'

When she'd gone, Vernon thoughtfully finished his whisky.

'I think I'll be off as well, if you don't mind, Claude. I'm getting a bit old for all this excitement.'

'Has it excited you, Vernon? You've certainly given no sign.'

'I like to play my cards close to my chest,' said Vernon in a strange voice. Then he gave a rather wistful smile. 'I'm one of the old brigade, you see. One of the old cloak-and-dagger brigade.'

With that, he levered himself up. I gave him all the letters except those directly relating to Byron, which I wouldn't have parted with for anything.

Frowning slightly, Vernon put the papers carefully in his inside pocket and patted his jacket three or four times, as though to convince himself that they were really there.

Then he began to pace towards the door. There was something even more precise than usual in the way he moved. Only when he reached the top of the stairs and swayed slightly, as though with vertigo, did I realise that Vernon was drunk.

When he'd gone, I read through the Byron letters again, wracking my brains to try and work out what the coded sections might contain. A simple love affair between Amelia and Gilbert would surely not have required such a degree of secrecy. If the Englishman had somehow got caught up in the labyrinthine Italian politics of the time – as Byron himself had been – why should he have bothered writing to Amelia about it? Unless the name Amelia itself was a symbol for something else . . .

In exhausted agitation, I got up and went to the window. The light was going, the streetlamps flickering orange ahead of me. Looking down, I saw that Vernon, slow as always, was only just leaving the shop. I watched him pace like a pall-bearer down the gloomy street, suddenly a stranger again: a small old man in a fawn overcoat, commuting back to a life of which I knew nothing, but which I sensed was numbingly lonely.

After two months of bitterness, Vernon and I were real partners at last. I watched him approach the end of the street with a new affection, but also with a strange care, as though examining his movements would reveal something about him. At that moment, I realised that Vernon himself was a mystery, with his quiet manner, dapper clothes and blade of a mind, another code waiting to be cracked.

Then, without warning, I had something like a vision. I saw Byron, sitting at his desk in Venice. Everything about him was clear to me, from his oiled ringlets to his foppish collar: a stout but handsome man, his features lit by a candle from below, scratching madly at his work and muttering as though in rage. The city was still; it was near dawn. Outside I could just hear the thick lap of stale canal water.

What's he writing?

Vernon's small, erect figure disappeared around the corner. The street was empty. I went and sat back at the desk. My mind seethed. It seemed to me that if I thought about Byron and Gilbert's code for an instant longer, the anticipation alone would drive me mad. Then I saw that what I needed to do was go home and tell Helen all about it. So I slipped the letters into my pocket, switched off the lights, and left the office.

Downstairs, the shop was already in twilight. The shelves seemed to have grown, hunching their shadowy shoulders against the walls. I went to the door and pressed buttons to activate the newly-installed alarm, which Vernon had so far refused point-blank to use.

Before I left, I paused and looked behind me. There was only one white object in the shop. The steady trickle of light from the street had gathered round it, so that it seemed to glow, floating on the gloom.

As the door creaked shut, I had the distinct impression that Byron's marble head moved a couple of inches, straining its blindness towards the sound.

3

NIGHT WAS FALLING by the time I got back home. The sky was just about blue, but the trees in the park were already black.

In those distant days, I lived in happiness and Greenwich. I'd considered Greenwich my patch ever since I'd had to leave Oxford in '59. Thirty years later, I owned a sizeable chunk of the place. I had two tall, Georgian terraced houses, one split into bedsits and the other into luxury flats. There were also two classy antique shops and a sandwich bar, each with flats above. All of it except the sandwich bar had been bought cheap in the sixties and was now worth a fortune.

My own residence was a large Regency villa of stately curves and symmetry. It was so regal that even I felt intimidated by it when I first moved in. I was only just thirty then and every time I walked up to the front door I'd find myself looking over my shoulder for the law. (People who deal in antiques and property have rather guilty consciences, it's an occupational hazard.) It took a long time for it to sink in that I actually owned the place.

The house was set disdainfully back from the road behind a semi-circular drive, where I parked my car that night just as I always did.

Try to be with me now. Try to hear as I can the purr and crunch of the Range Rover on the gravel, a sound full of England, of wealth and happiness and home. Now hear the reassuring clunk of the door. The tall middle-aged man walks towards the house. He has greying hair, just long enough to look artistic, a knife of a nose. His suit and early Patek watch give some idea of his wealth.

An unlikely type, this, to be carrying such a literary find in his tailored pocket, or even to be interested in books at all. To see him flicker smoothly through the shadows, moving with the ease of a man who's never failed, you'd think he was just another pinstriped shark.

On the lighted porch he pauses and turns towards the park, twisting the ring on his finger. For a moment he looks worried and worn, perhaps even in pain. His hands stop playing with the ring and lightly touch his stomach.

He composes himself and goes inside. The trees sigh in the park. The blue is gone from the sky.

Helen was in the kitchen. Alluringly buxom when we married, she had by now grown fat and developed heavy, post-menopausal breasts. She didn't wear make-up or dye the grey out of her hair; she invariably wore shapeless dresses and chunky sweaters. Because of these things, not in spite of them, affection still glowed in the ashes of middle age.

When I arrived, she put down the book she'd been reading and glided towards me with the majesty of a large woman. Then she put her arms around me and laid her head on my shoulder as though to cry or sleep. she had a soft voice.

'I love you, Claude.'

'Me too.'

There was nothing unusual about this. Each evening, Helen would hug me and tell me that she loved me. This was less to do with me than with her, for Helen loved everything. She seemed to consider the existence of things which it was impossible to love, like Victorian architecture and Mrs Thatcher, as proving some kind of moral shortcoming in herself, so that she would always cover up by calling whatever it was fine 'in its own way'.

Full of love, she was without ambition. All she'd wanted to do while the children were growing up was be with them. Now that they had all but grown up (through I still had serious reservations about our daughter, Fran) I had put Helen in charge of that sandwich bar of mine, where she seemed, in her own thoughtful way, happy.

She held me lightly, eyes closed, bosom heaving slowly, meditatively. Our bodies swayed as though anchored in a tide. That movement always reminded me of the last dance at a fifth-form disco: the lights down low and the polished wooden floor, marked out for netball, strewn with streamers and paper cups. Helen had somehow maintained that intensity and need.

Finishing those hugs of hers always made me feel a little guilty, but the fact was that one of us had to do it. It was a joke between us that, if she'd ever met a man with a temperament like her own, they would have done nothing but hug each other for days on end.

That evening I was too excited to stay still for long. When I'd released her, Helen surfaced, opened her eyes and smiled as though surprised to find that I was there. Meanwhile, I walked rapidly in the direction of the drinks cabinet. I felt like a stiff one, to celebrate and calm me down. As the flame fell into my chest, I turned around and found Helen standing just where I had left her. She was looking at me thoughtfully, head on one side, dimpled arms folded under her bosom.

'Something unusual happened to you today.'

'Did it now?' I said, smiling, but not surprised at her guess. Helen had a power of intuition which bordered on clairvoyance. Shortly after meeting her, I'd been forced to rethink my attitudes to the paranormal. 'What makes you think that, then?'

'Just a feeling, dear.' She settled herself at the table. 'Am I right?'

'As always. But can you guess exactly what it was?'

'No. Just that it was something . . . very unusual.'

'Helen, does the name Byron mean anything to you?'

'It rings a bell.' Helen had caught sarcasm from me back in the early days. 'I have a feeling you've mentioned it before.'

'Well, what happened today concerns that very same Byron.'

With that, I launched into the story of how I had found the letters. I sketched their contents for her, giving her a broad outline of Gilbert's character and his journey across the Alps.

Then, triumphantly, I took the two Byron letters out of my pocket.

As I read out the account of the opera and Gilbert's arrival at Byron's palazzo, Helen sat perfectly still, but I could tell that, unlike Vernon, she shared my pleasure. Helen knew my past, understood the distant catastrophe which still cast its ripples through my present calm. Vernon saw only a businessman, but Helen saw something far more complicated. She knew that my success could be interpreted as failure, the one route brilliantly followed no more than a symbol for so many others permanently blocked. She knew why Byron meant more to me than any other writer, since in him I found the conflicts of my own career played out on a heroic scale.

'*The meal over, Byron desired to converse with me Alone.*'

Over the top of the ancient paper, I saw Helen looking at me expectantly.

'And . . . ?'

I crossed the room and placed the sheet with its page of code on the table before her.

'And this.'

Where Vernon had been physically sucked in by the mystery, I was surprised to find that Helen seemed repulsed. As soon as she saw the page of symbols, she stiffened in her chair, moving away from them.

'What's that?'

'Some sort of code. Vernon's probably trying to crack it at this moment.'

'I don't like it.'

This irritated me a little. I had been looking forward to sharing the excitement with her.

'What do you mean you don't like it?' There was a look on her face which was almost fear. 'Don't you think it's fascinating?'

'There's something dirty about it. Take it away.'

In spite of myself, I was disturbed. As I stood there staring down at her, I was reminded of an incident from the early years of our marriage. We had been looking for our first house and went to view a place over in Camberwell. As soon as we entered the poky spare bedroom, Helen, to the astonishment of myself and the agent, absolutely insisted on leaving.

'Come on, Helen. It's just an old letter.'

'I'm serious, Claude. Take it away. I don't even want to see it.'

When we'd left the house, Helen had been so shaken that I'd taken her for a drink at the local pub. There the landlord told us that the property had been on the market for five years, ever since the previous owner had killed herself and her three children there. The landlord knew all the gory details. It was unnecessary to ask where the tragedy had happened, but I asked anyway, just to make sure, and he told me: in the spare bedroom.

As soon as the letters had disappeared back into my pocket, Helen relaxed.

'I'm sorry, love. You're probably right. I was just being silly.'

I was about to agree with her and add that this was by no means the first time, when the doorbell rang. Helen's hand immediately rose to her hair, which she made a futile attempt to rearrange. This was her invariable response to the sound of the doorbell, a vague nod in the direction of feminine vanity. Still fiddling with it, she went to answer. A moment later, I heard the door open and a voice like the crack of doom, which belonged to my pal Ross.

Alone for a moment, I stared around the kitchen. For some reason it had become the centre of our lives in that house. Perhaps this was because of the large French windows at the back, which opened on the garden. More likely, everything focused on the kitchen because that was where Helen preferred to spend her time. In many ways, it was she who was the real centre of our lives. The other rooms downstairs she considered 'too grand' with their antiques and chandeliers. The kitchen – functional surfaces, farmhouse floor, stripped pine – was where she felt at home.

Helen looked her serene self again when she came back in, smiling dreamily: she was even more fond of Ross than she was of everyone else. Ross himself looked as if he'd just come away from the funeral of a small child or a talk about jam-making at the Dorking Women's Institute. Ross always looked like that and had done ever since I'd met him up at Oxford. He was one of the terminally uneuphoric.

'Hi, Ross,' I said. 'How are things? Pretty bad?'

'Pretty bad,' he groaned, taking a seat. 'Pretty damned bad, I don't mind telling you.'

'Well, it could be worse, old son. You could have cancer or something.'

'I should be so lucky,' said Ross flatly. 'I'd give anything to get cancer. I'd even give up smoking.'

Ross, as should by now be obvious, was a writer. He'd taught until his early thirties, when, after seven years' trying, he'd finally managed to get a novel published. It had been a modest success and that had been that: he'd chucked teaching and refused to do a hand's turn ever since, for reasons of artistic integrity. The novels had become less and less successful, leaving Ross well and truly on his uppers. It now looked as if his publishers were finally going to dump him.

Luckily for him, he had me. He lived for a token rent in one of my flats and I was constantly giving him loans which could only be described as very long term. Though everyone in the family knew about them, these transactions were never mentioned. Like many poor people, Ross was rather touchy about money.

We all lit fags.

'Any word from those publishers of yours?' I asked cheerfully.

'Spineless Thatcher-boys,' growled Ross, who tended to get wordy when annoyed. 'They wouldn't know a work of passion and imagination if it − '

'Well, I thought your last book was very good,' chipped in Helen bravely, obviously wanting to stem the flow of this familiar diatribe. The fact was that Ross's novels weren't really her cup of tea. They had an alarming tendency to end in the suicide of the central character. 'It really was very good indeed, in its own way.'

This made me grin. Helen naively believed nobody could see through that little phrase of hers. She didn't realise how damning it really was.

'Thanks a lot,' said Ross in a tone of extra-deep misery which proved he understood it perfectly. 'Very kind of you.'

For a few moments we both looked at him sympathetically. He was a very stocky man, who tended to bounce pugnaciously up and down on the spot when excited or enraged. At other times, he had the capacity to sit entirely still and brood for hours. The baldness of his head was compensated for by a thick black beard. He had the reddish nose of a dedicated drinker.

For all his ugliness and poverty, Ross was powerfully attractive to women, and I could understand why. There was something about him which it was impossible not to love. His dark eyes, set deep, always held wistfulness or fire. However, his moody self-obsession alienated lovers as quickly as his charm had infatuated them. Each desertion seemed to leave him a little bleaker than before.

Looking at him now, I decided that what the geezer needed was a good feed, so I left the table, fag in mouth, and began supper. I loved cooking. It was the one household chore for which I'd never hired help, regarding it as creative therapy after a hard day on the make. While I was chopping things up, I told Ross the story of the letters.

'I don't believe it,' he said when I explained about the code. 'It's incredible! Let's have a look, quick.'

I carefully dried my hands and went back towards the table, reaching into my pocket. Helen left, ostensibly to go to the toilet, and I was again disturbed by the strength of her feelings about my discovery. Before handing the letters over, I said quietly, 'How are you off for money, Ross?'

'Not too bad. I'm expecting a cheque next week.'

This meant nothing. Ross was always expecting a cheque.

'Sure you don't need a sub?'

Instead of answering, he reached out and took the letters. Then he sat and gazed at them in silence, obviously not reading. I felt so sorry for him whenever we discussed money. As I stared down at his bald head, speckled like a brown egg, my mind went back some thirty years to Oxford. I remembered the nights we'd spent quoting poetry at each other and talking about women. I remembered the time I'd first seen him, standing in the corner at a party, a grim rock in a heaving sea.

'Fifty would come in handy, I suppose,' he mumbled at last. 'Just until that cash arrives.'

I got out my chequebook and wrote him one for a hundred, knowing that embarrassment always led him to underestimate his needs.

'Thanks, Claude.'

'It's nothing,' I said, matching his forced lightness. I meant it. Giving money to Ross was like giving money to a part of myself which had gone down another road, leading one of the lives I might have led if things had turned out differently. 'Have a read of those letters quick, before Helen comes back.'

'Why the big hurry?'

'She doesn't like them.' I pulled a face and put on my wife's husky voice. 'There's something nasty about them, Claude.'

We both laughed.

'God help us!' cried Ross. 'Feminine intuition again! The gibbering spooks!' Still smiling, he lowered his head and began to read. A moment later, the smile was gone, and he spoke in a completely different tone. 'I can see what she means, though . . .'

'Not you as well!'

'All this about Byron at the opera is fascinating, but as for the writer . . . well, there does seem to be something rather unpleasant about him.' As he spoke, Ross finished the page and saw the first section of code. 'Oh my sweet Jesus,' he said softly.

'Ross? What's the matter?' He just stared down at the fine brown paper, wide-eyed. 'What is it?'

'Evil,' he whispered. He looked slowly up at me as though in a trance. 'Evil.'

I tried to hide my shock, but Ross must have seen how he'd affected me. He suddenly burst out laughing.

'Look at you, you silly fool! I really had you going!'

'Very bloody funny,' I said, angrily taking the letters back and returning them to my pocket.

'Oh, Claude, you always have been easy to take for a ride! If you could only have seen yourself!' He rose up from his seat, twisting his face, bending his fingers like claws. 'Eeevil!' he wailed. 'Eeevil!'

Then he burst out laughing again, wiping his eyes. There was always something unnaturally manic about Ross when he laughed, the slight wildness of a man who'd spent too long alone.

'Oh, shut up, you demented scribbler.'

39

But Ross was helpless with mirth. As I watched him, I noticed what I had often noticed before, which was that laughter seemed to make his eyes more mournful and removed. They were like two cripples at a ball.

'So, tell us, Mr Wooldridge,' he said suddenly, mock-serious, 'how did someone as hopelessly gullible as you ever make it in business?'

'I'm not gullible, far from it. It's just that when I get home I leave my suspicion outside in the car.'

Ross stopped smiling.

'A good and true answer.'

With a sigh, I stood and went back to my cooking. I should have known that Ross wouldn't be interested in my little find, which, after all, bore no direct relation to his current book.

It was a pleasant evening, as it seems to me now those evenings always were. Helen came back down and, while the supper was cooking, the three of us smoked drank and chatted with the ease of people who'd known each other for thirty years. For all her irrational fear, Helen couldn't help getting drawn into speculation over the letters. Before we started eating, I opened another bottle of wine, with the result that Ross and I soon had some fairly wild theories flying around.

Just as dinner was served, punctual as always, Christopher gangled in. Both of my children were tall, but while Fran was all beauty and poise, Christopher was stooping and awkward. Though he'd inherited a lot of his mother's dreaminess, he'd got none of her grace, with the result that he was unbelievably clumsy. Against all commonsense, he'd insisted on studying philosophy at university, and now seemed to spend most of his time on another planet.

Though they got on well together, Christopher and Fran had been different even as babies. Christopher had been as good as gold, thoughtful even then. Fran, when she arrived five years later, kept us awake night after night, screaming as though she were in hell.

Once, at the age of twelve, Christopher was accused by the neighbours of opening the petrol-cap on their new Volvo and pouring in a load of gravel. This pleased me, partly because it revealed a surprising bravery in my son and partly because I'd never liked the bloody neighbours anyway. Hiding my pride, as a father sometimes must, I gave Christopher a proper telling-off. In the end, he suddenly burst into tears and admitted that it hadn't been him at all, but Fran. He'd been afraid to tell me. Only then did I realise that, though five years his junior, she was the real bully of the two.

Age failed to mellow her. At fourteen, she was apprehended by one of her teachers, in an incident whose precise details are still shrouded in mystery, letting off a fire-extinguisher in the male staff toilets. Only careful diplomacy, in the form of a hefty donation to the new sports hall, averted her expulsion. By some fluke she passed enough exams to stay on for her A levels. And then what did she do? Idled in her room listening to 'music' all day, that's what, and stayed out all night having sex with half of south London.

Unlike Helen, I felt it my duty to try to curb our daughter's worst excesses, and this tended to cause a little friction. My wife, during one of our many discussions on her *laissez-faire* approach, had once compared herself to a pacifist living with a war-monger and a nuclear bomb.

The bomb's brother, for all his irritating vagueness, made much more relaxing company. He was one of the main reasons I'd moved into books: in the two years since leaving university, he'd virtually taken over the antiques side of my operation, proving that he had a surprisingly good business head on his shoulders and, perhaps having inherited a little of his mother's clairvoyance, the ability to spot a fake through his fingertips. He lived in the flat above the larger shop, but often came round for dinner.

We got on well. In fact, Christopher, being such a tentative chap, got on well with everybody, including Ross, with whom he could chat away for hours about aesthetics, post-modernism, deconstruction and other idle fancies.

We ate in the kitchen, the dining-room with its long table and velvet curtains being rather imposing for everyday use. Gilbert and his letters naturally formed our main topic of conversation. Helen asserted once again that there was something sinister about the whole thing, to the amusement of myself and Ross. However, the letters themselves stayed in my pocket. This was partly out of respect for her feelings and partly because I knew that, if Christopher had caught sight of that code, we'd have lost him for the rest of the evening.

Towards the end of the meal, I found that I was already tempted to ring Vernon and see if he'd made any progress. However, I decided to discipline myself. It could do no harm to wait until the following day.

As we were starting on the cheese, Fran breezed in.

I could tell just from the sound of her footsteps in the corridor that she was smashed. All the excitement which had built up since the afternoon turned into irritation: it had been a unique day for me, and I didn't want it ruined now.

We all looked up as the kitchen door opened to reveal her standing there, stunning as ever, swaying as only a drunken teenager can sway. She was dressed, as usual, as though making a huge effort to disguise her own elegance. This was impossible, so the result was a sort of jumble-sale chic which I had always found intolerably affected. Her sweater was far too big, so that the sleeves obscured her slender hands. Her skirt was short but shapeless. Heavy, ethnic earrings were largely hidden by her blonde hair. Her climbing-boots were ostentatiously scruffy and masculine. All of it, I felt, had been specially chosen to get on my nerves.

Fran swayed silently for a moment, taking time off to

remember who the hell she was, no doubt, and then she said hello and giggled.

When we'd returned her greeting, there was an awkward pause. Fran giggled again.

'Come and sit down, love. Have you eaten?'

Ignoring her mother, Fran looked at me and her eyes seemed to snap into focus.

'Hello, *Daddy*. How are you, *Daddy*?'

It was the usual old thing. She knew I hated her coming home drunk and was determined to have a confrontation over it, to embarrass me in front of everyone. I decided to give her a taste of her own medicine.

'Very well, thank you, Fran. And how are you?' As I spoke, I noticed that tense edge which Fran always seemed to bring out in my voice, and was infuriated by it. 'You look as if you got through a lot of men tonight.'

'Claude!' moaned Helen, as though I'd punched her. This made me even angrier than before.

'Hope you remembered to put your knickers back on. I – '

'Claude! That's enough!'

The silence deepened, and I felt the beginnings of shame. This time I might have gone too far.

'Knickers?' said Fran, an edge to her own voice. 'Can't remember. Better just check.'

And with that she lifted up her little skirt.

Well, we all knew she was a tearway and almost insanely proud of her legs, but this broke new ground. The kitchen froze. Christopher's hand, holding a cracker, hung an inch from his lips. I felt a shame which made it impossible to speak. No matter how far I went, it seemed, my daughter would always go one further, and she would always win.

'Is there anything there?' said Fran, leaning forwards to try and see past her skirt and almost falling over. 'I can't see!'

To the relief of all present, the young lady was in fact wearing knickers, little white ones, as I shall never forget. However, they were very little indeed, so that some of her pubes had curled around the edges. The sight sickened me.

Just when it seemed that we would sit frozen in silent embarrassment all night, Ross came to the rescue.

'Oh, the grinding tedium of existence.'

I burst out laughing and Christopher bit into his cracker. Helen sat there, looking up at our daughter, her face full of concern. Fran herself just went on swaying, deflated and confused. Then she turned around and went upstairs.

There was never any doubt, in our family, about who took after who.

In those days I used to have my last cigarette and slug of whisky outside when the weather was fine. I would watch the traffic on the road beyond the drive and the black tops of the trees in Greenwich park swaying in their sleep.

At last the warmer evenings had arrived. When Ross and Christopher left, I went out and sat on the steps in front of the door for the first time that year. Helen had gone upstairs, presumably to mother Fran. I was beginning to have serious worries about her myself. Perhaps there was something else at work besides simple teenage rebellion.

It really was a fantastic night, mild, with ten million stars. One purple cloud slid sedately towards me, like some old hulk which had sailed too far and seen too much but just kept on drifting.

For ten minutes I sat there, forgetting Fran, forgetting even Gilbert's letters at times, happy. Eventually, I flicked my fag on to the drive, picked up my glass and went inside. As I closed the door, the trees whispered in the distance, a convocation of ghosts.

Upstairs, at the front of the house, there were two large rooms, of identical size and layout, with identical bay windows. The one on the left was our bedroom. As I reached the top of the stairs, I saw that there was no light coming from under the door, so I decided to spend a last few minutes in the other room, which housed my study.

Perhaps it could more accurately be called a library. The walls were lined with books, many of which had been bought from Dewson's before I'd taken it over. There was also, of course, a whole section on antiques. By the bay window was a large period armchair where, on Sunday mornings, I would sit and read for hours, breaking off occasionally to smoke a fag and enjoy the view of the park. It often seemed to me that what I'd worked for all those years was just that one room, with its quiet security, its air of learning, its perfect proportions, its green view.

Entering now, I went to the back of the room where, against the wall, was a glass display case. This had its own interior strip-light, which I now switched on. For some time I stood there in silence, staring at the familiar contents — a lock of hair, a small silver box, an illegible note on a scrap of paper, an old book open to show the scrawled signature on the flyleaf. Then I looked at the portrait above the cabinet: large chin tossed upwards, eyes liquid, perilously dark, ringlets thrown into confusion as though by a scornful wind.

At that moment, alone with the knowledge of my discovery, I felt that it had to be fate. Something had started happening between us.

Helen was asleep when I entered the bedroom. The light was off, but there was a gap in the curtains which admitted some of the silence from those perfect stars. My wife under her quilt was no more than a smudge of darkness, as vague and warm as the woman inside.

I quietly undressed and got into bed. She woke up and took me in her arms. As we began to make love, I felt the familiar pain. My caresses were driven by duty and guilt. All that day, as they did every other day, my eyes had followed the bodies of young girls. Now, in the dark, I remembered bending to pick up the box in the bookshop that afternoon and seeing Caroline's parted legs under the table.

Some time later, when my face screwed up and my body arched away from Helen's, Caroline stood behind the desk, staring at me, and lifted her skirt exactly as my daughter had done. That's a box, Mr Wooldridge. But what's this?

The cramp flowed from my body and I rolled clear, gasping like a man plunged into icy water. Helen rested her head on my shoulder.

'Hmm . . . that was lovely, Claude.'

'Yes.'

For a few moments there was silence. As my breathing stilled, I became aware of the silence of the black dome above the house, the impossible distances, the roaring stars.

'Claude . . . I'm really worried about Fran, you know.'

'Don't be silly.' Sometimes, I felt an irrational fury with my wife for having surrendered to middle age and fat. 'She'll grow out of it. She's just a wild kid.'

'I hope you're right.' There was a pause. I knew that Helen was wondering whether to risk another remark on the subject. In the end, she said gently, 'What do you think we should do to help her, though?'

'Helen, I'm tired. We'll talk about it in the morning, alright?'

'Alright, dear.'

She rolled away as gently as she could, trying not to disturb me, but she was so large that she couldn't help making the bed rock. At that moment, I remembered how Ross and I had made fun of her when she hadn't been in the room, laughing at her illogical fears. Helen herself would never have dreamed of mocking anyone. There wasn't enough malice in her. Nothing to her would have been worth the risk of causing pain.

'Helen?'

'Hmm?'

'I love you. I just want you to know that I love you,

really, and I always will love you. I could never have loved anyone so much.'

There was silence.

'You believe me, don't you?'

'Of course I do, Claude.'

Helen settled herself back down to sleep.

When I closed my eyes, the day rose through my mind. Freddie groping at the bright spring air. Vernon sighing after the motorcycle, some god of lightning and storms. That sounds like a crossword clue. All of us are cryptic. Perhaps he's trying to crack it now, working long into the night. All from the box in the bookshop, a bookshop box of books. Byron contacting me somehow. It must be more than chance. Fran lifting . . . the ghosts which congregate in Greenwich park. Trees turn black before the night has fallen. They seem to hold the night before the real blackness comes. With a sigh, they release it. The blue is gone from the sky.

Suddenly everything was light, and I realised that I was having my vision for the second time that day. It was clearer than before. I saw the young man writing at the window, but this time I could hear his quill scratching as he muttered over his work. He was wearing a loose white shirt. There was an empty glass on the table beside him. The shutters were open, so that the breeze seeped in, bearing the scent of stale canals. The candle fluttered, already redundant, pale in the light of the Venetian dawn thrown up from the water, clear and shimmering.

Suddenly, a strange thing happened: the picture acquired depth. I realised that I had the power to move into or away from it as I wished. I was free to walk towards the man at the desk and lean over his shoulder to see what he was writing.

My eyes snapped open. A few shapes were visible in the gloom. Suddenly I felt like a sleepless child, afraid of the eternal living dark. I heard my own voice like a stranger's.

'You do believe me, don't you, Helen? You know that I love you.'

'Hmm . . . ?' Perhaps she was only talking in her sleep. 'Yes, Claude. I know you love me in your way.'

4

THE FOLLOWING MORNING found me leaning against the French windows in the kitchen. It was another windy spring day. There was an edge to the light which left the colours naked. The garden was as luminous as an ancient painting from which layers of dirt had been removed. Each leaf and blade of grass swayed gently, in original brightness, a thousand drowsy signals on the breeze.

All of it seemed to demonstrate the absurdity of what I'd felt the previous night. Only drink and tiredness had led me to stand there in my study and believe that fate had led me to the letters. My three-dimensional 'vision' of the poet at his desk had been nothing but the phantasm of an overheated mind. More real than any of that were the two women lying upstairs, one of whom loved me too much, while the other was growing up to hate me.

The thought of what I had goaded Fran to do the night before caused me to sigh and light my third cigarette. I was still wearing my dressing-gown, and unshaven, with my grey hair, as it did each morning, doing its best to make me look like a mad inventor. In the kitchen behind me, the coffee percolator had started to chuckle.

As I stood there, I saw to my annoyance that next-door's black cat was on our lawn again. For once, however, it hadn't come to take a shit. It was stalking a sparrow which hopped in the shade of the bushes near the wall, unaware of its mortal danger. The cat took a step and froze so that it was the only motionless thing outside, one paw bent foppishly in the air. Its shadow fell a full yard across the dancing grass.

Putting my fag in my mouth, I opened the French windows and stepped out on to the patio.

'Fuck off, you horrid beast!' The cat's head snapped round, but the rest of its body stayed poised as before. It stared through wide, expressionless eyes, pretending not to recognise me, although this was by no means our first confrontation.

'Trespassers will be shot!'

There was no reaction. I was tempted to go and chase it off, but the grass was still beaded with dew, and I didn't want to get my feet wet. So I capered up and down the patio, waving my arms at my old adversary.

'Fuck off! Fuck off!'

This was so enjoyable that I started to do it more energetically. The cat watched, still standing on three legs. After a while, I found that I had started dancing a hornpipe up and down the paving-stones.

'Fuck *off*, fuck *off*, fuck *off*, fuck *off*, fuck off you horrid beast!' Reaching the end of the patio, I span round and took a deep breath. 'Fuck – '

'Good morning, Claude!'

I stopped in mid-step.

'Ah.'

The cat gave me a disdainful look and trotted calmly away. As I turned around, the breeze stood my hair on end. Helen was in the kitchen, smiling and shaking her head.

'Full of the joys of spring, I see. Or are you still excited about your letters?'

'The former,' I said, going back indoors. 'Well, maybe a bit of both. Coffee?'

Helen opened her arms.

'First things first.'

While we were hugging each other, Fran came noiselessly downstairs. Looking up, I saw her poised in the corridor, as still as the cat had been, staring at me over

Helen's shoulder. She was wearing a very short nightie, all black lace and frills, which I'd never seen before. There was recrimination in her eyes.

'I'll get that coffee.'

Fran unfroze and padded into the kitchen. Unlike Helen and myself, she managed to project a certain fuzzy elegance in the mornings. Glancing over my shoulder as I started to pour the coffee, I remembered the night before and decided that the nightie was a deliberate act of provocation. She was out to infuriate me again. This time, I was determined not to let her.

'That's new,' I said casually. Fran went to the cupboard and got out the Sugar Puffs, not deigning to answer. I gave Helen her coffee and we all sat down. 'Sorry, Fran, correct me if I'm wrong, but I could have sworn I just said something to you.'

'Roger gave it to me,' said Fran shortly.

'Who's Roger?'

'What's it to you?'

'Exactly. What right have I got to ask? I'm only your father, after all.'

'Now come on, you two,' said Helen with desperate cheerfulness. 'Don't row. Why don't we all just enjoy our breakfast?'

'It's impossible not to row with him, Mum. He only ever opens his mouth to get at me.'

'That's a bit rich. I only asked you who the bugger was and you jumped down my throat. You started it.'

'Claude,' moaned Helen. 'Don't be childish, now.'

'Pardon me, but she's the one who's being childish. I was only making polite conversation and – '

'Yes, she was being childish,' snapped my wife, 'but you're fifty-two and you ought to know better.'

'Ooh, pardon me! And what's bloody got into you this morning, might one ask?'

To the amazement of both Fran and myself, Helen cracked.

'I can't take you two at each other's throats any more. I can't take it, understand?' She picked up her coffee cup and hurled it into the corner, where it burst like a grenade. 'Understand?'

The coffee began to trickle in rivulets across the tiles. It was the only movement in the room.

'I understand your being sick of it, Helen,' I said softly. 'All the same, I won't have my teenage daughter kitted out like a tart by some man I've never even met.'

Helen's chin trembled.

'You just won't give up, will you, Claude? You always have to have the last word. You – ' Her eyes wandered towards the window and she leapt to her feet. 'Get away, you horrible creature! Shoo!'

With that, she rushed across the kitchen. Fran and I watched her in astonishment. She waddled out into the sunny garden, waving her arms in the air and screaming as though possessed, causing next-door's cat to flash over the fence like a bolt of black liquid. Her dressing-gown came apart as she ran. When she got to where the cat had been, she squatted down.

Leaving Fran to squint through the window, I went out to see what was going on. Helen was cradling something against her breast.

'What's happened?'

'It's dead,' said Helen flatly. She slightly opened her hands to reveal the floppy, broken body of the sparrow, feathers still fluttering. Its head lolled as though from complete exhaustion. It had left a pin-prick of blood on her nightie. She began to cry. 'Poor little thing!'

'It can't have felt much pain.'

'Do you really think so?'

The grief of people who are usually happy, people who feel love in its simplest form, is unbearable. To the rest of us, it's like the suffering of children.

'Leave it,' I said softly. 'It's only natural.'

I gently prised the tiny body from her hands. It was still

faintly and unpleasantly warm, like a telephone receiver someone else has just finished using. I laid it in the shade of the bushes. Then I put my arm around Helen's big shoulders and guided her back towards the house.

'What happened?' said Fran, looking up from the table.

'It was a sparrow,' I told her, 'killed by that bloody cat.'

'Oh.'

Helen leant heavily up against the worktop and tried to smile through her tears.

'I'm sorry. Silly me!' She wiped her eyes and sniffed. 'All that fuss over a little bird.'

As soon as she'd spoken, we understood that it had very little to do with the bird. Helen heaved a rather melodramatic sigh.

'I just wish we could live together peacefully and be happy.'

There was a silence, during which I clumsily rubbed her shoulder.

'Everybody wishes that,' said Fran, and quietly left the room.

When she was gone, I kissed my wife on the cheek.

'I love you.' In spite of myself, I was irritated with her, annoyed by her vulnerability, her strength of feeling, her very goodness. 'You're a better person than me.'

'No, no, Claude.' Her tears had stopped but she sounded desolate. 'You're a good man, in your way. But you're too hard on Fran. Can't you remember what it was like to be that age? Everything's just a mess for her. It's no good trying to push her around.'

'Maybe you're right.'

'Why don't you pop up and see her?'

'Oh God, here we go. Do I really have to?'

'Of course not. It's entirely up to you.' Arguing with Helen was like wrestling with a cloud. The frustration of it sometimes led me to the most amazing acts of savagery. 'I'd be happy if you made it up with her, of course,' my wife went on, 'but you do what you like.'

'Right. I think I'll have another cup of coffee and forget the whole thing.' While I started to make it, Helen watched me with her head on one side, big arms folded. Where there had so recently been tears, there was now a slight smile. I didn't even get as far as adding the milk. 'Oh, bloody hell.'

With great reluctance, I went upstairs and knocked on Fran's door.

The room was in its usual condition, with magazines, bras, make-up and cuddly toys busting out everywhere. Fran had changed into a white shirt and was doing up her school tie at the dressing-table. The clothes looked absurd on her now. She glanced over her shoulder when I went in, but said nothing.

Overcome by awkwardness, I sat on the edge of the bed, just as I had sat to read her stories as a child. I'd always looked forward to reading my children stories, but Christopher had let me down. Fiction had struck him as absurd. All he'd been interested in was planets, volcanoes and the stars. Fran, on the other hand, was encapsulated by tales of princes and magic, begging that I read her favourites over and over again. I think that one of the greatest pleasures I've ever known was that of stopping off on the way home from work to buy a new book for her.

She finished doing her tie and swivelled round on the dressing-table stool.

'I won't wear that nightie again. I mean, if you really don't like it . . .'

'Don't worry. I was just being silly.'

We shifted and fell silent. The spring light was behind her, a blonde aureole which seethed as she turned towards the window.

'Last night . . .' she began, and I lowered my head.

'It was my fault, Fran. I shouldn't have been so rude to you.'

As I spoke, I got up, and suddenly she was in my arms, hugging me with an astonishing fierceness. In the old times, after a day when the world had seemed against me, it had meant so much to see her before she went to bed. How I loved her then. She used to hug me each night with the greedy selfishness of children, who are unaware of any happiness they give.

As we stood there, I wondered if my paunch revolted her. Then I felt her breasts snuggling against me, rising and falling like a pair of warm, snoozing animals. Roger, or whatever his name was, would feel them just like that. I saw his head, dark and faceless, bending towards them. Suddenly I released her and stepped away.

Fran looked at me in surprise.

'It's difficult . . .' I said, then found myself unable to go on.

'I know it is. I understand.'

For a moment it seemed she might, though I could barely understand myself. The sun blazed through her white shirt, silhouetting her breasts. They looked smaller than they had felt and were shaped like teardrops. With a small nod, I moved stiffly to the door. When I'd opened it, I stopped.

Fran had turned towards the window. She was pulling on her school blazer, just as she had done in the days when there had been nothing but terror in the world beyond my arms.

How I loved her then.

Before I went to see how Vernon was getting on with the letters, I had a business engagement down in Kent.

Kent, of course, is not somewhere I would normally go except in case of dire necessity. What drew me down there that day, as it did on a regular basis, was the presence of Clive the crafty craftsman. Clive was one of my occasional employees. As far as my family knew, he was a restorer, but he was actually a bit more than that, which was why I liked to keep him at arm's length.

I got into my Range Rover and crunched down the drive.

These visits to the country were always a pleasant break from routine. After twenty minutes, I had begun to cheer up. I was going back into the simple world of business, where I knew my way around and was always in control.

There wasn't much traffic going out of London that morning and I belted along the sunny roads with the window down, squinting at the clean sky. The unfamiliar spring brightness made me feel as if I'd just removed a pair of sunglasses. I had a tape of *The Canterbury Tales* in the car and, since I was heading in that direction, I shoved it on. Shoals of clouds swam above me, impossibly serene. They were embodiments of the whiteness which teeth and paper echo, visitations from an absolute world, yet they looked almost close enough to touch. Cool lakes of shadow slid beneath. As I flashed through them, I began to feel that old Chaucer was speaking to me directly from the back seat in the gentler language of his age, resting his chin on his staff and staring sagely through the window.

Clive lived in one of those stagnant villages which so typify the Home Counties. At least, they look stagnant. In fact, they are hives of activity, what with people making jam, writing to the *Radio Times* about that word they heard last night, having perms and knifing each other in the back. Clive's own gaff, with its leaded windows and wall-roses, was nauseatingly typical.

The man who opened the door was a rangy, grey-haired type in overalls, with a dead roll-up grafted to his lower lip. You wouldn't have thought it to look at him, but he was a goldmine, one of a dying breed. There were very few craftsmen left in the country who could actually build antiques from scratch. All most of them could manage was to make an existing piece look older than it really was.

'Morning, Crafty,' I said. 'All ready for me, is it?'

'I think so, Mr W,' said Clive, causing his roll-up to wag admonishingly. 'About as good as I can get it, any rate.'

'Show me, show me quick, before I come in my pants.'

Kent had always brought out the worst in me.

Clive led me through the house to the large workshop in the back garden. When we got there he opened the door with the calm modesty of a master. Inside, besides his carpenter's tools, were the raw materials of Crafty's trade: piles of timber in various stages of treatment, endless boxes which contained handles, hinges and locks for all the major periods. In one corner a large object covered by a dust sheet towered like a pantomime ghost. Walking with ritual slowness, Clive crossed the room and jerked the covering so that it fell among the woodchips and sawdust on the floor.

'There she is.'

It took my breath away. It was a George III mahogany tallboy with the full works: detailed cornice, ogee bracket feet, fluted angles. To find such a fine example, which hadn't been separated to make a chest of drawers, was a stroke of luck, to say the least.

'Crafty!' I said admiringly. 'You have excelled yourself!' For some time I moved round, examining the thing from all angles, awestruck by the talent of the man. 'Yes, yes, this is your masterpiece.'

'Very kind, Mr W.'

I hadn't been exaggerating, either. That tallboy was the finest of all Clive's 'reproductions'. To start off with, as I say, he had built the thing from scratch, which put him on a par with the honest Georgian carpenters who'd made them in the first place. But then he'd had to start being dishonest, and this put him in a different league.

First of all, he'd yanked the drawers in and out thousands of times to mimic a couple of centuries' wear. Then he'd left the tallboy out in the garden for a month. Having ruined it, he'd taken it back in and restored it. Then – and this was a real inspiration – he'd removed the original handles and replaced them with early Victorian ones, slightly heavier and more ornate. Even the sharpest dealer would be taken in by that. He'd spot that the handles weren't original, feel very clever, and unscrew them to have a look. Underneath he would find the lighter patches the Georgian handles had left during their time in Clive's garden. The verdict? Original, of course, had to be. Very fine piece.

If you believe you've got an original, it's as good as having one, that's what I say.

'Crafty, you're a genius. How much?'

'Well, things have been a bit tight recently, Mr W. I was hoping for seven fifty.'

'Come, come, Clive, be serious. Consider my margins. My overheads have rocketed this year. If I pay seven fifty, the profit won't cover my petrol down here. Call it five hundred.'

The fool accepted. Good with his hands, bad with his brain, that was Clive.

Gasping and groaning, we loaded the tallboy into the Range Rover and I went back to Greenwich. Christopher was alone in the shop when I arrived, polishing a rather nice William and Mary breakfast table. The vagueness of his movements gave the impression that he'd been doing the same small area all morning while internally wrestling with something knotty and metaphysical. The sound of the door caused him to jolt upright, almost upsetting five hundred quid's worth of telescope.

Christopher, of course, knew that it was impossible to make money in antiques without selling the occasional fake. What he didn't know yet was that I actually employed a man to make them. I hadn't told him because I wasn't sure how he'd respond to such cold-blooded deception. However, he had a head on his shoulders, and it was only a matter of time before he began to wonder how I came up with such gems month after month.

'Morning, Christopher. Any movement?'

This was a bit too elliptical for my son. He pursed his thin lips and thought deeply for a few seconds about what I had said and the other mysteries of existence. His Adam's apple jumped up and down like a frantic castaway. At last he got it.

'Well, I did sell those chairs this morning.'

'What, not the Regency ones?' They'd been the most expensive thing in the shop and almost certainly genuine. 'The rosewood jobs?'

'Yes.'

'Bloody hell! What did you get for them in the end?'

'Two thousand and fifty.'

'Nice one, son.' It was shaping up to be a good day. For a moment I stood there, savouring the smell of furniture polish and Brasso which always reminded me of my youth. 'Very nice indeed. I've got a new article outside. Want to give me a hand in with it?'

We lugged Clive's wooden lie into the shop.

'This is a good piece, I think,' puffed Christopher when we'd put it down. 'Where did you get it?'

'Auction out in Essex. Had to pay through the nose for it, but I think we'll make something back.'

'Oh,' he said, stooping to examine it. 'These handles are a bit late, aren't they?'

'Probably been changed. They often were.'

'Hmm . . .' said Christopher dubiously, proving once again that he'd inherited his mother's intuition. 'I'm not so sure . . .'

'Well, try it on anyway and see if we get any takers.'

'What shall I price it up at?'

There is a simple technique for these calculations. Think of a fair price. Triple it. Add fifteen per cent for the VAT, in case you decide to pay it. Add another twenty per cent for the crass ignorance of the populace and bingo!

'Two and a half grand.'

'Sounds fair.'

'Does it? I must be slipping. Make it two seven fifty.'

Remembering that I'd paid only five hundred, you may feel this was a bit steep. How much did you expect me to pay? The bloody thing was a fake, for God's sake.

'Right.' I moved rapidly towards the door. 'That's enough hard graft for one morning. I'm off to see how Vernon's getting on with that little decoding job.'

On the drive up to the shop, the excitement of the previous day took hold of me again. Even before they'd given up all their secrets, the Byron letters were the most dramatic find I'd ever made. The coded sections might reveal something entirely new about the poet's life, a new affair, for example, which would astound the literary world.

It took ages, as usual, to find a parking space near the shop. As the Ranger Rover, all hot rubber and metal, crawled through the spring streets, I had already begun to fantasize. The cryptic paragraphs would change our view not only of Byron, but of the entire romantic movement. Vernon and I would have our photographs on the front of all the Sunday reviews, be asked again and again to repeat the story of our amazing find. The letters themselves would be worth a fortune, but I would never allow them to move from their rightful place in my display cabinet at home.

By the time I'd parked, I had half convinced myself that Vernon would have already cracked the code. I walked rapidly towards Dewson's, almost running the last few yards, and burst breathless through the door.

There was only one customer, an American with a brash jacket and an outrageously phallic camera, feet planted apart in the carpet while Caroline climbed the library-steps. She was wearing the short skirt of the day before and, even with so much else to think about, my eyes lingered a moment on her pale thighs.

Vernon was sitting at the back of the shop, bent over

a confusion of papers on the desk. Hearing the brass bell, he raised his head and looked towards me. His eyes were empty.

'Ah, yes! Here it is!' Caroline began to clamber gawkily down the steps, clutching a large volume with an embossed gold spine. 'I think you'll find it's in very good condition, sir.'

'Come upstairs, Vernon,' I said, moving past the American, aware of Byron's marble stare, 'and tell me how things are going.'

The old man nodded and began to lever himself up. Reaching the desk, I looked down and saw the small pile of Gilbert's letters surrounded by sheets torn from a modern pad, startlingly white in comparison. These were covered in a neat, bookkeeper's hand, and I noticed that there were as many numbers and sums as there were words and sentences.

'We might as well take all this up, too,' I said, beginning to collect the papers. 'The office is a quieter place to work.'

'Thank you.' As he paced towards the stairs, Vernon cast a disapproving look at our only customer. 'It has been rather distracting down here.'

Holding the papers in one hand, I took his elbow in the other and helped him up the first step. His knee creaked, not just audibly, but almost melodramatically, like a door in a horror film. I guessed that before long the old man would be confined to a wheelchair.

'Any joy, then, Vernon?'

'Very little, Claude.' Only when I heard him use my first name did I remember the new warmth which the letters had brought to our partnership. 'Code-breaking can take time.'

We continued in silence, because I felt suddenly awkward with him. It seemed to me that our old relationship, with its barely suppressed bitterness and rivalry, had been somehow easier to live with. What he had said the previous day was true: we had very little in common. We came from different generations, different worlds.

The office was sunny and quiet. The ancient piles of books stood as they had always done, structures apparently as timeless and cryptic as Stonehenge: all the sophistication of European culture reduced to a collection of primitive totems. Byron posed in the frozen wind of the beach. Dubious Dave's books were still spread out on the desk as we had left them, along with the bottle and glasses.

We negotiated the room at Vernon's crawling pace and sat as we had the day before, facing each other across the desk, me with my back to the window so that the spring sun warmed me like a shirt hot from the iron.

'Vernon, I'd like you to feel free to come up here whenever you want from now on.' The old man gave a peculiar little bow across the desk. 'I know it means a lot to you, but to me the legal ownership of this shop is unimportant. All I care about is making it profitable. Look on it as ours.'

'That's very kind of you, Claude.'

'Right. Now tell me about these letters.'

Without answering, Vernon spread his papers out on the bright desk, squinting down at them. As often happened, I began to feel he'd forgotten what I'd said. Just as I was about to repeat it, he spoke.

'The code, as far as I can see, is somehow numerical,' he said, without looking up from the papers. 'However, it seems almost impossible to crack. I was at it till the small hours last night and I started again early this morning and I've made no progress at all. I've looked at it from every conceivable angle, yet all that comes out is gibberish.'

'Surely it's only a matter of time, though?'

He raised his eyes, gazing at me severely over his glasses.

'Claude, has it yet occurred to you that this might all be some kind of prank?'

'How do you mean?'

'Think about it. Here we have purported Regency letters containing long sections of code which make them virtually unique. There are three possible explanations for that. The first is that the code is genuine, in which case Gilbert had something which he needed to write but wanted to keep very secret. The second is that he inserted the coded sections as some sort of a joke.'

'Hardly likely though, is it?'

'Now is the first explanation, in my opinion. After all, what could this Amelia have needed to know that was so explosive?'

'Hmm . . . what's the third possibility?'

'I would have thought it was obvious. The letters are forged.'

'Ridiculous. There'd be no motive. The only reason one forges something is surely for some kind of financial gain.'

'Indeed, indeed,' muttered Vernon, bending back towards the faded papers. 'It just seems to me that all the explanations are unlikely. Every time I look at these blessed symbols I can't help feeling that somebody's pulling my leg.'

'You'll keep at it, though?'

I needn't have asked. By the time I'd finished speaking, he was frowning at his pad again, scribbling, lost to the world.

'Eh . . . ? Oh, yes, I'll . . . keep . . . ah . . .'

Vernon left the sentence hanging. This time, however, he didn't finish it. Five minutes later, he had stopped writing and was staring at his work, obviously unaware of my existence.

The air of concentration with which he filled the room was such that I was almost afraid to breathe. Vernon's thoughts seemed to swirl over the silence like rainbows over a film of soap. Any noise would destroy them. My chair had belonged to his father. It was an old leather one which swivelled on a wooden pedestal, and the slightest movement tended to make it squeak and groan, so I sat there, perfectly still, and wondered what to do next.

In truth, I was approaching a time in my life where there wasn't really much left to do. My main office in Greenwich, which dealt with paying wages, chasing up the rents from my various properties and so on, virtually ran itself, with a little help from Christopher. The antiques side was entirely in his hands: my own little trips to auctions, to house clearances, to Crafty Clive, were matters of amusement, not necessity. What with Helen doing the sandwich bar, I seemed to have delegated myself out of a job.

Taking over Dewson's had been less of a business venture than a search for something to do, yet, a mere two months after my moving in, the place was already completely renovated, up and running. Vernon and Caroline had no need of my presence.

Sitting there, motionless in my creaky chair whilst Vernon pored over the letters, the awareness suddenly struck me, as it must strike us all sooner or later: my career was winding down. Yet this realisation was confused by my excitement over the letters, which vividly recalled my youth and the early deals that had started everything moving.

Vernon was writing again, as though suddenly inspired. Leaning a little across the desk, I found to my surprise that he was engaged in a complicated long-division. What this had to do with cracking a code was anybody's guess. As I watched he shook his head and scored a neat line through the entire calculation.

Twisting my wedding-ring, agitated by not being able to help, I looked around the room. Everything – the strong-box, the print of Shelley's cremation, the solemn piles of books, the sunlight gleaming off Vernon's watch-chain – had taken on the frozen quality of a still-life.

My mind wandered. I saw Caroline's legs under the desk. I saw Fran, only yesterday a little girl, raising her skirt – why? – to prove her womanhood. I saw Helen, waddling into the garden, waving her arms above her head. My career is coming to an end. Ross, charging into my university room without knocking, then stopping suddenly and rubbing his beard. Listen to this. What did he want to read me? Some poem he had found.

In my early twenties, I had visited an old woman in Clapham who had antiques to sell. None of them were of much value – a lot of late Victorian stuff which had been altered and mucked around with. To her, however, they were priceless, which made it difficult to reach an accommodation. While we were haggling over the contents of her spare bedroom, I noticed that she had hidden something away behind the wardrobe, as though ashamed of it: a pale Chinese screen. With my heart in my mouth, I casually asked to have a look. It was just a bit of old junk, she said, and as far as she was concerned I could take it away for free. In the end, out of the goodness of my heart, I forced her to accept thirty quid.

The screen made the cover of Christie's catalogue that month. It fetched twenty-five thousand in the sale and allowed me to move into property.

A pang from my stomach brought me back to earth. I found I was still fiddling with my ring, restless with the same thrill which had addicted me so many years before. Yet it was leading nowhere now; I was feeling it for the last time. Suddenly, I felt an obscure desire to escape. A part of me wanted to sell everything I owned and leave, go abroad, away from the career which was finished, the passionless marriage, the children who had outgrown my love.

I stood up and went to the window. The sun embraced me. Freddie was on the pavement below, supporting himself on the bin and staring down into its depths as though waiting to vomit. The restlessness still grew in me, the sense of a great change on the way.

'Vernon.' There was a catch in my voice, but Vernon didn't hear it. He barely glanced up from his work. 'There's

65

nothing I can do here. I'm going out. If you make any progress, try ringing me at home.'

'Very well.' He had already started again, writing rapidly. 'I'll do that, Claude.'

I strode out of the room and down the creaking stairs. There were no customers in the shop. The American had gone. Hearing my footsteps, Caroline looked up from her book.

'Mr Wooldridge?'

'Hmm?'

'What's going on? What's all the excitement about? Vernon wouldn't tell me.'

'I'll explain later,' I said, hurrying past her, though I had no idea of where I was going. 'Can't stop now.'

The sun seemed cooler outside. In front of the British Museum, I turned left and headed in the direction of Soho. Then the idea leapt into my mind. I slowed my pace, wondering at myself, but I didn't stop. I just seemed to float on, drawn like a mote of dust on the current of the street. A detached part of me was fascinated to see how far I would actually go. After wandering the red-light district for a while, I stopped and read a sign in an open doorway.

EIGHTEEN YEAR OLD MODEL. WALK UP.

Lifting my head, I saw four flyblown windows with grey net-curtains. Above it all, the same clouds still glided, a dream of whiteness, impossibly serene.

Suddenly I found myself climbing the stairs, and I realised that the decision had actually been taken back in the shop, or perhaps even earlier. I felt no anticipation. There was none of that craving for young flesh which had dogged me for most of my married life. Twenty-five years of fidelity and sacrifice came to an end quietly, in sorrow.

66

5

WHEN I OPENED the front door that evening, home from my first betrayal, Helen was cooking supper. The aroma of food had already invaded every recess of the house. In the kitchen, my wife was moving from cupboard to hob in a print dress like a tent. Seeing me, she came over, gesturing at a few loose wisps of hair. The sight of her filled me with the insufferable nostalgia which, in a relationship like ours, often stands in the place of love.

'Hello, dear.' For a moment she looked at me, obviously seeing that there was something wrong. This time, however, her intuition failed her. Helen must have had a kind of blind spot when it came to infidelity. Perhaps her gift didn't function where it would have caused her pain. She completely misread me. 'No progress with the letters, then.'

I shook my head. It suddenly occurred to me that the girl might somehow have left her smell on my clothes and body, so I quickly sat down at the table before Helen could come any closer. As soon as I'd done it, I realised that this deviation from our nightly routine would be more suspicious than any smell.

But Helen didn't seem to notice or to mind. She simply went back to her cooking. To me she had never before seemed so innocent and weak. For some time she stood with her back to me, while I sat there and wondered what madness had come over me that afternoon.

'Claude!' Helen suddenly turned from the cooker, as

though she'd just noticed something. 'Whatever's the matter with you?'

'Eh? How do you mean?'

'You haven't got yourself a drink!'

For a moment I stared into her beaming face, tinted like a carol-singer's in the heat.

'No. I don't feel like one.'

'My God, things must be bad!'

Unable to answer, I looked past her, out through the French windows, overcome by the sense of futility which follows sex. Darkness was descending on the garden. Above the roofs, through mournful bars of cloud, the daylight shrivelled and dissolved. Across the immeasurable complex of streets and throughout the darker countryside beyond, the lights were coming on. It was like some ritual, elegant and profound, a gigantic signal no one would ever understand. A plane inched across the darkness, lights flashing as though to monitor the beating of a hidden heart.

'This is for you.' Helen was standing by the table, holding a small package out to me. 'To say thank you for this morning.'

'What?' I said blankly. 'What happened this morning?'

'I don't know. All I know is that you went up to Fran's room and she was in a really good mood when she got home. I haven't seen her so happy for ages.'

'It was nothing.'

Helen smiled warmly and gave me a peck on the forehead.

'I know you, Claude. I know what it costs you to apologise.'

In silence, I opened the package. Inside was a velvet box containing a pair of hideous gold and black cufflinks. Helen looked down at me apprehensively.

'Well?'

'They're lovely.'

'Do you really like them?' She sounded uncertain. 'I thought they were quite unusual.'

'Yes.' Helen loved to buy me clothes, but she always got it wrong. She had no understanding of vanity or style. Forgetting everything, I got up and took her in my arms. 'They're lovely, Helen. Really lovely.'

I could have wept.

'Good.'

'Where is Fran, in any case?'

'In her bedroom.' Helen stepped back and gave me a significant look. 'Doing some revision.'

'Oh.'

'Well, aren't you pleased? She's actually doing some work!'

'Of course I am,' I said, managing a smile. 'Very pleased.'

Under other circumstances, it would have been a perfect evening. Helen and I exchanged the usual pleasantries about how work had been. After an hour or so, Fran came down, smiling, and actually kissed me on the cheek. Ross and Christopher turned up around supper time. Even Ross seemed in a good mood that night, drinking all through the meal, his dark eyes gleaming from their recesses as he poured out stories and jokes. In his happy moments he was the most entertaining person I knew.

All of them were talkative and cheerful. My own silence almost vanished in the noise. Only once did Fran lean towards me, her clean beauty lit from below by one of the candles Helen had laid out, and say,

'What's the matter, Dad? You seem a bit down.'

'Nothing. I'm just tired.'

When we went to bed that night, I didn't want my wife. She cuddled up to me and, sensing my lack of desire, went contentedly to sleep with her head on my shoulder. I lay there for hours, hardly moving, afraid to wake her. In the end, I lost all sensation in my arm, but still I didn't move. Never in all the years of our marriage had I felt so alone. I was almost grateful for the warmth in my stomach, a kind of company, a small part of the payment I deserved.

* * *

69

The following dawn found me at my usual post, leaning against the French windows and watching the light harden. The night melted across the lawn until it remained only in isolated patches under the trees and bushes. All the while, I smoked and watched, thinking.

Something had broken in me the day before and only now that it had snapped did I realise the strain it had been under all those years. Fidelity must always be a strain. The girl I'd found up the stairs had been succulent and cheap. After so long with the bruised-fruit softness of my wife, I had forgotten how firm young flesh could be.

All the same, there had been no real desire. Her youth had only served to emphasise my age. Now, as I stood there, smoking and staring out at the garden, I saw the extent to which the girl had merely been a symbol, a coded message about my life.

In due course, Fran and Helen came down for breakfast. They chatted at the table, but I was silent, watching them. It felt like watching a television documentary. Now I could see quite clearly that Fran was almost grown-up. Perhaps that had its part to play, as well. Children have their function. They give a kind of meaning to our lives. My wife herself was a cheerful, overweight woman, her fine hair greying. Watching her, I felt a certain guilt about the day before, but it was distant, something relayed from a stranger's life. My action hadn't hurt her.

My wife and daughter ignored my silence, taking this for one of my normal moods. When she'd eaten, Fran disappeared upstairs. I left the table, went back to the window, and lit another cigarette.

'Aren't you going to get dressed, love?'

'No. Why should I? I've no reason to go out.'

Helen was surprised by this.

'You're not going up to the bookshop?'

'The bookshop can run itself. It's all in order now.'

'What about the letters, though? Vernon might have decoded them.'

'He'll ring me if he does.'

A moment later, I felt her hand on my shoulder.

'What's the matter, Claude?' she said gently. 'I know you haven't been sleeping.'

'I'm feeling old, Helen. Getting so worked up about this Byron thing has proved it to me. You know, this is the sort of buzz I used to get out of making twenty quid on a wardrobe. Now it takes something this enormous. I can't help feeling it's the last find. After this, I won't have the drive to carry on.' I smiled, feeling a fool, but needing to tell someone. 'I've passed the baton on to Christopher. I'm useless now.'

'Of course you're not, my love. Perhaps you should start a new business, branch out or something.'

'I'm sick of business, that's the whole point. It's too easy. Any fool can make money.'

Helen laughed.

'You realise that this is the position you always said you wanted to be in, with enough wealth to retire in luxury.'

'Having money and nothing to do is only any good if you're young. To me it feels like death. I'm afraid of the emptiness.' A cloud passed across the sun. The air in the garden shrank. 'My father . . .'

Without looking round, I knew that Helen had gone still behind me.

'Put that right out of your mind, Claude. It's the last thing you should be brooding on now.'

I looked up at the cloud, which was drifting away from the sun so that the brilliance exploded in white turmoil around the edges.

'I've been running all my life.'

'Bye Mum! Bye Dad!'

We said goodbye to Fran, who had paused at the front door in her school uniform. As the door closed, a terrifying sadness swept over me.

'How I love that girl.'

'I know you do, Claude. That's exactly why you mustn't

let yourself get all miserable. It's an important time for her.'

I said nothing and for a moment Helen stood there with her hand on my shoulder. Then she went upstairs to get dressed.

All morning, I wandered around the house. I was too depressed to read or listen to music. There was nothing to do but move from room to room. Perhaps because of my inactivity, my stomach-ache seemed worse. I half-heartedly resolved to go and see a doctor if it hadn't improved within a week.

At about two o'clock, the cleaning lady arrived. To avoid her, I decided to take a stroll in the garden. There, under the bush where I had left it the day before, I saw the body of the sparrow, its feathers blasted. Somehow it seemed wrong just to leave it for the gardener to find. I went to the toolshed, got a trowel, and buried the corpse in the soft soil of one of the flowerbeds, being careful not to touch it.

As I stood upright, I wondered why I had bothered. The breeze had stiffened by then and the sky had curdled. I felt something like the grief of a real funeral. My eyes closed and my mind went back to the Christmas vacation of my last year at Oxford. That morning I was awoken by a scream. My mother was standing white and rigid on the landing outside my room, my father hanging from the banisters by the cord of his dressing-gown.

Twelfth night had not yet arrived and there was still tinsel all around the banisters. In his last clumsy moments, Dad had managed to dislodge some of it, which now lay draped mockingly around his shoulders. It made even his gargoyle's face, fat tongue and bulging eyes, look absurd. The corpse was absolutely and unnaturally still. You felt that the slightest draught Would have been enough to set it slowly turning on its cord, just like the paper Santas and snowmen on the Christmas tree when you opened the living-room door.

The phone was in the hall downstairs, on a round inlaid Victorian table directly below my father. His feet, suspended just above eye-level, were as pale and translucent as a waxwork's. It was early and the house was cold. The bakelite seemed to freeze against my ear. As I dialled, I was vaguely afraid that the cord would come loose and drop the dead weight on my head. But it stayed completely motionless, in eternal silence, the corpse of a bankrupt and a coward.

I returned the trowel to the toolshed and began to walk slowly back towards the house.

Halfway there I heard, coming and going on the buffets of spring air, the sound of the telephone.

There was a portable phone on the worktop in the kitchen. I pulled the aerial up, drifting back in the direction of the garden as I answered.

'Hello?'

'Claude? Vernon.'

My heart jumped.

'Ah. Good afternoon, Vernon.' As I spoke, the time of day came home to me: it was getting on for three, and there I was, wandering around the windy garden in my dressing-gown. 'What news?'

'I've cracked it.'

'Christ. What does it say?'

'Well, I've only decoded the first letter so far.'

'And?'

There was a noise which might have been interference on the line or one of Vernon's gentle coughs.

'I think you'd better brace yourself for a disappointment.'

'Surprise, surprise.'

'The first thing you should know is that, as I predicted, the code is indeed numerical and astonishingly elaborate. Unfortunately this means that it does not convey much information per page, since each letter is represented by a separate calculation. The clusters of symbols which one at first sight takes for words in fact stand for individual letters. Thus a page of Gilbert's code boils down to a short paragraph of normal writing.'

'He went to a lot of trouble, then.'

'An incredible amount.'

'To hide what?'

'Judging from the first letter, nothing of much substance. It's a love letter, Claude, pure and simple.'

'Oh.' I stopped in the middle of the lawn and stared up at the sky. It looked as though we were in for a spring storm. 'You think that's bad news, then?'

'Not good, certainly. I was hoping for something which would make secrecy essential and so go some way towards proving the letters genuine. Love alone doesn't do that. What interests me now is to decode the Byron letters. You're coming up to the shop today?'

'Within the hour. I'll bring them with me.'

I pushed down the aerial like an admiral closing his telescope and stared for a moment at the dark clouds massing on the horizon, a range of mountains on the move. Then I almost ran into the house, letting my slippers slip off as I went and leaving them on the lawn.

In the bedroom, I thought for a moment and decided that it was too late to pretend this was a working day. Perhaps my working days were over. So I dressed in casual clothes: loose corduroys, open shirt, suede loafers and a short anorak. Then I went into the study, lifted the glass top of the display case, and took out the two Byron letters.

As my fingers touched the paper, I felt a powerful intuition, though I couldn't have expressed it in words. It was just a feeling that their secret was in some way connected with myself: my crime of the day before, Helen and Fran, the anxiety of a man with nowhere left to run, all would be decoded.

While I was driving up to town, the clouds moved

in, darkening the world as noticeably as curtains darken a bedroom. Car sidelights lent a forlorn gleam to the afternoon. When I arrived at Dewson's, I decided not to bother looking for a meter. I parked the Range Rover on the pavement outside, glancing around the gloomy street to check for wardens, and went straight in.

There were a couple of browsers in the shop, which would once have pleased me. Caroline, though evidently surprised to see me in my weekend clothes, refrained from making any comment.

Upstairs in the office Vernon was still stooped over the desk in the weak light from the window; he seemed to have moved as little as Byron on his timeless beach. When I lowered myself into the creaky seat opposite him, he glanced up, his face an impassive mask.

'Claude. Good afternoon.' The old man allowed himself a small smile. 'I've rather been looking forward to explaining this to someone.'

'Fire away, then,' I said, leaning forward.

From a neat stack of papers, Vernon produced a new white sheet and turned it to face me.

'I made copies of all the coded sections. This is the one from the first letter. Each of these symbols represents a number. This rising arrow, for example, is a two, this half-moon a five. All ten digits are represented. You are perhaps familiar with the most basic code of all, which simply allocates each letter of the alphabet a numerical value: 'a' is one, 'b' two and so on. Well, Gilbert's code is a far more elaborate version of that.'

Vernon paused dramatically, pushing his glasses up his nose with his pencil, obviously pleased as punch at having outsmarted our Regency friend.

'Of course, each number does in fact correspond to a letter. However, to find out what each number is you first have to do a calculation. Besides the digits, we also have coded symbols which mean subtract, add, multiply and divide. So, for example, this cluster here reads 'two plus seven minus four' giving the answer five. Clear?'

'Perfectly.'

'You would have thought, then, that this cluster stood for the letter 'e', the fifth letter of the alphabet. Logical enough?'

'Indeed it is.'

'That's what I thought, too. But no matter what values I gave the symbols, I couldn't make it work. All that came out was gibberish. That was why, when you saw me yesterday, I was starting to think the whole thing had to be a practical joke. Then, this morning, quite out of the blue, it suddenly struck me.'

Once more he paused, staring at me across the desk. Never in all our acquaintance had I seen such a look on his face, elated and alive, the watery eyes glittering.

'What did?'

'Each letter to Amelia contains a hidden numerical key, usually in the paragraph before Gilbert starts using the code. For example, in this first letter, as you remember, he is describing how he went to bed, blowing out the candle, looking at the stars above Paris and so on. He gives the time as midnight, so twelve is the key to the section of code which follows. All you have to do is add twelve to the result of each calculation and the whole thing comes out making perfect sense.'

'Vernon, you're amazing,' I said, staring down at the baffling scrawl and wondering how I would ever have made a start on trying to decipher it. 'And I was impressed that you could do *The Times* crossword!'

'Don't you want to know what it says?'

'Of course.'

'I've clipped a translation to each of the original letters.' He shuffled through his papers for a moment, avoiding my eye. 'Here is the one we've just been looking at.'

Still refusing to meet my eye, he handed me the page of code from Gilbert's first letter. Neatly clipped to the top was a white slip with the decoded message. After the elaborate Regency English of the letters themselves, the secret words had a strange starkness.

FIRST NIGHT WITHOUT YOU TO DO IT AS YOU ALWAYS DO SO I THOUGHT OF YOU TILL SOLDIER STOOD AND MADE HIM DANCE MYSELF

I unclipped the sheet to look at the original from which it had been translated, and saw that Vernon had been right. Those few words took up about twenty lines of Gilbert's symbols. He had gone to incredible lengths to keep his obscene little message a secret. Once more I noticed the controlled violence of the calligraphy, the neat slashes of the quill across the page. Then, as it had done on my first discovery of the letters, the sheer sense of the man overwhelmed me: Gilbert, that sneering, cultured aristocrat, taking such trouble to secrete in the midst of his elegant prose those little smudges of smut.

'Claude? What do you think?'

Though their secret was trivial, the symbols now struck me as more occult and sinister than before. I remembered how Helen had taken one look and refused to be near them.

'Claude?'

Still with a faint disgust, I put the letter down on the table and pushed it away.

'There's something very unpleasant about it.'

'Our friend Gilbert was hardly a great romantic, I'll admit.'

'It's not just that. There's something really, deeply nasty about him. Can't you feel it? Horrible.'

'You think it's all real, then?'

'I'm sure of it, Vernon. I don't know why he did it, but I'm convinced that in 1817 a man called Gilbert wrote coded letters from the Continent to a woman in England. Perhaps they didn't need any ulterior motive. Perhaps the code itself gave them both some kind of kinky thrill. What are the other messages like?'

'They're all in a similar vein: baby talk with a very adult meaning. This is actually one of the milder examples. Would you like to see some of the others?'

'I'd rather not, thanks. Why don't we just get on with the Byron letters?'

Vernon smiled, pulling his chair closer to the desk.

'Why not, indeed?'

I took the letters from my pocket and pushed them across the table to him. The dark clouds were now directly overhead; Vernon switched on the Anglepoise and shone it down on to the page before he began.

'The first thing to do,' he said, scanning Gilbert's account of the opera, 'is to find the key number. While I'm looking, would you mind writing out the letters of the alphabet?'

Glad of something to do, I ripped a sheet from his pad and began. As I got towards the end, Vernon said, 'Aha! That's the boy! Listen. '*We must have gazed at each other a full five seconds, during which an understanding passed between us.*' Then he breaks into code. The key is five, then, Claude. Could you now write five under the letter 'a', six under 'b' and so on?'

As I wrote the numbers, I realised that it was the first time we'd really worked together. To my surprise, I, the richer and more successful man, felt honoured by this, like a first-year befriended by a perfect. Dealing with codes, poets and old documents, we were very much on Vernon's home ground. There was about him that air of confidence and command which I was more used to carrying myself.

When I'd finished my little job, I glanced up at him. He'd pulled the cone of the Anglepoise right down so that it was no more than six inches above the ancient paper. As he lowered his head, two bright images of the desk below were visible in his glasses. Leaning above that harshly-focused light, he had the precise calm of a dentist or a surgeon.

'Ready? Good.' From his papers he produced a list

of Gilbert's symbols and the digits to which they corresponded. 'I'll do the sums and tell you the results. You write down the letters and we'll be done in no time. The first is . . . twenty-eight.'

After that, he decoded the sums and worked out the answers so quickly that I barely had time to produce one letter before he'd fired off the next number. The key was obviously only for reference: Vernon had already memorised the meaning of each symbol. Working at that speed, it was impossible to make any sense of what I was writing.

WEWERETWOAPARTASITMUSTALWAYSBE

'Read it back to me, then,' said Vernon when we'd finished.

'WE . . . WERE . . . TWO . . . APART . . . AS . . . IT . . . MUST . . . ALWAYS . . . BE. Is that it?'

'Hmm. I'm afraid that's all the code in the opera letter. Two apart. I wonder why he said that?'

'Two aristocrats, perhaps? Two men of genius? What's more puzzling is why he felt he needed to put the sentence in code. It seems innocuous enough to me.'

'Indeed, indeed.' Vernon gave a dry sigh. 'It's the first coded message with no sexual content. That in itself is remarkable. It's like a code within a code.' He looked across the the desk at me, his old face, suffused in the glow which rose from the brightly lit papers, suddenly resembling a skull. 'Do you still think all this rings true?'

For a moment I considered, feeling the stillness of the gathering dark outside.

'Yes. I think it does.'

'Very well, then,' said Vernon in a soft voice which was nevertheless full of a sense of occasion. 'Let us proceed to the second of the Byron letters.' He picked it up and began skimming through it. 'This sentence must be the key. *The reason for his ill humour was a low Neapolitan woman with whom he had a three-day liaison.* Same procedure as before, then, Claude, this time with the number three.'

I scribbled out the numbers, half-listening for the first

clap of thunder. The weight of the air had grown until it seemed certain to buckle at any moment. Even the sound of traffic was muted, as though, like birdsong, it fell silent before a storm.

The second Byron letter took far longer to decode. We soon fell into a rhythm, Vernon calling out the next number just as I'd finished looking up the last. There was no sound other than that of his soft voice and the occasional rustle of paper. The mechanical process of looking up the numbers and writing the letters made me lose all sense of time. It seemed we were there for ages, yet, when the voice at last fell silent, I had the confusing impression that we'd only just begun.

Looking back at my work, however, I found that I'd produced long lines of block capitals.

'So,' said Vernon, leaning away from the brightness of the camp, 'what does it say?'

'NOTHING ... IS ... CERTAIN ... BUT ... OUR ... LOVE.'

'Hmm. Most unlike Gilbert. I have a feeling he's going to wax lyrical in a minute.'

'Yes. That's what meeting those romantic poets did to a man.'

We laughed, then both stopped abruptly, because the sound had been loud, almost hysterical. Glancing across at Vernon, leaning back in the gloom beyond the Anglepoise, I sensed that he, like me, was more excited than he cared to show. I gave a little cough and continued.

'NOTHING IS CERTAIN BUT OUR LOVE ... I ... FEEL ... WE ... MAY ... NEVER MEET ... AGAIN. My God, Vernon, I've just realised!'

'What?'

'This is the last letter of the series, isn't it? Now, either the rest of the letters are lost or Gilbert simply stopped writing.'

'True enough. After Venice, most travellers would have moved on to Florence and Rome ...'

'Yet the letters end in Venice. Perhaps his premonition was correct, then. Perhaps he and Amelia never did meet again.' When I looked back down, it was with the unsettling knowledge that I might be the first person since 1817 to decode Gilbert's last recorded thoughts. As on first reading the letters, I felt like a man desecrating a tomb. In the gloom beyond the desk, the low piles of books seemed to be listening intently: a still, shadowy class. My voice sounded unnaturally loud. 'NOW I . . . LEAVE . . . OUR COMPANY . . . AND GO TO . . . NAPLES . . . ON . . . AN . . . hang on, I think we must have made a mistake here. Yes, that's definitely a 'D' ON AN . . . ERRAND . . . FOR LORD B.'

'I don't believe it. Gilbert running errands?'

'Hang on, Vernon. Let's see what he's got to say. I AM . . . SWORN TO . . . SECRECY AND ONLY TELL YOU . . . LEST . . . SOMETHING . . . SHOULD . . . BEFALL ME THE . . . KNOWLEDGE MAY BE OF SOME USE THE . . . WOMAN . . .'

'Claude?' With unnatural slowness, Vernon leaned forwards, settling his elbows in the pool of light. 'Well?'

But I just sat there, staring down at the sheet without seeing it. There was a red pulse before my eyes, I felt queasy: I was waiting for the first clap of thunder. By rights, that was the moment when it should have happened.

'Well?' said Vernon, almost raising his voice. I've never known him so rattled, before or since. 'What does it say?'

'THE WOMAN HAS STOLEN HIS MEMOIRS.' When I stood up and moved to the window, I found that my legs were weak. The light outside had gone brown in the coming storm. Freddie was in the street below. Like a cow that sits down before the rain comes, the old tramp had already gone to mutter in a doorway. It felt like the end of the world. 'The woman has stolen his memoirs.'

In the silence which followed my voice, I suddenly heard the first large drop of rain splat against the window-pane. It made me flinch.

'Ah, well,' sighed Vernon tiredly. 'That's that, then.'

'What!' Spinning from the window, I was astonished to see him gathering up his papers as though preparing to leave. 'Where the hell are you going?'

'Downstairs.' He was quite calm. 'Back to work. There's nothing more to do up here.'

'But I haven't even read you the end of the message yet!'

'There's no point,' he replied, separating the Byron letters from his own papers and leaving them in a neat pile under the lamp. 'These letters are fakes.'

'How can you be so sure?'

'Come, come, Claude. We knew there was something odd about it from the start but, as you said, the only reason to forge something is financial gain. Now we have that reason. These letters are merely the bait, designed to draw you on towards a huge hook: forged memoirs of Lord Byron, asking price in the low millions.'

There was such certainty in his voice that I was unable to argue. I just stood and watched him lever himself to his feet. As he began to walk slowly towards the door, I turned away.

The roofs outside were black, the sky gunmetal grey, one huge ship preparing to fire. The odd drop of rain still exploded like a shot against the glass. As I stared out, I suddenly remembered my vision: the young man writing furiously at his desk, muttering, while the light of dawn shimmered at the window. This time I knew what he was writing, but my curiosity to see over his shoulder was even more urgent than before, because now I felt that, in some way which I could not yet understand, he'd been writing it for me. Then there was a moment of complete clarity. Everything went blindingly white as the first bolt cracked the overcharged air, a symbol of power, of genius, of divine creativity.

'Vernon!' I bellowed. 'The letters are genuine!'

I swung around, the thunder and my voice seeming

to roll away together, and found that the old man had paused at the head of the stairs. Slowly, he turned. As though obeying a hidden signal, the rain opened fire.

'Come back,' I said in a quieter voice. 'At least listen to the end of the message and talk the thing over with me.'

With a sudden feeling of exhaustion, I went and slumped back down in my creaky old seat. After a moment's hesitation, Vernon himself walked slowly-back towards the desk. As I waited for him to arrive, I remembered: I was wearing weekend clothes because my working days were at an end. Perhaps I was willing to believe in any nonsense which would fill the sudden void.

'Very well, then.' He settled himself back down just outside the glow of the light, elbows on the arms of the chair, fingertips lightly touching. In the faint light from the papers there was something almost Mephistophelian about his calm old face. 'The rest of the message.'

Still with that strange feeling of tiredness, I picked up the sheet with its lines of capitals and started to read the message once more from the beginning. It was necessary to raise my voice against the roar of the rain, and I had the absurd impression that the storm had been summoned in a vain attempt to drown out this last revelation.

'NOTHING IS CERTAIN BUT OUR LOVE. I FEEL WE MAY NEVER MEET AGAIN. NOW I LEAVE OUR COMPANY AND GO TO NAPLES ON AN ERRAND FOR LORD B. I AM SWORN TO SECRECY AND ONLY TELL YOU LEST SOMETHING SHOULD BEFALL ME. THE KNOWLEDGE MAY BE OF SOME USE. THE WOMAN HAS STOLEN HIS MEMOIRS. I AM . . . CHARGED . . . TO RECOVER . . . THEM . . . SHOULD I FAIL . . . IT FALLS TO YOU TO DO AS YOU WILL . . . WITH . . . THE . . . KNOWLEDGE IT MAY BE THE . . . GREATEST BOOK OF THE AGE THE . . . WOMAN . . . IS . . . IGNORANT AND KNOWS . . . NOTHING OF ITS WORTH . . . NOTHING . . . IS . . . CERTAIN BUT OUR LOVE ALL . . . OUR LOVE IS THERE.'

When I'd finished, I saw Vernon in his shadowy seat

looking at me over the tips of his fingers, one eyebrow sceptically raised. A gust rattled rain against the windows.

'Claude,' he said softly. 'This is absolute nonsense. You know what really happened to Byron's memoirs?'

'Yes.'

'They were burnt,' Vernon went on, as though not ready to believe that I really knew, 'on his death, by – '

'John Murray, his publisher,' I interrupted, annoyed at his presumption in lecturing me, 'who considered them too smutty for public consumption, although some who read them maintained that they contained only a few "improper passages".'

'I forgot. You know your Byron.' Vernon's tone suggested that knowing one's Byron didn't really count for much. 'Very good. A moment's thought will tell you that you are being tricked.'

'How so?'

'To begin with, we've discovered no reason as yet for Gilbert to write in code. Even if there were such a reason, his story is full of holes. Why did the woman steal the memoirs?'

'Because Byron had included her in them, perhaps. She was a low-born Neapolitan girl, remember, and we know that the memoirs were frank. The last thing she'd want would be for her sexual peculiarities to be published by some debauched Englishman.'

'Very well, suppose all that is true. Why didn't Byron just follow her and get them back?'

'Come, come, Vernon!' I said, laughing maliciously. 'I thought you knew your Byron better than that! The man was notoriously lazy. It would take more than that to make him up sticks and leave Venice.'

'Notoriously lazy, perhaps,' said Vernon, with that perfect calm which meant he was starting to feel irritated, 'but also notoriously attached to his papers. You will remember how the mere suspicion that one of his letters had gone missing threw him into a frenzy. Here we are talking about an entire book, and an explosive one, at that.'

'Gilbert does say he was in a very ill humour.'

'Indeed,' said Vernon drily. 'Gilbert also expects us to believe that the poet confided the whole amazing story in him, whom he'd only just met.'

'Alright, I admit there are a lot of holes in the story. But Vernon,' I said, lowering my voice and leaning forwards, 'I'm convinced that it's true. My nose tells me so.'

'Your "nose" may have served you admirably in the world of antiques, Claude. However, this is another world, to which my own instincts are well attuned, and they tell me you're being duped. You do make the perfect target for this particular forgery, with your undisguised love of Byron and rather obvious wealth.'

For a moment, we sat and stared at each other over the egg-shaped radiance of the anglepoise. The room abruptly filled with silver light.

'Vernon.' As I stood up, the thunder began to roll towards us, a broadside from the big guns. 'I admit you're right. You know much more about all this than I do, and it certainly does look like a trick. But I can't just let it go.' For a moment, I stared down at the street. There was white leaping water in the gutters. Again I remembered the new emptiness of my life: wandering around the house in my pyjamas all day, my children grown up, my wife unlovely and unloved. 'I can't.' I turned from the window, making an effort to keep the desperation from my voice. 'Even if the chances are a million to one, I can't let it rest. Will you help me track the memoirs down?'

'It's a wild goose chase, Claude.' I could hear from his voice that he was mollified. 'There have been so many cons like this. Once you get caught up in the search, its very difficult to remain sceptical, that's the problem.'

'Precisely why I need you.'

Vernon gave a tired smile, his yellowish teeth glinting in the gloom.

'Very well, I'll give you what help I can. Now remind me. You originally found the letters in the spine of an old bible.'

'That's right.'

'Which you found . . . ?'

'In a box of books Dubious Dave tried to sell me.'

'Dubious, indeed? The sobriquet merely confirms my suspicions, I'm afraid. The first step is obviously to contact this Mr Dubious and find out how he came by the bible.'

Accordingly, I rang Dave, who told me he'd got the box of books as a job lot from a place called Millbank Hall in Hertfordshire, a stately home where he'd gone in the hope of cheap antiques. Beyond that he couldn't, or wouldn't, tell me very much.

'I suggest a division of labour, Claude. You go up to Hertfordshire and snoop around a bit, try and find out if Gilbert and Amelia ever even existed. For my own part, I'll get George Conway to have a look at the letters.'

'Who's George Conway?'

'Head of manuscripts at the British Library,' said Vernon, as though the holder of that post were automatically a star, 'and an old friend of mine. He should be able to convince you that the letters are fakes, even if I can't.'

'Excellent. Thanks very much, Vernon.'

'It's nothing. And now, if you don't mind, I think I'll go and have a bite to eat. What with all this decoding nonsense, I've had nothing all day.'

Once more, he got up and paced towards the door.

'Vernon!' At the top of the stairs, he turned slowly around, a short, dapper man, precise in dress and mind. 'What do you think our chances are?'

'Of finding Byron's memoirs? The great lost treasure of English literature? The Holy Grail of antiquarian books?' At that distance, the dry voice was barely audible over the roar of the rain outside. 'Nil! Of being lured out to

Naples and offered an expensive fake? Very good!' He turned away and began to descend the stairs one by one, jerking his hand down the banister. 'Just don't do anything without consulting me!'

6

THE RAIN CONTINUED. It battered young leaves and petals
to the ground, leaving them to spin in puddles or be swept
into the gutters. Windscreen-wipers, almost overwhelmed
by the sheer volume of water, signalled like drowning
arms. While Helen and I sat in the prematurely dark
kitchen, discussing my plan of action for the following
day, the thunder and lightning moved away, but the rain
went on. At three in the morning, as I lay in a state
of confused wakefulness, the downpour seemed louder
than before. In its roar I found that all the separate
parts of my life – Helen, Byron, Fran, the girl in Soho
– seemed obscurely joined, like streams converging to
feed the same swollen river. Then the rain stopped and,
as though its sound had been the only thing disturbing me,
I fell fast asleep.

Five hours later, I was already in the car and well on
my way to Hertfordshire, trying to forget the vaguely
unsettling incident which had occurred as I was leaving
the house.

As I had walked towards the stairs, a loud click made me
jump. The bathroom door opened and Fran emerged into
the corridor right in front of me, so that I almost bumped
into her. She was stark naked.

'Oh!' Recovering from her own shock, she put her
hands on her shoulders so that her forearms covered her
breasts. 'I didn't think you'd be up!'

'Well I am.' Her pubic hair was only slightly darker than

the familiar blonde of her head. 'You might at least have put some clothes on.'

She turned away from me.

'Sorry!' With a little giggle, she trotted down the corridor towards her room, her firm buttocks shivering as she moved. 'I thought you were still asleep!'

When I began to walk down the stairs, I realised that my legs were weak. I felt sudden nausea, as one sometimes does early in the morning after a bad night's sleep. At that moment it seemed to me that a man's love for his daughter must not only diminish, but utterly die. I wanted Fran out of the house.

Pausing halfway down the stairs, I looked over my shoulder and caught a last glimpse of her long, slim nakedness as she closed the bedroom door.

Millbank House lay just outside a village called Denholm, some forty miles to the north-west of London. The house wasn't hard to find. It was set off the main London road behind a high wall whose length suggested substantial grounds. At first I could only catch a glimpse of the building itself because the road was a dual carriageway and I was travelling in the wrong direction. As the gate flashed past, I saw an eighteenth-century house of pale stone, just large enough to be called a stately home, its windows a row of yellow slabs in the morning sun.

Speeding up, I drove to the nearest roundabout and turned back the way I had come. A few minutes later, I was pulling off the dual carriageway and on to the private road which led to the house. The gates were locked. I stopped the Range Rover and got out.

The air was cool, for it was not much after eight. A damp freshness rose from the earth and leaves, still wet from the night before. As soon as I stepped down from the car, I was struck by the roar from the road behind, which lent an air of anachronism to the old house. When I went and peered through the bars of the gate, the impression of two overlapping times was strengthened: a large yellow dumper-truck was parked by the side of the building. Some way off, at the bottom of a shallow slope, I could just make out the lazy glitter of a broad ornamental lake. On the other side of this, at the edge of some woods, was a muddy JCB with its jaws lolling in mid-air.

A little mist, not yet dissolved by the sun, lingered theatrically above the grass. Everything was completely still. There was a look of timeless abandonment about Millbank House which made it difficult to imagine life ever having gone on there. The JCB could have been standing next to the lake for years, asleep or paralysed, an enchanted dinosaur. I couldn't believe that a woman called Amelia might have trailed her fingers in that water, thinking about Gilbert, or decoded his latest letter in the light from one of those tall windows. Nor, now that I saw the elegance of the building, could I really believe that a Regency aristocrat would have been capable of sending such smut to its mistress.

There was no bell, no sign giving useful advice for visitors. In any case, it was too early yet to go disturbing whatever inhabitants there might be, so I decided to have breakfast.

Some ten minutes down the dual carriageway, I found a little transport café – no more than a hut in a lay-by – where I ordered egg and bacon. The waitress was a huge, snub-nosed girl with wobbly buttocks and dimpled calves. When she brought me my food, I asked her what she knew about Millbank House.

'Big old place up the road.'

'I know, I've just seen it. But what's going on there?'

'Making it into a golf-course, they are. The locals been fighting against it for months, getting up petitions and that, but they've just gone right ahead.'

'Nobody lives there now, then?'

'Dunno. Don't think so.'

'And who used to live there?'

'Dunno.'

Since she was obviously not an expert on local history, I let her go and see to her other customers. In any case, the house itself was a dead end. During our discussion the night before, Helen and I had decided that my next move should be to visit the local church and search for an Amelia in the parish records.

Denholm, when I rolled into it about half an hour later, turned out to be both quaint and prosperous. Although I'm no great fan of these English villages, this one had a certain charm. The pillar-box on the sleepy main road was an absolute red. The graves in the churchyard seemed to have been arranged at those drunken angles on purpose, just so, as though to imply that death itself was something picturesque and a little absurd. The crooked whitewashed cottages, perfect, stainless, shone like souls in the early sun.

At the centre of all this, a few yards down the road from the church itself, was the vicarage. I walked up the path towards the front door with an unaccustomed feeling of humility. On my way, I noticed that the garden was large, the daffodils already in bloom beside the path, green arms spread questioningly. The entire garden was sodden, drying slowly, so that the very air seemed wet enough to wring.

There would no doubt be tea-parties in this vicarage on Sunday afternoons. While the mothers, in their best hats and frocks, chatted inside, the bored boys would lie on their fronts for hours by the pond in the corner of the garden, peering into the idle world of frogs and waterboatmen. As I approached the front door, I felt that the roses around it in summer would be the largest and reddest in all England.

As soon as I knocked on the door, dogs started barking behind it. A moment later, I could hear their claws scrabbling against the oak, which made me rather apprehensive about the moment when it would open. I needn't have worried. They were two English setters with almost identical brown and white coats, and all they seemed interested in doing was licking my wrists.

Bending to stroke them, I looked up and found that their owner was a man of about sixty-five. He was narrow-shouldered and white-haired. His food-stained cardigan was unravelling at the right sleeve. He was leaning towards me very slightly, very still, as though peering at some rare butterfly which he didn't want to scare away. There was a gentle but rather dotty air about him which his first words did nothing to dispel.

'Good morning, my dear.'

'I'm terribly sorry to trouble you, but I need to have a word with the vicar.'

The man made a vague but expansive gesture to indicate the house and garden. 'Vicarage,' he said and then, with a soft laugh, pointed at himself. 'Vicar! How can I help you?'

I stopped stroking the dogs and stood up straight.

'Would it be possible to have a look at the parish records?'

'Nothing simpler. Are you a friend of Tim's, by any chance?'

'No.'

'Not local, then?'

'I've come up from London.'

'London!' I couldn't help feeling that there was something rather affected about his awe, as though he were over-doing the part of eccentric country churchman. 'London, no less! You must come in, then, my dear. Do come in.'

There was a powerful but not unpleasant smell in the house, a mixture of dogs and damp cinders.

'Who's Tim, if you don't mind my asking?'

'President of the local history society.' The vicar opened the door of a small room with a disproportionately large fireplace. The walls seemed almost entirely lined with books. 'They're always coming round here wanting to

93

look things up in the records, you know. We're great friends, indeed we are.'

This didn't surprise me in the least. I imagined that the vicar was great friends with everyone in the village.

'My name's Claude Wooldridge, by the way.'

'Peter Golding.' He held out his hand, looking at me for a moment straight in the eye, his dottiness evaporating. 'Call me Pete. My dogs like you.'

'Ah.' His directness made me awkward. 'What are their names?'

'Yin and Yang,' said the Vicar flatly, still staring straight at me. 'Dark and light, you know.' Abruptly, he moved away and started bumbling around again. 'I was just making tea when you arrived, my dear fellow. Would you like a cup before we get down to business? Good! Make yourself at home for a moment here, then, and I'll see what we can do.'

While he was gone, I took the opportunity of looking round the room. Peter's books strengthened the impression that he was no ordinary vicar: besides volumes on Christian theology, there was a collection of works covering all the major religions, as well as a whole shelf of logic and philosophy. Interesting though all this was, it paled into insignificance beside the carriage clock on the mantelpiece, which drove even Byron temporarily from my mind. Without thinking, I crossed the room to have a look.

Carriage clocks are unusual in that their design has hardly been changed since they were first made. This causes a most regrettable confusion. It is all too easy for unscrupulous fakers, far less talented than Crafty Clive, to take a fairly modern example and make it look much older than it really is. The confusion works the other way, as well. A man ignorant in antiques – a country vicar, for example – has no way of knowing whether he's in possession of a gem or the sort of thing you find advertised in the Sunday supplements.

Carriage clocks, in other words, are a dealer's dream, and

they had made me countless thousands over the years. It was with a quickening of interest, therefore, that I picked this one up from the vicar's mantelpiece, with the idea of rapidly assessing its value before he returned.

The trick with antiques is to pick them up naturally. If the thing is old, it will have been grasped thousands of times in the same way, and should therefore be worn under your fingers. This clock passed that test. The enamel on the dial was also convincingly smooth. There were only four digits in the serial number. After a few seconds' examination, I was in little doubt that the clock had been made shortly before Gilbert set off for the Continent. Being an English one, it was a very valuable example indeed, because few were made outside France before 1820. Best of all, it was 'clean': there had been no later additions or modifications, such as the glass sides which ruin so many old carriage clocks.

Antiques by that time had been my livelihood for so long that I had rather come to look on them as mine, all of them: they were simply being held in trust by other people, waiting for me to go and collect them. In any case, I'd always felt that if you didn't appreciate the true value of a piece, you had no right to possess it. My function was to transfer these things of beauty from the hands of philistines to those of connoisseurs.

Before the vicar came back, I replaced the clock exactly as I had found it and sat down on the sofa. Through the diamond-leaded windows, the colours of the garden were strangely bright in comparison with the cluttered and rather gloomy room. Thin steam spiralled above the drying vegetation like the smoke from a thousand sticks of incense. The dogs, which had settled themselves in front of the fireplace, watched me incuriously. I noticed that the sofa was frosted with their fine white hairs.

A rattle of bone china announced the vicar's return.

'So,' he said, having poured the tea in reverential silence, 'what's your interest in our humble parish records?'

95

'It's to do with Millbank House – '

'Tragic, tragic!'

'Eh?'

'The Japanese are turning the place into a golf-course. Bought up all the surrounding fields to make room for it and – But I'm sorry. Do go on.'

'Not at all. What I need to know is whether a woman called Amelia lived there at the beginning of the last century.'

The vicar smiled, leaning forwards to sip his tea.

'And why do you need to know that, my dear chap?'

'Can you keep a secret, Vicar?'

'All in a day's work.'

'Very well, then.' I gave him a brief account of how Vernon and I had found the letters and decoded their contents. 'If Amelia and Gilbert existed and had some reason to hide their love, the survival of Byron's memoirs is all the more likely. So, while the British Library run tests on the letters, I'm doing some historical research.'

'Fascinating! The mythical memoirs of Lord Byron, no less!'

'So, if we could just have a look at the records for – '

'That will not be necessary!' cried the vicar, raising his palm with all the pomp of an Italian traffic-policeman. 'The first thing I can tell you is that your box of books almost certainly did come from Millbank House. The place was only recently sold to our Japanese friends, the previous owner having been a Lloyd's name with enormous debts to pay. A couple of weeks ago, there was a large auction in which most of the contents were disposed of.'

'That fits Dubious Dave's story. And what about Amelia?'

'It just so happens that I know a little about that particular case. Tim told me her story and, for once, it stuck in my mind. The young lady caused something of a controversy for one of my distant predecessors.' He seemed about to tell me more, but, as though on a sudden impulse, he stood up, sloshing tea into his saucer. Yin, or it may have been Yang, raised a sleepy brow. 'Come with me!'

With that, he hurried from the room, only just giving me time to put my own tea down and follow him. We went down a corridor to the back of the house. On the way, I noticed again his unravelling right sleeve and wondered whether, if I were to grab hold of the loose wool and quickly tie it to a chair, he would just wander around without noticing until the entire cardigan had come undone.

'There!' We were standing in the kitchen, whose rustic homeliness would have delighted Helen, and looking out of the window. The back garden was larger and more unkempt than the one at the front of the house. There were bushes at the bottom, giving way to a dense wood from which a woodpecker was broadcasting in broken morse. 'What can you see through those trees?'

'Almost nothing,' I said, peering forwards. There was by now a slight breeze and, as the leaves stirred, I saw a flash like a mirror signalling in the sun. 'Water?'

'Water! That's right! And can you guess what the relevance of that water is to your Amelia?'

For a moment I was silent, mentally retracing the route I had taken between Millbank House and the village.

'That must be the lake in the grounds of the house.'

'Correct. Soon to be an interesting feature of the eighteenth hole. So, let's test your logic. What's the connection with Amelia?'

I stood quite still. I had already guessed the connection, but I didn't want to hear that I was right. The vicar took my silence for bafflement.

'Come on, my dear, come on! Think! A controversy in the church, a woman, a lake!'

Suddenly I felt irritated with him for turning such a tragedy, however distant, into a game of twenty questions. It was as though, with his self-conscious eccentricity, he felt himself immune.

'I don't know. You tell me.' If the vicar heard the anger in my voice, he chose to ignore it. 'What's the connection?'

'Suicide!' he said with undisguised relish. 'One cold morning, Amelia Millbank failed to appear for breakfast. She wasn't in her room or anywhere in the house. Her distraught mother rushed into the grounds, calling her name. Right in the middle of the ornamental lake was an empty rowing-boat. The child – she was only sixteen – had almost certainly thrown herself into the icy water. So, why the controversy with the church?'

'The family wanted her buried in consecrated ground,' I said flatly.

'Quite right! Very good!'

'I know, because we had the same problem with my father. He had to be cremated in the end.'

All the animation and amusement died from the vicar's face, giving way to such a convincing look of pain that I at once felt ashamed of my sadistic revelation.

'Your father!' he whispered, as though he'd just seen the dead man plodding across the lawn in his dressing-gown. 'How absolutely unforgivable of me!'

'Don't worry. You weren't to know.'

The vicar turned and looked me straight in the eye, as he had before, his dottiness gone.

'I'm a fool,' he murmured. 'How can anyone reach my age and still be such a blundering fool?'

With that, very tentatively, as though afraid of offending me further, he raised his arm with its unravelling sleeve and patted me on the shoulder. It was impossible not to feel an irritating affection for him.

'How about another cup of Earl Grey?'

'But, my dear, dear fellow, of course! That's exactly the thing!'

As we walked back into the living-room, that carriage clock hit me in the eye again. Some deep part of me, which functioned almost on the same level as breathing and heartbeat, was already working out the profit to be made on its reclamation: the best part of a grand.

'Amelia existed, then,' I said as the vicar topped up my cup, 'that's encouraging. You've never heard of any Gilbert, though?'

'No, but then I'm not really the person to ask. I only happen to remember her because of the, ah, church angle. By far the best thing you can do is speak to Tim. I'm sure he'll be able to give you the full story.'

'And how can I contact him?'

'I happen to know that he's on a trip to France with our local primary kids today, but I'll give you his number before you go and you can ring him tonight. He'll be only too pleased to speak to you, I'm sure.'

'Thanks.'

We were silent for a moment. Birds were singing in the drying trees outside. The light was growing. Yin and Yang watched lazily from the frayed rug before the hearth.

'Claude, do you mind if I ask you a personal question?'

'Not at all.' It was a lie: although this vicar didn't seem the type to suddenly try and convert me, there had been something slightly unsettling about his tone. 'Go ahead.'

'Why are you so desperate to find these memoirs?'

The absurdity of this completely floored me for a moment.

'Well, I mean, they'd be worth millions, for one thing.' A glance at the vicar's face told me that he was not satisfied with my answer. I felt suddenly defensive. 'In any case, I've always been interested in Byron.'

'Why?'

I thought for a moment.

'There are aspects of myself, on a far grander scale, in him.'

'Ah!' cried the vicar softly, happier this time. 'That makes more sense. It's not the memoirs themselves you're after, then?'

I shrugged.

'I'm not sure what you're driving at.'

'Forgive me, my dear,' he said in a completely different voice. 'I'm a nosy old fool.'

'Not at all. In any case, I really think I'd better . . .' As I stood up to go, I casually glanced over at the mantelpiece. 'Oh! That's rather a nice clock you've got there!'

Of course, there was absolutely no excuse for this, but, as I say, it was pure instinct. My blood was up. In a perverse sort of a way, I'd have felt guilty if I'd left that clock, as though I'd somehow done myself down.

'Do you like it? It's been here ever since I moved in.'

'Mind if I have a look . . . ? You may not believe it, but I could probably get a couple of quid for this in one of my shops. It's a modern one, of course, but all the same – ' I paused for a moment, pretending to consider, then turned to face him. 'Look, I'd like to thank you for everything you've done. How about this. The clock's worth about fifty quid. I'll give you a hundred for it, fifty for you and fifty for the coffers of the church. What do you say?'

The vicar seemed delighted by this.

'Well, that really is most generous of you, my dear fellow. Most generous. I can't say that I'm actually terribly keen on that clock and, of course, a little extra money is always welcome.'

A few minutes later, I was walking down the sunny garden path, past rows of mournful daffodils, with the local historian's number in my pocket and the carriage clock under my arm. At the garden gate, I hesitated, feeling the damp moss beneath my palm and staring into a spinning blue sky. Then I turned around and went back up the path.

When I knocked on the door, the vicar opened it immediately, as though he'd been waiting on the other side. The dogs came leaping out once more.

'Claude! Back already?'

'I can't take this,' I said, holding the clock out to him. 'I came to return it.'

The vicar smiled comfortably, as though my words had been proper but entirely predictable, like a response at evensong.

'You'll be wanting your money back, then?'

'No. Keep it. The money's a gift. Just take the clock.' The vicar didn't move. He just stood there, squinting silently at me, his white hair outshining the whitewashed walls. Suddenly I realised that this was the first time in my life I'd ever turned down a deal. Then it seemed to me that the clock in my hands symbolised everything: all the lies and tricks by which my fortune had been made, the great game I'd always relished, my whole career. The damned thing weighed a ton. 'Take it.'

'Why?'

'The price wasn't fair. I cheated you.'

As I spoke, the vicar reached forward and effortlessly took the clock.

'Yes, I know.'

'You knew? Why did you sell me the bloody thing, then?'

He shrugged.

'That I don't know. I just did it. God may have been guiding me. Perhaps that sounds absurd to you. In any case, I knew you wouldn't really go away with my clock. I knew you'd bring it back.'

'How could you? Believe me, it was most out of character.'

The vicar just stood there, quite still, gazing at me, white hair blazing. Suddenly, I felt that I had misjudged him: he was by no means affected or a fool. There was something benign about him. At last he said, 'Is there anything else you want to say to me?'

'What do you mean? No, of course not.'

There was another silence, and suddenly I found that there were in fact a thousand things I wanted to tell him: the full story of my father, my marriage, my career. I felt that if I could just find a way to include him in my life, his cultured innocence would make everything alright. Helen and I would fall in love again. I'd find reasons to go on.

'You're quite sure? Nothing at all?'

'No.' I began to back away. 'I've got to go.'

'When you arrived this morning, I thought you looked like a man carrying the world on his shoulders.'

'I've been under a lot of strain recently. This Byron thing . . .'

'But when you took my clock, I knew you'd bring it back.' As he spoke, I turned around and walked off down the path. His voice pursued me. 'Goodbye, my dear chap! Keep in touch!'

Without a backward glance, I stormed out of the garden, suddenly furious at his presumption. I got into the Range Rover, slammed the door and roared out of the village.

Ten minutes down the dual carriageway, I parked in a lay-by, rested my head on the leather-bound steering-wheel, and wept.

Vernon, when I told him the story of Amelia's suicide, was far from impressed.

'The woman existed, then. That's good, as far as it goes. But the important thing is to pin Gilbert down and find out why he wrote those letters.'

'Perhaps this Tim fellow will be able to help us with that when I ring him this evening.'

'Perhaps.'

We were sitting upstairs in the office, just as we had sat the day before to do the decoding. The sun was streaming over my shoulder; it was early afternoon. The piles of books surrounded us like a miniature Manhattan, dreamy in the sunshine.

Vernon was wearing a bow tie and a claret waistcoat, complete with watch-chain. Comparing him with the man I'd met that morning, I felt I understood something more about his character. He and the vicar were of about the same age, and both eccentric, but where the vicar was vague and warm, Vernon was dry, sharp and precise. In comparison with the vicar's openness, Vernon's air of compulsive secrecy now looked almost perverse.

'Did you take the letters to your friend at the British Library?'

'Yes.'

'And?'

'And he didn't immediately say they were forgeries. That means nothing, of course. We shall have to wait for the results of the tests.'

'So we shall.'

This was something I only said to humour him, because my faith in the letters was stronger even than before. I was convinced that they were genuine.

Shortly afterwards I went home, where I spent the remainder of the day in my study. At first I was unable to do anything except think about how I had returned the clock that morning. Like my visit to the prostitute, it seemed to mark a turning-point. Both incidents, momentous enough in themselves, had also been encoded signs of something even bigger, mere twitching weather-vanes.

I picked up the phone.

'Christopher?'

'Oh, hi Dad!'

'You remember that Georgian tallboy I carted in the other day?'

'Yup.'

'Remind me: what did I price it up at?'

'Two seven fifty.'

'Right. Mark it down to five hundred and put a big sign on it saying "reproduction".'

'What!'

'The thing's a fake, Christopher.'

'That's what I thought, too. But I took the handles off this morning, just to check, and they've definitely been changed. It's got to be original.'

'When I say a fake, I mean a proper fake, a professional one, designed to take in experts.'

It was the first time I'd ever hinted at the existence of Crafty Clive.

'Surely you're not trying to tell me that someone – '

'Not just someone. A professional, Christopher. A master, in fact.'

My son fell silent for a moment. I could almost hear the implications whirring through his mind. While he worked it out, I thought about patches left by handles, codes, and letters slid down the spines of bibles. Eventually, Christopher spoke.

'You mean you know somebody who actually *makes* antiques?'

'We'll talk later. Seeya.'

After this conversation, my stomach-ache suddenly bit. To distract myself, I stood and went over to the display case. My career might be almost over, but not quite: the biggest find was still to be made, the biggest game was only just beginning to unfold.

I read through the letters, my new knowledge of Amelia constantly in my mind – the young girl to whom those dirty messages had been addressed had drowned herself. When I finished, I put the letters down and tried to piece together all my knowledge in order to explain the mystery of the code: Gilbert's character, my own and Helen's instinctive revulsion for him, his admiration for Byron, Amelia's suicide, her youth, the pornographic content of the letters.

I felt so close to the truth that I simply couldn't understand why the answer hadn't emerged. After half an hour of puzzling, it seemed to me that perhaps the answer had emerged after all. The truth was there, staring me in the face, but some perverse part of me simply refused to see it.

In the end, I got stiffly up and went downstairs to pour myself a drink.

Through the door of the sitting-room, I heard the sound of the TV. Peering in, I found Fran there watching a cartoon. She was curled on the sofa with her heels tucked under her bottom, eating a bowl of cereal.

'Hello, Fran.'

'Hi, Dad,' she said, glancing towards the door. 'I didn't think you'd be back so early.'

I stood stock still, silent, because her words had stirred some memory in me, and I sensed intuitively that it was of huge importance. My mind groped blindly for a moment, then suddenly got it: Fran emerging naked from the bathroom that morning, explaining that she hadn't thought I'd be up so early, raising her arms to cover her breasts . . .

At that moment, I saw the truth and understood also why I had refused to see it for so long. Desperate now to know for certain, I left the room without saying anything further and rushed upstairs.

Back in my study, I picked up the phone and began punching the buttons with a sort of feverish horror, in which there was nevertheless an element of pleasure, the elation of discovery. I had intended to give the vicar's friend time to finish his supper, but there was no question of that now.

'Hello? Can I speak to Tim, please?'

'Speaking.'

I found that, unable to keep still, I was moving jerkily in the direction of the window.

'Sorry to bother you like this. My name's Claude Wooldridge.'

The voice on the other end of the line became suddenly friendly.

'Hello, yes! Pete's told me all about you.'

'Pete?'

'Peter Golding. The vicar.'

'Oh. Of course.'

In the park outside, some boys were playing cricket,

using a tree in place of stumps. The sun was low, and the boys' shadows were impossibly long, the shadows of slender Titans.

'You're interested in Amelia Millbank, I hear. Fire away.'

'There are only a couple of things I need to know.' One of the shadows slid with a surreal grace along the grass, raising an arm to bowl. 'Did she have any brothers?'

The receiving shadow swung.

'No. She was an only child, as far as I remember.' It made me feel airsick to watch the ball, which rose and fell so slowly I felt that it would never return to earth. 'Hello? Are you still there?'

'Sorry. Yes.' With a sudden longing to be told that I was wrong, I asked my second question. 'What was her father's name?'

'Gilbert.' One of the fielders, with a dramatic dive, had caught the ball. I could just hear the distant shouts of jubilation. 'Gilbert Millbank. He died in the same year that she killed herself.'

'Which was . . . ?'

'Eighteen seventeen. Her family had to leave Millbank House that winter.'

'And what do you know about Gilbert's death?'

'Not much . . . it was all rather mysterious. Made him a local legend for a few years, in fact. All we know for certain is that he was on the Continent at the time, down in the south of Italy.'

'Naples?'

'I'm not sure. I'd have to check. What else do you need to know?'

'That's all for the moment, thanks.'

'Look, if you want me to send you some bumph on the family, just give me your address.'

'Yes, that might be of great help. You're very kind.'

'Any friend of Pete's, you know.'

'Pete?'

'The vicar.'

When I put the phone down, I found that all the pieces had fallen into place. The whole thing made perfect sense. I understood, too, why Gilbert had felt so strongly about Byron. The decoded phrase from the opera letter drifted through my mind.

WE WERE TWO APART AS IT MUST ALWAYS BE.

Then it hit me. All along, as though refusing to see it out of sheer wilfulness, I'd been ignoring the most obvious clue of all: Byron himself had used code in some of his letters. They had been letters to his sister. Both men had written in code because they were driven by a passion so unnatural that it had to be kept a secret at any cost, yet so urgent that it had to be expressed.

7

THE FOLLOWING DAY was Sunday, and I lay in late, catching up on some of the sleep I'd missed since my discovery of the letters.

When I eventually awoke, I knew at once that it was another sunny day: through a chink in the curtains a dusty rod of light bisected the room. Helen's side of the bed was empty but still warm. In the distance outside, church bells were ringing. The sound carried perfectly on the bright air, as clean and tiny as the notes of a musical box. From downstairs came the smell of bacon, and I smiled: a cooked breakfast was Sunday's biggest consolation. A few moments later I was in my dressing-gown, squinting and shuffling, surprised that everything could still be so normal.

'Perfect timing, as usual,' said Helen, as she slipped a glistening egg on to my plate. She slid the frying-pan into the sink; steam hissed through the sunshine. 'Miss the work, reap the reward. It's a fine art.'

We were still eating when Fran appeared, dressed to go out: an ostentatiously scruffy cardigan and stockings that were a few inches too short for her skirt, leaving tantalizing garters of thigh. Wishing us good morning, she opened the fridge and poured herself some orange juice.

'You off out, then?' I sand lightly.

'That's right.'

'And remind me: when's your first exam?'

Helen gave me a warning look across the table.

'Two weeks.' Fran bent and brushed her lips across my cheek. 'Don't worry. Everything's under control.'

Some part of her body touched my shoulder. Helen was still staring at me, willing me not to start a row.

'All under control, eh? Well, I'll take your word for it. Have a nice time.'

Tension drained from the room.

'Thanks. Bye, then. Bye Mum.'

Leaving her dirty glass on the worktop, Fran swung elegantly down the corridor and left. Helen went back to her breakfast.

'That was for your benefit, I hope you understand. If I had my bloody way, we'd lock her in her room and make sure she did a bit of work.'

This was the opening gambit of our usual argument over Fran, but Helen chose not to accept it.

'Do you know what I think?' she said conversationally, slicing the fat off her bacon. 'I think you're jealous of her.'

'What, Fran? Me? Nonsense!'

'Just a feeling.'

I was about to tell her what I thought of her feelings when the phone rang.

'That'll be Ross,' said Helen smugly as I got up.

'Will it now?'

'Bound to be.'

'Hello? Oh, hi Ross, fuck it.'

Helen started buttering herself some toast.

'Just a feeling,' she murmured. 'That's all.'

Ross, it turned out, was bored.

'He's coming round,' I explained when I'd put the phone down, 'to inflict himself on us, the bastard. I did everything I could to dissuade him, but – Hello? Hello? Are you still with me?'

'I was just thinking,' said Helen, chewing ruminatively, 'about that poor girl throwing herself into that lake. What was her name again?'

'Amelia.' I had told Helen the whole story as soon as she'd got in the night before. 'Amelia Millbank, daughter of Gilbert.'

'What a terrible thing! To be driven to that by your own father! As soon as I saw those letters, I knew there was something dirty about them. That was just a feeling, too.'

'Yes, you're very clever with your feelings, but I think you've got this one wrong. I don't think he drove her to suicide. She killed herself after he'd died, remember. I think she did it out of grief. I think she did it because she loved him.'

'Don't be ridiculous, Claude. No girl could love a monster like him.'

'Couldn't they? I'm not so sure. And I'll tell you what else I think. I think your monster was murdered.'

'What makes you think that?'

'The last thing he said to Amelia was that he was going in search of the memoirs. I think he got too close to finding them.'

I had expected Helen to laugh, but instead she was silent for a few moments. 'What was in the memoirs, then,' she said at last, 'that you think people would kill to conceal?'

'The truth.'

'About what?'

'That's what I'd give anything to know.' Turning to face her, I felt a sudden hopelessness. 'I doubt if I ever shall, of course. Even if the manuscript had survived, the chances of our finding it would be millions to one. If we did, though . . . if we did.'

'Perhaps it's best left undisturbed. Perhaps the letters would have been better left, as well. After all, what have you gained by finding out that poor girl's story?'

'I can't just leave those memoirs.' I turned towards the window, seeing again as I did the luminous veils thrown upwards from the water, the young exile stooped before the light, writing madly. 'There's nothing else left worth finding.'

The hopelessness of the task made me gloomy for the rest of the day. In any case, I've never much cared for Sundays. Ross came round as planned and helped cook lunch. He was in a buoyant mood, reaching the end of his book, declaring himself a genius. After lunch, we went out into the bright garden, where we drank Pimms and played the first croquet of the year. Helen and Ross threw themselves into the game, Helen because she enjoyed it, Ross because he always had to win. While participating good-humouredly, I kept myself a little to one side, thinking of the memoirs with hopeless longing, wondering about the thickness and texture of the paper, the colour of the ancient ink, the opening sentence. The final version delivered to John Murray had comprised seventy-eight folio sheets. I wondered how many Maria Apuglia had managed to escape with, though it didn't really matter: even one of them would be a monumental find. The more I thought about it, the more I despaired of ever holding those priceless pages in my hands.

Helen played with her usual vague grace, baffled by each failure to get a ball through a hoop. With me not really paying attention, Ross's ruthlessness ensured an easy victory. This was just as well, because, genius or not, he got in a foul mood when he lost at croquet.

Fran came back in the early evening and went upstairs, supposedly to work. I made up my mind to have a word with her the following day, but said nothing to Helen. Ross didn't go home till late. He and Helen made most of the conversation over dinner.

At last we went to bed. Helen made no advances to me and soon she was asleep. I lay awake, thinking of the memoirs, overcome by the emptiness of a day without work. If my career was really over, then only this lay ahead: a descent into the twilight of autumn, silence settling like gloom, the emptiness of Sundays.

*   *   *

Though the next day was Monday, I lay in late again. One question was starting to obsess me: why had John Murray, Byron's publisher, burnt the memoirs? None of the explanations which had been offered since were really convincing. Byron's incest with his sister, for example, was common knowledge by the time of his death. Mere confirmation of it would not have been motive enough to burn the memoirs of the greatest poet of the day. Nor, for that matter, would racy accounts of his various affairs. It seemed to me that there had to be something more.

On my way into town, I made a short detour, just out of interest, past the antique shop. Christopher wasn't there. The woman behind the counter was a stranger – my son was by this time entirely in charge of hiring and firing for the two shops – and the sight of her made me realise the extent to which my own business now went on without me. However, what really interested me was Clive's tallboy. Carefully dusted and polished, the fake now had pride of place in the window display. Nobody with any sort of eye could fail to be attracted to it. Despite my orders, Christopher hadn't changed the price.

At first, I was amused by this: the lad was following in his father's footsteps, after all, willing to bend the rules of Kantian morality for the kick of making a deal. On the way to London, however, it began to depress me. Somehow I felt that, a generation on, the Wooldridges should have progressed to something less grubby. An upright son would have been some justification for my own career. Instead, it seemed that the suns or the fathers had been passed on.

In town, I achieved the miraculous feat of finding a parking space just off Long Acre, and continued on foot. My first stop was a reference library near Leicester Square, where they keep telephone directories from all over the world. There I sat and copied out the addresses of all the Apuglias living in Naples: with any luck, one of them would be the descendant of that Maria who, according to Gilbert, had stolen the memoirs. If this didn't lead me directly to the book, it might at least mark the beginning of the trail.

Writing down the addresses didn't take long, since there were only twelve Apuglias in the whole city. This, in my opinion, was not a good sign: the more long and complicated the search, I felt, the more likely its object was to be genuine. Forgers, wanting to be certain of leading me to the memoirs, would obviously have chosen an unusual name.

When I'd finished in the library, I made my way up Long Acre to Stanford's. In the shop windows on the way, my reflection looked grey and haggard. I bought myself a map of Naples and set off for the bookshop. Vernon was dealing with a customer when I arrived, patent shoes placed neatly together on the carpet, just warming up to recommend Blackwall's across the way.

'We don't have it, sir, but – ' Noticing me come in, he gave a short, solemn nod, and continued in his usual thin voice: 'At least, we don't have it just at the moment. However, you could always try again next week. And have you considered one of the slightly later editions? They are just as collectable, really.'

For a novice, it was an impressive performance. Only someone who knew Vernon well would have guessed he was putting it on. However, there were a couple of tell-tale signs – watery eyes wandering, a wizened finger vaguely rubbing the side of his nose – which made me feel sorry for ever having tried to change his ways.

Moving past, I got an even bigger shock than that of hearing Vernon trying to sell a book: Caroline was not alone. A long, gangling man was perched awkwardly on the edge of her desk with his back to me. The way she was gazing up at him through her thick lenses left no doubt that he'd been giving her the full treatment. More staggering still was the identity of her admirer.

'Morning, Christopher,' I said as I reached them. It was difficult to keep a straight face. 'Taking a bit of time off?'

Christopher sprang away from the desk as though it had bitten him, and span round, flapping his hands.

'Oh! Dad! Hi! I was just passing, just on my way back from the auctions up in Camden, you know, when I thought I'd pop in and have a chat with Caroline . . .'

Inspiration failed him. Meanwhile, the young lady in question, blushing painfully, started doing complicated and important things with paper-clips.

'You two know each other, then?'

'We've spoken on the phone a couple of times,' said Christopher. 'But we've never actually met, not actually in the flesh.'

Their embarrassment was infectious. As is perhaps natural for a father, I was so obsessed with my daughter's sex life that it never crossed my mind to think about my son. He had a little bachelor flat, courtesy of yours truly, where I assumed he just did what young men had always done. The idea that he, or anyone for that matter, could fall for Caroline was astonishing and rather touching.

With a paternal hand on his elbow, I steered Christopher away from the desk towards the glass-covered display case holding the most expensive volumes.

'I see,' I said softly, 'that you didn't bother marking that tallboy down as instructed.'

There was a slight but perceptible change in his manner, suggesting a sudden increase in confidence. I realised that Christopher was already more at ease with his business affairs than his emotional life.

'No, I didn't. Granted, it's a fake, but it really is an exceptionally good one. I'm sure that in your youth, Dad, you wouldn't have – '

'Don't worry,' I said, still speaking in a low voice so that Caroline wouldn't hear, 'there's no need to explain. The shop's in your hands now. You make your own decisions. However, I can't help wondering what old Immanuel would have said.'

'Old who?'

'Kant, Immanuel, of the categorical moral imperative.'

'Oh, him,' said Christopher, with a touch of derision. 'Well, I don't think he'd have lasted long in antiques, do you?'

'Probably not. Just one word of advice, though.'

'What?'

'Take Caroline to *Lear* at the National. It'll slay her.'

After that, of course, he came over all awkward and bashful again, so I pressed a fifty quid note into his clammy palm, told him to have one on me, and went towards the stars. Vernon was still dealing with that customer. On my way across the shop, I left instructions with Caroline to send the old man up to the office as soon as he'd finished.

Upstairs, I cleared a space on my desk and unfolded the map of Naples, intending to start marking the addresses of the Apuglias. Instead of that, though, I found myself just sitting and staring out of the window in sudden depression. It took me a moment to make the connection with Christopher. The shops were in his hands now. He could make his own decisions. My role had become that of a respected observer.

My fingers turned my wedding-ring. My mind wandered in its now familiar way: Christopher chatting up Caroline! Who'd have thought it? Come to think of it, they rather suit each other, in a way. He's just the type to do the dirty on me, get married and make me a granddad within a year. And what if he does? That must have its consolations, too. It's the reason we all go on. Playing with my grandchildren in the garden at Greenwich, Helen spoiling them, doting. You get all the pleasure of kids without the grind. A little girl would be nice, another little Fran. They all escape you in the end.

'Claude?'

'Come in, Vernon. Sit yourself down.'

Like a priest approaching an altar, Vernon paced between the piles of books. Watching him, I was struck afresh by the unique atmosphere of the office, an aura of sadness, sanctity and age. The very air had the calm of a pensioner in an armchair, lost in a book, perhaps, or just allowing his mind to flick through the dog-eared past, the last magazine in the waiting-room. The distant drone of London only seemed to emphasise the silence: Dewson's was an island in that sea.

Vernon creaked into the chair opposite me, and the sun came out in welcome.

'What's this? A map of Naples? You're surely not thinking of going out there till we've got the results of George's tests?'

'No, don't worry, I'm going to do it your way. However, I must admit that I'm getting ready: that historian gave me some interesting news.'

Vernon linked his hands, raising his index fingers against each other like a steeple.

'Indeed?'

'Gilbert was Amelia's father.'

For a moment Vernon was silent, tapping the steeple against his chin. Then he smiled.

'That's clever.'

'How do you mean?'

'I mean that our friends have taken a huge amount of trouble to lay their trail. The deception really is admirably elaborate.' He raised his head towards the ceiling, glasses glinting. 'To find a young suicide from Byron's day, then forge coded love letters from her father! Marvellous imagination! This whole thing is almost a work of art.'

'Vernon, does it ever cross your mind for one moment that the letters might be genuine?'

'Not seriously. Not since we decoded the one about the memoirs. It's just too obvious.'

'You know what I'd do if I was going to forge Byron's memoirs? It's quite simple. I'd forge the things, then hawk them round till I found someone to buy them. Failing that, I'd offer them to newspapers and publishing houses.'

'And end up without a penny because nobody would

believe you for a minute. Don't you understand, Claude? Byron's memoirs have to be one of the biggest literary cons going. The biggest, perhaps, short of a new Shakespeare play.'

'Sort of King Con?'

'Ha, ha,' said Vernon drily, 'most amusing, Claude. If I were to take the trouble of forging the memoirs, I'd chose my mark carefully, then wrack my brains for some way of duping him before he'd even seen them. You see, everyone believes, quite rightly, that Murray burnt the only existing copies. The forger's first job is to reverse that belief. Then he has to lead his mark on to the manuscript. The letters we've found do both things very cleverly. You, for example, already believe that a woman called Apuglia some or all of Byron's memoirs.'

I was silent, staring down at the map of Naples, filled with the sudden fear that he might be right. If that were so, then it seemed to me that my life would have no meaning left at all. Vernon's voice when he next spoke seemed to have been distilled from the silence of the room.

'Tell me the truth, Claude. You believe it, don't you?'

'Yes, I do.'

'If it weren't for my influence, you'd probably have set off for Naples already, wouldn't you?'

'Almost certainly.'

'There you are, you see.' Now he was almost whispering. 'The letters have served their purpose.'

'This is a pointless argument, anyway. Your friend at the BM will settle it once and for all.'

'George will only be able to spot a forgery if the forgers have made a mistake. As I'm sure you know from your own experience of antiques, a real craftsman can always take in the experts. You can only be certain if something is a fake. The genuine always leaves a little doubt.'

'Then it'll be a case of trusting to instinct, I suppose.'

'Not much to rely on with such huge sums of money at stake.'

'Hmm. How long will it take this George to examine the letters?'

'Not long. He might even finish it this week.'

'We'll just have to wait and see what he says, then. Meanwhile, why don't we get on with marking these addresses on the map?'

I tore off the bottom half of the list and gave it to him. With a shrug to show that he considered the task pointless, Vernon turned the map so that we could both see it and started work.

The Apuglias were spread all over Naples. As I sought out their addresses, fluorescent marker-pen poised, I found myself wondering what the city would be like in reality. Though I'd spent time in Italy in my youth, and even learnt the language, it had all been up North. Naples to me was still a rather exotic and mysterious place. I knew that those brown squares, the size of postage-stamps, represented blocks of houses whose architecture would have a rather Moorish influence. That curve, half a blue beachball, was one of the most famous bays in the world. Just over Vernon's shoulder, hovering above piles of books, my mind sketched the huge outline of Vesuvius, a knee raised under a blanket.

'That was your son downstairs, I understand.'

'Hmm?' I was wandering through the imaginary streets. 'Yes.'

'There is little resemblance.'

I shot him a look, wondering if this was one of Vernon's coded remarks.

'So people say. What about you, Vernon? Have you got any kids?'

Vernon affected not to have heard me, staring earnestly over his glasses, searching for the last street on his list.

'Ah! There it is!' Leaning forward, he drew a neat circle on the map and shook his head. 'And you actually believe that the memoirs might be there, hidden away on that very spot at this very moment!'

However, I was not going to be sidetracked. My old curiosity about Vernon's private life had been aroused. Putting down my own pen, I leaned back in my creaky chair.

'Well, have you or haven't you?'

'What?'

'Any kids.'

For the first time in our acquaintance, Vernon looked decidedly awkward.

'No, Claude.' With an aggressive little jerk, he pulled his waistcoat towards his hips. 'I haven't.'

'You were never married, then?'

'Oh, I was. Ages ago, it seems. Back in the forties. My wife left me.'

There was silence while I waited in vain for him to volunteer more information.

'Why was that, then?'

'She found out about my lover.'

This was so astonishing that I couldn't immediately reply. It was still windy outside, the sky opening and closing like a huge, slow signal, filling things with dreaminess.

'Well, Vernon!' I said at last. 'Who'd have thought it? So, there was another woman, eh?'

'There was another,' breathed Vernon, staring straight at me, 'but it was not a woman.'

It was a moment of revelation similar to the one in which I had guessed Gilbert's incest. Everything suddenly made sense and was seen in a new light: Vernon's dapper clothes, his soft voice, his precise movements, his lonely air. My mind went back to the day the box had arrived. Seeing a motorcycle courier roar past the shop, Vernon had murmured at the window, something about the vandal being taken for a god. In those words I had mistakenly heard an old man's disapproval of the modern world. I'd missed the longing in them, the admiration of youth and male power.

'I hope it doesn't upset you, Claude.'

'No, no, Vernon, not at all! Do forgive me. I was just thinking . . .' I picked up my pen and began to fiddle with it, tapping it on the map. 'You're gay . . .'

'Not a word which I have ever considered very suitable. Perhaps, for the new generation, it may be. In my day, however, our condition had very little to do with gaiety.'

I nodded sympathetically, but I was thinking that modern homosexuals would have objected to his terminology just as he did to theirs. It could no longer really be described as a condition. Then the word 'gay' started going through my head as though it had some hidden meaning.

'My God!'

'Claude?'

Ignoring him, I started rummaging wildly through the drawers of my desk.

'Where is it, where is it? I know it's here somewhere. Ah, yes, here it is! Now, look at this. How would you describe that face?'

When he saw the postcard I handed him, Vernon smiled.

'It has been described so many times before. Childlike or angelic are the adjectives most commonly used.'

'Not the ones I'd choose, though. How would androgynous strike you? Or effeminate, even?'

Vernon raised an eyebrow.

'Possible, I suppose.'

He handed the postcard back to me, and I stared for a moment at the aesthetic, large-eyed face, framed by a woman's hair.

'What was that phrase from Gilbert's letter?' I stared upwards and quoted it from memory. 'This gentleman is called Shelley, and is also a Poet of whom we may one day hear. B described him as quite the most beautiful human being he had ever met.'

'What of it?'

'Don't you see?' I cried, leaping to my feet and thumping the desk. 'That's it! The key to the riddle!'

Vernon looked at me solemnly.

'You are quite, quite mad, Claude, if you think – '

'Look, this morning I was trying to work out why the memoirs had been burnt. There seemed to be no good reason for it, not in Byron's life as it has come down to us. But of course we wouldn't know the real reason: the memoirs had been burnt precisely to conceal it.'

'Byron and Shelley lovers, though? It's – '

'Vernon, when you told me you were gay, I wasn't surprised. You just can't completely hide a thing like that. Not even a hundred years later.'

'It's just about possible, I suppose.'

The sun went in again.

'More than possible. All you have to do is open your eyes and read the signs: Byron, the sensualist so jaded that he was willing to break even the taboo of incest for a thrill. There have always been unproven whispers about what he got up to in Greece. Then Shelley, the shocking atheist and proponent of free love. Their admiration for each other in a platonic sense is famours. So – '

'So you hope that the mythical memoirs, when you find them, will astound the world. Really, Claude, I do think you're getting a little carried away.'

With a sigh, I flopped back down into my seat.

'Vernon, why must you always be such a wet blanket? What does it take to get you excited?'

'I am excited.'

'Oh, obviously.'

'You don't understand.' Vernon gave a long sigh, as though to slow himself down. 'I am excited. I have been ever since you found the letters. I find your theory about Byron and Shelley more exciting still.'

'Why don't you give any bloody sign of excitement, then?'

He stared at me for a moment over the temple of his fingers.

'My nature has forced me to become adept at hiding

what I truly feel,' he said quietly, tapping the steeple. 'Perhaps that is unfortunate . . . In any case, I do it without thinking now, even when there isn't any need.'

As he spoke, I remembered how he had once described himself before: one of the old brigade, the old cloak-and-dagger brigade. That phrase haunted me, like a catchy tune or a nagging crossword clue, for the rest of the day.

Nobody came round for supper that evening. Christopher was probably out with Caroline. Ross was buried in his work. God alone knew where Fran might be. Helen and I, too lazy to cook just for ourselves, went down to the steak house in Greenwich.

As was not uncommon for a Monday night, the place was deserted when we arrived. The waiter lit a candle at our table, as though to emphasise the gloomy emptiness around us. While we were waiting for our food, I ran over the day's news for Helen. The story of our son's interest in Caroline delighted her. Since she'd never met Vernon, the revelation of his homosexuality was rather less exciting.

'Well,' she said lightly, picking up her wine glass, 'it only goes to show: you never can tell.'

'No. It's funny, isn't it, how a person's sexuality can be the key to their entire character. I felt it about Gilbert, and now about Vernon. That one piece of knowledge colours everything else. What strikes me most about poor old Vernon, though, is the thought that he's spent all of his life living a lie.'

'Along with most gays of his generation, I suppose, poor dears.' Helen raised her glass. 'God bless the sixties!'

'Quite. But do you know what else it made me think about? Byron.'

'Well, blow me down.'

'Him and Shelley, you see! Once you've got that key, everything falls into place, just like with Vernon. That's why the memoirs were burnt.'

'You're probably right, love.' The kindness of her voice

made me feel like an old man lost in an impenetrably personal fantasy.

'All this doesn't mean much to you, Helen, does it?'

'I can see that it's important, but I could never get as worked up over a mere book as you seem to. The sooner you find the blessed thing, the better, that's all I can say.'

'Why am I the only one who seems to take this seriously? It might turn the world of English letters upside down, for God's sake, yet you just pat me sympathetically and tell me not to get too worked up.' Smiling, I picked up my glass. 'And as for Vernon, he's convinced that the whole thing's a . . .' The glass stopped on its journey to my mouth. '. . . Con.'

'Claude?'

'Vernon,' I said softly. 'Vernon. Why am I so bloody slow?'

'Whatever are you talking about?'

'I should have seen that Dubious Dave could never have dreamed it up.'

'Who's Dubious Dave, for God's sake, and what is it?'

Helen was still smiling, but as I replaced my glass I felt my hand tremble with the rage and horror of doubt.

'Dubious Dave is the one who brought me the box of books in the first place. If he had the imagination to think up a con like this, he wouldn't still be trying to flog boxes of paperbacks at his age. And in any case, I've known him for years, and he's never really tried to cheat me. The whole thing is just too big for him.'

'So?'

At that moment, the waiter arrived with our steaks. I watched in silence as the plates were laid in front of us, my mind racing.

'Vernon has always borne me a grudge,' I said when we were alone again. 'My taking over his shop was a terrible humiliation for him. He sees me as a kind of uncultured wrecker. He's the one with the motive and the inside knowledge to try and con me.'

'But I thought he was the one who constantly tried to persuade you that the letters were fakes.'

'And every time he does so, I argue against him. Every time he tells me not to believe, I end up believing a little more. Don't you see? It would be a most poetic irony for him, the bastard, telling me not fall for the stunt, and all the while laughing into his hat. Do you know what he said today?'

'Go on.'

'He said the whole con was so elaborate that it was virtually a work of art. Then he got me to admit in so many words that I'd fallen for it.'

'Claude, I really do think you're being too Machiavellian.'

'No, it all fits. For him it would be the perfect revenge. He's always sneered at my admiration for Byron. He even incorporated codes into the lettes, using his own little hobby to intrigue me. As he said, it really shows marvellous imagination.'

'Well, I think you're being too hasty. From everything you've told me until today, he sounds like a rather sweet old man. I think you should give him the benefit of the doubt.'

'Maybe you're right.'

We were silent for the rest of the meal. I was stunned by the possibility of betrayal. I cut my steak with gloomy aggression, looking back over my relationship with Vernon, sickened by doubt. To play out such an elaborately vicious deception on someone close to you, whilst all the time affecting increased friendship and warmth, would require a degree of hatred which I could only dimly imagine. Surely the mere fact that I had taken over his shop, and perhaps treated him brusquely at times, would not have been enough to inspire such bitterness and duplicity. The man would have had to be mentally ill.

Then I suddenly realised that the whole thing was absurd; Vernon had to be genuine. I was the sick one. How else could I have suspected a cultured old man of such evil? The appearance of the fantastic letters, combined with the end of my career, had begun to turn my mind. Paranoia and obsession were setting in. Then again, Vernon was certainly odd. Those piles of books in the stock-room hardly suggested normality. Anything might happen to the mind of a sexual outcast, grown to old age in that depressing shop . . .

By the end of the meal, I was beginning to hate Vernon and myself by turns.

'Don't think about him, Claude,' said Helen, pushing her plate away. 'You'll only work yourself up for no reason. In any case, it's unfair to convince yourself without any evidence.'

'You're quite right,' I said, trying to sound cheerful. 'It's probably just my morbid imagination. There's so much at stake, you see. Let's talk about something else.'

'Well, I think your news about Christopher was far more interesting. What's this Caroline like?'

I poured myself another glass of wine.

'Bookish, but mainly from timidity, and probably a virgin.'

Helen laughed.

'Oh, really! And how would you know?'

'Male instinct,' I said lightly. 'Just a feeling.'

'Ha bloody ha.'

I got out my cigarettes and offered her one.

'In any case, I should think she's perfect for Christopher. How would you feel about being a grandmother, old thing?'

Helen smiled softly, suddenly serious.

'I can't wait.'

For a moment we looked at each other in silence, the cigarettes unlit in our hands. I became aware of the waiter hovering in the background, and thought how many couples he must see, young and middle-aged, who came in and sat with nothing to say. Apart from our silence over Vernon, Helen and I had been chatting and laughing since our arrival. Now I realised, to my surprise, that she could still make me forget my troubles, as she had in the old days. Everything except her face was driven from my mind.

'It's been a long time, hasn't it, Helen?'

'What has?'

'Us. Our being together.'

We smiled. Without taking her eyes from me, Helen leant forwards to light her cigarette at the candle's flame. Suddenly I wanted her more badly than I had done for years. For a moment she stayed like that, poised above the flame as though inhaling the scent of a flower, looking up into my eyes through the wavering glow. Then she straightened behind an arc of smoke.

'There are going to be a lot of evenings like this, aren't there, when Fran finally leaves home. Just you and me together. I'm looking forward to it.' My wife said nothing; her eyes shifted momentarily from mine as I lit my own cigarette. 'Well?'

'I was just thinking,' she said, 'about Christopher going out on his first date with Caroune. It reminds me of us, right back in the old days.'

In the old days, Helen's beauty had been of the sort which transforms its surroundings. She had never lost her magic while travelling on a bus or eating in a cheap café. Rather, those places had been caught up in her enchantment and elevated beyond the ordinary. The weeks after our first meeting had been sleepless with happiness. We had both known that we wanted to spend our lives together.

'We were happy then, weren't we? Right back in the old days.'

Looking at her now, in the kind light of the candle, I suddenly felt the old love and happiness again. Replete after my meal, warm with wine, I wanted her with a young man's need.

'Yes. We were very happy then.'

Both of us understood what was happening. We paid

and left without another word. On the way home, under the yellow drizzle of a streetlight, I stopped and took her in my arms. It was years since we'd kissed on the street. Her tongue was as hesitant as a girl's, too shy to probe, a trembling invitation.

Arm in arm, we seemed to float towards the house.

'I still can't believe that we actually live in this place. It seems so grand.'

When she spoke, I understood that she, too, had been transported to the past.

'Too grand for you, perhaps. But I couldn't move, not now. I'd miss my study.'

Inside, we went straight up to the bedroom and got undressed. We climbed into bed and went through the first motions of love. But calm and happiness gradually gave way to a drowning desperation. There came a point where, without needing to speak, we simultaneously moved away from each other. The ritual was dead.

For some time we lay there in the twilight, in silence, in the agony which follows that failure. It had never happened to us before. For a long time, sex to me had been no more than a nocturnal exercise, a duty which was easy to perform. Now, in that sudden excess of nostalgia and love, I had failed. There was no magic, after all. It had died many years before. All that remained was two middle-aged bodies lying in a room, heavy and breathless, worn thin inside. Like a floundering priest who had finally lost the struggle for faith, I suddenly felt myself to be a lump of flesh and nothing more.

Still neither of us spoke. The window was open, so that we could hear the trees stirring in the park. Lifting my head, I saw them stroke the pale sky as though to calm or console. The clouds slid by, impassive visitations. The curtains shifted in a breeze which was mild, dark, and sweet with spring. A car approached a corner on the far side of the park, brake-lights glowing like fiendish eyes, and passed on into the night. At that moment, all of it seemed full of mystery and meaning. Only the two objects on the bed were physical and nothing more, exiles from the spiritual world.

'You don't love me any more, do you, Claude?'

I could have hit her.

'Don't be stupid. I've just had too much to drink. Of course I love you.'

'No you don't. Do you know when I first admitted it?'

I lay in silence.

'The year Christopher went to university. There was such an emptiness in my life, but you didn't even see it. You just went on with your work.'

Part of me was sickened, perhaps because I saw so much of my own pain in hers: the sudden emptiness of life which no relationship can fill. Still I lay in silence.

'How could you love me, after all? How could anyone? A great big fatty like me.'

'Oh, shut up. Shut the fuck up. Spare me your sodding pathos.'

With a jerk, I turned to face with wall and closed my eyes, stunned.

After a few minutes, I found myself thinking of Gilbert: all the signs had been there, yet I'd refused to decode them. In the same way, it had taken me ages to admit the possibility of Vernon's betrayal. For the second time that day, I was overcome by the rage and horror of doubt. It seemed to make the silence deeper.

'Helen?'

'What?'

Just from that one word, I could tell that she was crying.

'Have you ever been unfaithful to me?'

'Would it matter if I had?'

The trees stirred against the pale sky. At that moment I felt that, if it were true, I would be shut out from my only consolation.

'It would matter.'

Helen's hand groped in the dark warmth of the bed, found mine, and clasped it.

'That's something, anyway.'

8

THE MORNING AFTER a row always has its own atmosphere, as distinctive as the air of Sundays. A sodden cloud
of resentment sags above the breakfast table. Cornflakes
crunch in crisp accusation. Stale bitterness and hurt, like
smoke after a party, take a day or so to seep away. Perhaps
a little rancour remains each time, as smoke does, slowly
yellowing the walls.

The feeling woke me earlier than usual that day. After
my two late mornings, I now found it impossible to get
back to sleep. So I went downstairs and stood in the usual
place, leaning against the French windows in the kitchen,
and smoked and watched the dawn. The pale light grew
slowly firmer and more sure. Kindness and trust should
grow like that, becoming fiery as time goes on.

When she finally came downstairs, my wife looked
more pathetic than ever. Instead of joining her at the
table, I stayed where I was, staring out of the window.
Behind me I could hear the small sounds of Helen having
breakfast, a little symphony of rejection and pain. I knew
that she was waiting for me to speak, feeling that I was the
one who'd been vicious to her and that it was therefore
my responsibility to reopen relations.

When Fran came in, I didn't move my head. Our
daughter was immediately subdued by the atmosphere.
She said hello in a small voice. There were a few timid,
muted sounds, and then she left. A moment later Helen
also went upstairs to get ready. Only then, as though a

gun had been withdrawn from the back of my head, did I realise that every muscle in my body was tensed.

This was more than a normal argument. Our sudden nostalgic affection the night before had been a false dawn which only served to underline the darkness. This might really be the beginning of the end.

I was still thinking about it when I heard Helen's footsteps on the stairs again. I listened carefully, wondering if she would go straight out. Instead, the footsteps came down the corridor towards me and stopped at what I guessed was the kitchen door. There was a silence. My arms and legs were so tense that they ached.

'I hope you're proud of yourself.'

Helen waited in vain for me to reply. Then her footsteps slowly dwindled back down the corridor. As the front door closed, my body relaxed almost to the point of collapse. I moved weakly from the window and sagged into a chair.

A sense of the large, silent rooms engulfed me. The house had the pointed emptiness of a playground during lessons. For the first time since my marriage, I felt utterly alone. However, I didn't sit there long; action had always been my answer to these moods. As soon as I found myself beginning to brood, I went upstairs and dressed.

The first thing I did on arriving in town was to book myself on to a flight for Naples the following week. Five days had already passed since my discovery of the letters and I had now begun to suspect that Vernon was using his friend at the British Museum as a pretext to stall me for some reason. In any case, authentication of the letters, even if it could be relied on, meant nothing: there was no reason why genuine letters shouldn't lead to fake memoirs. Everything hinged on what I found in Naples. Seeing it in that light, I couldn't understand why I'd let Vernon keep me in London so long.

Ten minutes after buying my ticket, I was striding through the bookshop, inviting Vernon upstairs for a drink. In the office, I faced him across my desk and plied him with whisky, hoping he would make some kind of slip. He talked, more freely than ever, of his past: the difficulties of being a homosexual during the war, the death of his parents, how he had decided to carry on the bookshop mainly out of respect for his father. It had all come to nothing, of course, because the values of the past were gone. The world had turned its back on literature. All that mattered now was to be like me, slick and without scruples.

Vernon made no secret of his resentment or pain, and this did something to restore my trust in him. After about an hour, I realised that the long-delayed revelation of his homosexuality had opened the floodgates. Now he was loquacious as the old and lonely often are. He was also so frank about himself that it became more difficult to doubt him.

One phrase sank into my mind like a dart into balsa wood. While we were discussing secrets, codes and the war, I asked Vernon if he thought it a coincidence that such a high proportion of British traitors had also been homosexuals. He became perfectly quiet and still, and it occurred to me that I might have given away my suspicions of him. After a few moments, he crossed his legs in that precise way of his which I now saw was really a piece of high camp, touched the fingertips of his left hand delicately against those of his right, and spoke.

'Betrayal is a terrible thing.'

When Helen got home that evening, I was standing almost exactly as she had left me, leaning against the window and watching the glow sink into the garden. Without moving my head, I listened to her footsteps approach along the corridor, ready to repeat that morning's performance and simply stand there in silent stillness. The footsteps reached the kitchen door, but didn't stop. Instead they started across the tiles. I had a mad fear that she was going to attack me. This made my back feel so vulnerable that, at the last moment, I span to defend myself.

'Claude!' Helen flung her arms around me, dropping her bag as she did so, sending a pen and some coins skittering over the floor. 'What a horrible day!'

I was taken aback; it took me a moment to return her embrace.

'Why? What happened?'

'Us not talking this morning, of course. I've been upset ever since. It's been awful, Claude.' Helen rested her head against me and closed her eyes. 'Promise me we'll never have a row like that again.'

I stared over her shoulder, slowly shaking my head.

'You're like a child.'

'Am I?' She held me closer, nestling needily, so that I felt the desire to push her away. 'Maybe I am. Just promise me.'

'How can I promise that? Nobody can say what will happen in the future.'

'No. I suppose not.' A moment later she released me with a sigh and bent down for her bag. I picked up the coins and the pen and gave them to her.

'I went up to the bookshop today. I wanted to see if I could get Vernon to make a slip.'

'And did he?'

'No. He seemed more friendly than ever. That only makes it worse, in a way. All along, he might have been acting a part while my feelings were genuine.'

As I spoke, Helen unplugged the kettle and took it to the sink. Her voice came over the roar of water.

'Even if he had forged the letters, would it necessarily be a betrayal of your friendship?' The roar abruptly stopped. Helen moved back towards the worktop. Her tone was conversational. 'I mean, his liking for you might be perfectly genuine. He may be driven by circumstances you can't understand.'

'Betrayal is betrayal,' I said flatly.

Helen had switched the kettle on. She walked across the tiles, serene as a swan, and took both my hands in hers. I wondered whether she could feel that they were trembling.

'He never really meant you any harm.' Her voice fell kindly on my ears, as sad and soft as the dusk outside. I listened intently, as though to decode her words. 'Try to think the best of people. I don't believe there's really any harm in them.'

'I don't agree. There's endless malice in the world. People like Vernon feel that they've been wronged by me. They use their own pain as a justification.'

Helen released my hands and gave a small shrug. Then she moved away to carry on making her tea.

'Ross is coming round tonight,' she said lightly.

'Oh yes?'

'Hmm. He popped into the shop for a sandwich today and I thought I'd ask him over.'

'I see.'

Helen poured boiling water into a cup, concentrating as though it were nitroglycerine. When she'd finished, she didn't turn towards me, but just stood there, staring down into the steam. Her dimpled fingers fiddled with a teaspoon. I flew across the room and grabbed her shoulders with all my strength, spinning her round to face me.

'Claude! That hurts!'

'What are you trying to tell me, Helen?'

'I don't know what you mean! Let me go!'

'You know perfectly fucking well. Last night when I asked you, you wouldn't give me a straight answer.'

'Asked me what?'

'If you'd ever – '

As we stood there, staring at each other and panting, the doorbell rang. Helen gave a desperate little laugh.

'Saved by the bell!'

I redoubled my grip on her arms, squeezing pain up into her face.

'Why can't you just have the guts to come out with it?'

With that, I thrust her away from me. Her expression of pain gave way to one of fury.

'It's taken you long enough to ask, hasn't it? All these years you've never even noticed me enough to wonder.'

Then she became suddenly calm. Her hands, as they always did when the doorbell rang, rose up to fiddle with her hair. A moment later, she went to the door, apparently composed.

My own composure was more difficult to feign. The blood was swarming in my head; my breath was short. I went quickly to the worktop and started gathering the ingredients for supper before Helen and Ross came in.

When they did, they didn't behave in the usual way. Normally, they would both sit at the table while I cooked. Now it was only Helen who sat there. Ross came to lean against the worktop, watching as I chopped carrots, onions and peppers, and tried to engage me in a conversation about my search for Byron's memoirs, an activity for which he had so far shown nothing but thinly-veiled scepticism.

Since my side of the conversation consisted solely of monosyllables, Ross eventually gave up and went to take his usual place at the table with Helen. I heard his voice over my shoulder.

'Claude Wooldridge, antiques dealer and man about town, is not his usual chatty self.'

Smiling the sort of broad smile I usually reserved for business negotiations, I turned to face him. He was sitting with the sprawl of a champion after an easy first round: legs spread, arms hooked over the back of his chair. The checked shirt which clothed his stocky torso looked as if it had been deliberately dirtied and crumpled to express a vicious disregard for the formalities. Its higher buttons were open over a springy mat of hair which was almost a direct continuation of his beard, conspiring with his bushy eyebrows to mock the baldness above. The deep-set eyes were slightly blearier than usual, the nose a little redder: Ross had already been at the whisky.

'How are you off for money, Ross?'

The smile which he had assumed in answer to mine wavered a little as I spoke, becoming vague around the edges.

'Fine,' he said coldly.

'You're not here for a handout, then.'

The weakened smile collapsed completely, razed to a grim horizontal. Helen needed no paranormal abilities to sense that something unpleasant was about to happen. Without speaking, she stood, her pine chair squeaking loudly against the tiles, and left.

The silence continued for a moment after her departure. Then Ross, with a voice as tart as a cooking apple, cut through it.

'How dare you speak to me like that in front of Helen!'

He remained perfectly still as he spoke. Even his lips barely moved.

'Do you think she doesn't know? It's no secret that I give you money.' In all the time I'd known him, I'd never had this kind of argument with Ross; my pulse was racing in outrage. Now that I'd started, though, I felt compelled to go all the way. 'We all know your crummy little books aren't enough to support you.'

'If anyone else said that,' said Ross, still without moving, 'I swear I'd kill them.'

'But as it is, you're dealing with the goose that lays the golden egg.'

'Don't you come it with me, you jumped-up little bar-row boy!' He leapt to his feet, sending his chair clattering across the tiles. 'Don't you fucking push it! Jesus Christ, all you care about is money, isn't it?'

'If you say so.'

'Look at the way you live!' With unveiled violence, he hurled a heavy arm through the air, then started pacing towards me. 'You've spent your entire life cheating and lying to get here, and now you think it gives you the right to lord it over people with your fucking patronage. Why can't you see that I'm worth fifty of you?'

'Your having to say that proves you don't believe it.'

Ross stopped pacing and laughed.

'Listen to him! Now he thinks he can analyse me with his amateur psychology! Look, mate, the nearest you can get to an understanding of humanity is knowing the lowest price some old dear will take for her family heirlooms.'

'Perhaps. And you're the one who's been happy to live off my expertise.'

About to reply, Ross suddenly stopped and slapped his palm against his forehead, as if to wake himself up. The anger on his face gave way to desolation. It was an emotional gear-change which only he could have completed so smoothly.

'What is happening?' He looked at me in astonishment, suddenly seeing the whole thing from my point of view. 'Why did you start all this, Claude?' Reaching out his arm, he took the last step forwards and slapped me on the shoulder. 'We're meant to be friends, for Christ's sake!'

'Just remembered who owns your flat, have you?' The hand fell from my shoulder. 'It would be difficult for you to get by, wouldn't it, without my help?'

'That's all our friendship means to you, is it?' Ross's regret was no less forceful than his rage. There was just as much power and passion in his eyes. All his emotions burned with the same brightness, and this was part of his charm. 'After all this time, is that really what it means?'

'How can you talk about our friendship? We're not friends, you and I. Not the way we used to be. When did we last have a conversation? I mean a real one, like the ones we had at university?'

Ross shook his bald head at me.

'What do you expect, Claude? What do you expect from friendship or love? Do you hold these things to be eternal?'

'Once I did.'

Ross came right up to me so that his face was only a few inches from mine. His voice fell to a croak.

'Then you should have worked at them a little harder.' After staring at me for a few moments, he turned and walked towards the door. 'You had other priorities, though.'

'Ross!' He was moving away down the corridor. 'Come back, you stupid fool!'

Ross didn't even pause or turn around. I detected that there was still a little anger in his stride, which made me suspect that, when he got to the front door, he would slam it. Instead of that, though, Ross did a strange and somehow moving thing: he left the door wide open, so that I could see the roof of my car and the distant trees of the park.

When I eventually went upstairs to look for Helen, I found her lying in our bedroom with the curtains drawn. It was as though she were sick. She refused to get up for supper. No more words passed between us that day.

By the time I awoke the following morning, Helen and Fran had already left the house. On the doormat, among the day's bills and junk mail, I found a large buff envelope.

When I opened it upstairs in my study, the envelope turned out to contain Tim's promised information on the Millbank family. The first sheet I looked at had been photocopied from something called *A Brief History of Denholm and Environs*. Tim had highlighted the following passage:

MILLBANK HOUSE

Millbank House, which remains as one of the finest Georgian buildings in the area, was built by Gilbert Millbank Esq. at the end of the eighteenth century. Little is known about this enigmatic and ill-fated man or his family, whose name now survives only as that of the charming house they have bequeathed to us. We do know that Gilbert Millbank owned cotton mills in Yorkshire and moved to the South of England in his middle years, perhaps in an effort to further social or political ambitions. The story of how these were tragically cut short remains one of the most colourful in Denholm's history and a knowledge of it can only make a visit to Millbank House all the more interesting.

In 1817, mysteriously leaving his wife and daughter in Hertfordshire, Gilbert set off for the Continent with two other successful businessmen. The exact motive for the trip is unknown, although Gilbert's wealth would suggest that it was simply idle pleasure. All was well until the group reached Venice, where Millbank abruptly parted company with them. Accompanied by a single manservant, he set off down the Mediterranean coast in the direction of Naples, travelling so rapidly that, a few days later, he was standing on the hills above the city and gazing out across its famous bay.

What was the reason for his fateful journey? If it was mere tourism, then Millbank was a strange tourist indeed to travel so quickly to Naples, not allowing himself time to even glance at the countless natural and architectural splendours along the way. A strange tourist indeed: a tourist possessed! It seems obvious that some other purpose drew him south to the teeming city, famous even then for its footpads and brigands, a purpose which, alas, we shall never know.

On his return to England, Millbank's servant related that he and his master had taken rooms in a hotel on the sea-front. Though they arrived late at night and in bad weather, with huge waves and driving rain out on the bay, Gilbert insisted on leaving the hotel again as soon as he had changed his clothes. He went alone. He never returned.

For some time after his disappearance, Millbank's family continued to hope that he might still be alive . . . it is easy to imagine how empty that fine house must have felt without him, how forlorn those splendid gardens! No body was ever found, no motive for his strange flight to Naples and death was ever uncovered, although it seems likely that, a rich Englishman wandering the city on such a night, he met his fate at the hands

of common thieves. Eventually, in the winter of 1817, his family
gave up hope . . . alas, the blow was too much for his daughter,
Amelia. One freezing morning her body was found floating in
the ornamental lake – where the visitor can still take a rowing
boat out today. Although there was no positive proof, there seemed
little doubt that, mad with grief, she had taken her own life. This,
at least, was the view of Vicar Daniels. Burial in the churchyard
was refused on grounds of suicide.

For some time after reading the passage, I sat perfectly still.
Here were facts, external, objective, and incontrovertibly
true. At last the doubt which Vernon had sown in my mind
on the day we decoded the letters had been dispelled. The
official version of Gilbert's story tallied exactly with the
contents of the letters. I was sure of everything now.
Gilbert had been conducting an incestuous affair with
his daughter. In Venice, he had met Byron and heard the
story of the stolen memoirs; the secret had been entrusted
to him alone because of the sympathy between the two
men. Gilbert, without a word to his companions, had
sped south. The only explanation for his departure was
contained in a coded message to Amelia.

In my mind's eye, I could clearly picture him, setting
out from his Neapolitan hotel into the wild night of his
death: hooded eyes squinting against the rage of the wind,
hair blasted, cloak flapping about him as his obsession drove
him out into the storm. The author of the Byron letters
would have met his end with cold bravery, a patrician
sneer on his face, a last look of chilling arrogance for his
murderers. Perhaps they had hesitated before they struck,
unsettled, as Helen and I had been on reading his letters,
by an overwhelming sense of the man's evil.

My mind was still full of him when I felt the envelope
on my lap and realised that it wasn't empty.

Sinking my hand inside as though into a lucky dip, I
pulled out a small sheet of paper. To my disappointment,
this was only a handwritten note from Tim, telling me

that he hoped the information enclosed was of use and to contact him if I needed any further help.

The next page I withdrew was blank except for the name 'Amelia Millbank' written in Tim's hand. For a moment I stared at it in confusion, wondering if this was another coded message. Then I realised that, of course, I was looking at the back. Turning the sheet over, I found a picture which looked as if it had been photocopied from a book, perhaps the same one from which Tim had got the information about Gilbert.

It was only a simple pen and ink sketch, yet it left me in no doubt that Amelia had been a strikingly beautiful girl. The artist had economically conveyed an impression of symmetry, liquid curls and languid eyes. For all its extreme youth, the face seemed to me to have a haunted look about it. However, I only glanced at this picture for a moment, because there was still one more sheet in the envelope, and I suddenly realised what this must be: a picture of Gilbert himself. At last I was to see the man who had put me on the trail of the memoirs, whose presence had chilled me through his letters, whose code had led Vernon such a merry dance. Placing Amelia's portrait on my lap, I pulled out the sheet, which, as I had guessed it would, had Gilbert's name handwritten on the back. A moment later, the absolute faith which had come to me so suddenly on reading his story was abruptly destroyed.

Like Amelia's, Gilbert's picture had been copied from a book. Unlike hers, though, his was a proper portrait, done in oils and ornately framed. Gilbert, resting most of his weight on a stick, was standing in front of Millbank Hall. A dog sat on either side of him, each staring adoringly up at their master: a small, chubby man, with a round face and bright button eyes.

This buffoon was so far from the image of Gilbert which had built up in my mind that at first I simply couldn't believe it. For a long time, I sat there and stared at the portrait, trying to convince myself that this gouty-looking fellow had been capable of incest, that he could have invented a complicated code, that Lord Byron might have entrusted secrets to him. The more I stared at the picture, however, the more I became convinced that none of these things could be true. Far from being evil and intelligent, Gilbert Millbank had obviously been pleasant, good-humoured and rather dense.

In desperation, I stood up, went to my display cabinet and got out one of the Byron letters. Lying it on the glass, I placed the portrait next to it and stared at each in turn, as though this would somehow help me to believe there was a connection between the man and the words. All that happened, though, was that I was struck for the hundredth time by the careful violence of the handwriting, and convinced that the man in the picture couldn't possibly have produced it. Then I looked above the display case at my picture of Byron, head tossed back, large chin jutting arrogantly forwards, unwelcoming and hard. The poet would never have let a fool like Gilbert past his front door.

Suddenly enraged, I snatched Gilbert's portrait from the display case, screwed it up, and hurled it into the corner of the room.

'It's all a trick,' I muttered. 'Somebody's having a great laugh at my expense.'

Then I felt exhausted, as though drained by that brief moment of anger. I left the study, crossed the corridor, and entered the bedroom, where I undressed and slipped into bed like a reptile slipping into a swamp. There I lay all afternoon in an amphibious half-world, neither asleep nor properly awake, brooding the nature of betrayal.

When Fran got home, I was still lying there, my mind in twilight. Lying in the gloom, to me like the gloom of a sickroom, I heard her moving around downstairs. There was a speed and sharpness about the sounds which convinced me it couldn't be Helen. She went to the kitchen and made herself tea. Then I heard the familiar creak of the stairs and the click of the bathroom door. A few moments later there came a distant roar. Fran went into her bedroom.

In due course, my wife came home. I heard her exchange greetings with my daughter, the voices calling cheerfully. Neither of them knew that I was there. The roar returned, accompanied by the thunder of distant pipes: Helen was running herself a bath.

Stealthily, I got up and got dressed. I felt a storm coming which would rent everything in two, so I was going to make things up with my daughter once and for all: to tell her I had been too hard on her, to show that I loved her unconditionally and would continue to love her whether or not she passed her exams. She was all I had left to cling onto.

I crept past the bathroom, for Helen would still be in a bad mood with me and I didn't want her to know that I was in. The door to Fran's room at the end of the corridor was closed; I tapped on it lightly. There was no reply, so I gave another, firmer tap. A moment later, I opened the door a crack and peeped in.

My daughter was leaning against the window-sill with her headphones on. The first thing to strike me about her, as usual, was the length and elegance of her body. She was wearing jeans full of tears, which I assumed must be fashionable, and had most of her weight on one leg so that her hips slanted at an irritatingly insouciant angle. The second thing to strike me was that she was smoking.

At first I felt the righteous fury which I would have felt on any normal day: I had expressly forbidden Fran to smoke, and she had sworn time and again that she didn't. It was her dishonesty that annoyed me more than anything else. Then I remembered the reason for my visit, and it seemed to me that her smoking was in fact an opportunity. Here was my chance to replace rage with kindness, to prove my love for her and lash her to me.

The immediate problem was to attract her attention; because of her headphones, she hadn't heard me open the door. I coughed, but there was no reaction. She just stood there, nodding her blonde head slightly in time to the music and puffing at her cigarette. The air outside the window was sunny and still. The smoke flickered brightly from her hand and lolled in lazy clouds from her mouth, floating like incense.

After standing there stupidly for a few seconds, I walked into the room and around the bed, picking my way through underwear and magazines. When I tapped Fran's shoulder she almost jumped out of her skin.

'Jesus Christ!' As she said it, she span round and pulled the headphones from her ears. 'You scared the shit out of me!'

'Sorry, Fran. I didn't know how else to let you know I was here.'

Fran looked down at the cigarette in her hand like a murderer remembering a smoking gun. Her arm jerked, and it was gone.

'What do you want, in any case?'

'What was that?' I asked, sniffing. 'What did you just throw out of the window?'

'A cigarette.'

Even if I hadn't heard the defensive note in her voice, I would have known. I could smell it quite clearly now, as sweet and musky as a bonfire.

'Yes, but what was in it?'

'Tobacco, of course. What else?'

'Don't you bloody lie to me!' I bellowed. 'I want the truth!'

'Alright, then,' she said, as though addressing a child. 'It *wasn't* tobacco. Happy now?'

'How dare you take that tone with me!'

Grabbing her shoulders, I whirled her round and threw her on to the bed. She landed bouncing on her bottom, staring up at me in half-laughing amazement.

'That Roger gave it to you, didn't he? I swear I'll kill the bastard!'

'Roger had nothing to do with it – '

'Shut fucking up!'

My fury almost silenced her, but she found the courage to mutter: 'Christ! You did ask me a question, after all.'

Ignoring this minor act of rebellion, I began to rave at her. There would be no laws broken in that house, not while I was still the master of it. If I ever caught her smoking that shit again, she would be out on her ear, no questions asked. She was to stop seeing Roger. There would be no more going out, full stop, until she'd done her exams. Her mother had let her have her own way for too long, and this was where it had got us. Well, the easy days were over now, and no mistake. It was time for me to put my foot down, to try and restore some honesty and decency to the house before it was too late.

Even as I spoke, I knew that I wasn't handling the situation well, that I would only succeed in alienating her, yet somehow I couldn't stop. She had tapped a bottomless rage in me. I stood there in front of her bed haranguing her with all the passion of a fanatic at Speaker's Corner.

Fran listened seriously to the whole thing. Her behaviour up till now had been so normal that you wouldn't have thought she'd been smoking pot. When I at last fell silent, however, she stared sombrely up at me for a moment, then, unable to keep a straight face, burst into fits of giggles.

'You're potty, you know that?' She began to shake her head weakly, helpless with mirth, and I just stood there, horrified to see my daughter so altered. 'Potty! Potty!'

The word seemed hilarious to her. Suddenly all the rage, frustration and impotence of the past few days flowed through me. I raised my hand above my head as though she were eight instead of eighteen and I could regain her respect by spanking her. Fran's giggles stopped as though at the flick of a switch. She now sat completely still, staring up at me in defiance, daring me to do it. For a moment the only movement in the room was that of my rigid arm, jerking above her head as though in a high wind. Then my daughter suddenly looked so beautiful, composed and young that the arm came crashing down. At the last minute it stopped as though it had run into an invisible shield, and I ended up giving her a light pat on the side of the head.

'You bastard!' Fran buried her face in her hands and began to sob. 'I hate you.'

'Nice to be appreciated.'

As though this were a second blow, Fran rolled over and curled herself into a ball on the bed, sobbing harder. I wondered whether her tears, like her giggles, were helped along by the drug. Her voice was muffled.

'You've never really loved me. You've never approved of anything I've done. If I really was a junkie, it would only be because of you. I can't wait to get away from you.'

'The feeling is mutual, believe me,' I said, moving towards the door. 'The sooner you spread your little wings and fly the nest, the happier I'll be. Don't stick around on my account.'

Out in the corridor, I stood still for a moment, astonished at myself. Then I saw that I had to keep on being angry. I strode furiously off and hammered on the bathroom door.

'Helen! Let me in!'

A moment later, I heard the click of the lock. When I opened the door, Helen was quivering back into her bath.

'Whatever's the matter, Claude?'

'Fran's taking drugs in her room, that's all,' I said, walking round in circles.

'Don't be ridiculous. What drugs?'

'Cannabis is the only one I've found so far.'

Helen gave me an angry look.

'I hope you haven't gone and upset her.'

'Well, yes, I think I have, actually, if that's alright with you. What did you want me to do, for God's sake, fetch her an ashtray?'

My wife sighed, as though in acceptance of some inevitable problem. Then I understood and was stunned.

'You knew about this, didn't you? You knew she was smoking that shit even before I came and told you.'

Helen looked away from me, absently rubbing her breasts with a flannel.

'Yes, I knew.'

It took my breath away. Lifting a towel, I went and sat down on the chair by the bath.

'You knew,' I gasped, 'and you didn't even bother to tell me.'

'Because I could guess how you'd react, Claude, and you've just proved me right.' Helen smiled, as though suddenly feeling she was being too hard on me. 'There's no point in bawling at her and making her feel bad. We have to let her make her own mistakes.'

'Oh, and of course you know that, don't you? You know that with such an absolute certainty that you don't even need to consult me on these little family matters. In fact, the less I'm involved the better. Is that right?'

'You know that's not true, love,' said Helen in her softest voice.

'All of you are living secret lives behind my back. That's what it comes down to.'

'What's got into you, Claude? Whatever are you talking about?'

'Betrayal. I'd have thought that was obvious enough.' A look of concern filled Helen's face. About to speak, she reached out a dripping arm to me. 'Get away from me!'

The arm recoiled.

'Claude!'

I jerked up from my seat, holding my hands out as though to ward her off, and began to back towards the door.

'Keep away!'

Outside in the corridor, I was unsure of what to do. After a moment's hesitation, I decided to go and lie down in the gloomy sickroom where I had spent the afternoon. When I had slipped back into my swamp, I began to think again and again of something Vernon had said about his friend at the British Museum. The friend would only be able to spot a fake; he couldn't tell you for certain if something was genuine. It crossed my mind that people might be like ancient documents, that you could spot a bad fake, but never a good one, which would condemn us all to lives of constant doubt.

After a few moments, I heard Helen's bath draining away. I was sure that she would ignore me and go to comfort Fran instead, and I was already feeling bitter and hurt about this when the bedroom door opened.

'Claude? Goodness, it's dark in here!'

Through half-closed eyes I looked up at her. She had one towel wrapped under her arms and another around her head in that high turban whose construction had always bewildered me. It made her look tall and regal, a tribal queen. Her large shape seemed to float through the twilight towards the curtains.

'Leave them! I want it dark.'

Helen gave a small shrug and floated back. Lying there watching her, I felt like a sick man watching his nurse, or a child watching his mother. She seemed the source and centre of my world. When she sat on the edge of the bed and started pushing her hand through my hair, I didn't move away.

'Tell me what's the matter, Claude. Get if off your chest.'

The movements of her hand were so kind that I felt tears rising in my throat. The suspicion of betrayal is similar to love. It produces the same pain and need. I felt I loved her then.

'Are you having an affair?'

Helen lifted her turbaned head and gave a soft laugh. 'Of course I'm not!'

'Why didn't you just tell me that when I asked you before?'

'Because it's so ridiculous!' She looked down at me, suddenly serious. 'And I was angry with you. You can be a very hurtful man sometimes, Claude.'

When she spoke, I felt that people were not like ancient manuscripts at all. They could be full of feeling and warmth, and so inspire faith. All my doubts dissolved into nothing before the sound of her laugh, her touch, the kindness of her voice. I was the real traitor. The flaws in our love were all my own. Now I realised that I'd only started to doubt her after my visit to Soho, which I'd made and covered up so easily.

'I don't know what made me think it.' I began to sob with relief. 'It just leapt into my head, then, last night, when you were defending Vernon, I thought you were trying to tell me . . .'

Helen shook her head at me as though I were insane.

'What a state you've got yourself in, Claude!' She opened her large arms for me. As she did so, the towel slid down across her damp, scented skin. 'Come here. Come here. It's all in your mind. None of us would ever do anything to hurt you.'

Cradled against her warm breast, I began to weep freely.

'I'm sorry, Helen. I don't know what came over me. I really thought it. There have been so many lies in my life. And now, at the end of everything – I mean, can you understand this emptiness? I've nothing to do but wonder. First I wondered about Vernon and the letters, then the doubt somehow spread even to you . . . I think all this may be having a bad effect on me, you know.'

'It's alright, Claude. It's been a difficult time for you, that's all. I understand.'

I felt I loved her then. I suddenly clung to her with violence.

'Help me, Helen. I'm going downhill fast.'

9

BEFORE THE PLANE had even slowed to taxiing speed, the Italian mob in Economy Class were already on their feet, tugging bags down from the luggage containers while continuing the vehement conversations which had been going on since Heathrow. Over the intercom, first in Italian and then in absurdly accented English, a stewardess told them to remain seated until the plane had come to a complete standstill. Nobody took any notice. The stewardess obviously didn't expect them to: she had rattled off the message like a child on her fifteenth Hail Mary.

Up in Business Class we did things according to the book: everyone sat tight. Of course, there were fewer of us. We didn't need to stake our places in the mad scramble for the exit. As the roar which had carried us from England fell into a nasal whine, I sat and stared out of the sunny plastic porthole. The runway was a patchwork of repairs over which the plane bumped audibly. Swinging suddenly into view, the airport buildings looked small and temporary.

When the whine dwindled to a sigh, even some of my co-travellers in Business Class cracked and left their seats. I watched them, one eyebrow raised in surprise and mild reproof, determined to be more English than anyone on board. That's the effect the Italians have on us, and always have done, since the time of Byron and before. A part of us sneers at their lack of civilised reserve, yet somewhere deep inside we cannot help but envy them their anarchic souls. This causes us to make a great show of being more civilised and reserved than ever.

Only when the sigh had shrunk to a whisper and the plane was categorically at a dead standstill did I undo my safety-belt and take my briefcase from the luggage compartment. Inside was the map of Naples on which Vernon and I had marked the Apuglias the previous week. The case also contained transcripts of all Gilbert's letters and copied samples of Byron's handwriting from his Venetian period, which had been supplied by Vernon's friend at the British Museum. Only the day before, the friend had sent a report on headed paper saying that the letters had passed every conceivable test. As far as he could tell, they were the real thing.

At Heathrow, we had boarded the plane by way of a high-tech motorised gangway. We now left it, past the professional smiles of the hostesses, via a rather rickety set of airport steps. The evening sun on my cheek was still hot. In Naples, summer had already arrived. It made me feel young and light-hearted, as though this were not my last business trip, but my first foreign holiday.

At the bottom of the steps we were all herded together, regardless of ticket class, in an orange airport bus. The noise of so many Italians in such a small space was deafening. As we rumbled off towards the terminal, clinging on to railings and leather straps, I thought of Byron. His own impressions on arriving in Italy would have borne some similarity to mine. He too would have been struck by the rowdy exuberance of the people, the hollow clarity of the light. Like me, he would have felt the sense of his own Englishness increased, would have stared at everything around him with a heightened awareness of himself and who he was. Little had really changed since his arrival. Fundamentally, the same meeting of cultures was being repeated. He might almost be said to be arriving in Italy again through me.

As these things crossed my mind, I had for the first time

that sense of Byron's presence which was never to leave me while I was in Naples. It couldn't have been more intense if he'd been physically there, swaying from the leather strap next to mine and scanning the jabbering faces around us with that pale sneer of his. I felt he was there, summoned to watch over my quest for his lost work, his treasure, his final vindication. Then, through the back window of the bus, I saw him.

About a hundred yards away now, the last group of passengers from the plane was boarding another orange bus identical to our own. What I saw was this: a short, rather portly figure emerged from the shadow of the wing, quickly walked a few steps, and vanished behind the bus. Even at that distance, there could be no mistaking his startlingly pale skin and glossy chestnut curls. His most instantly recognisable feature, though, was his limp. The man walked as though trying to disguise it, just as Byron had done, half-gliding. He was wearing a white shirt, open at the neck. The rest of his clothes I do not remember, though I am sure that they were modern.

The apparition was so solid and ordinary that at first I only felt a thrill of recognition, the excitement of seeing a long lost friend in a crowd; I wanted to call out to him, to somehow stop the bus and run back across the tarmac. Indeed, I had to stifle a cry, telling myself to be logical. The whole thing had been a trick played on my mind by the Italian light, to whose intensity I was still adjusting. I had only to wait until we arrived at the terminal to see a man who bore a passing resemblance to Byron get off the bus behind ours.

When I waited at the terminal door, however, and watched the passengers from the bus file in, the pale figure was not among them. Nor were any of the male passengers wearing open-necked white shirts. Yet he had been as real as the bus itself, or the weeds which pushed through the cracks in the runway, and I was left, not with a feeling of fear or confusion, but simply with one of grief that he had so completely disappeared.

Only as I drove my hired car towards the city did the fear and confusion arrive. The limping man had obviously been a technician or a member of the cabin crew; that I could have believed it was Byron, even for a moment, had been nothing but a sign of my own growing instability.

As Gilbert had done, I put up in a hotel overlooking the bay. It may even have been the same hotel; it certainly looked old and crumbling and grand enough. Evening was falling by the time I tipped the porter and was left alone in my room. Opening the rattling windows, I stepped out on to a small balcony. Long light was falling east across the city. A hydrofoil rode it out in front of me, turning slowly, ploughing the sunset in plumes off the bay. Below me was the main road which follows the huge curve of the sea-front, a wild, weaving race-track, roaring and hooting. In the far distance on either side were the silent hills which loom above the city.

Looking to my right, to the steep heights north of the bay, I was struck by a house perched near their summit. From where I stood, it was just a tiny rectangle, yet its two rows of windows mysteriously caught the dying sun and flashed down at me as though broadcasting in code. I could tell that the long facade was of pale pink plaster, and it suddenly struck me that, if he had ever made his home in Naples, that palazzo would have been the residence Byron chose. Far above the ants' nest of the city, flashing its message nightly from the hills, the building would have made a fitting home for one who had so towered above his time.

Night fell while I was standing there. The windows of the palazzo ceased to flash, and soon the building was lost from view. The great hills themselves then fell into darkness and became no more than flat shadows pasted on the purple sky, sustaining galaxies of lights. I could understand why Gilbert had been tempted to rush out and start his search immediately. Even without the hope of finding the memoirs, the city would have had a mystery and excitement of its own. All the same, I stayed where I was, leaning against the railing and staring out across the dark water. I was thinking of what I had seen at the airport, wondering. Of course, it had been a technician or a member of the cabin crew. Yet perhaps people do see ghosts, and in the most unlikely places.

The following morning, I set off in my hired car and began visiting Apuglias.

The first lived in a block of flats in the south of the city. When I got out of the car I found myself in a street which, in comparison with the rest of Naples, had a strange air of desertion. On one side was a row of old buildings with cracked plaster and peeling shutters. On the other was the block of flats: a series of balconies stacked on top of one another and crowned with a thicket of aerials. The sun was already warm against my back as I crossed the street. From the distance came the roar of traffic and the braying of horns, as though some vast mechanised hunt were in progress, yet everything around me was empty and still. As I walked towards the flats, I was struck by the full absurdity of my own hunt. I couldn't help wishing that this Apuglia lived in the older buildings on the other side of the street, which looked somehow more likely to harbour ancient manuscripts.

All the same, when I saw the name 'Apuglia' neatly printed by one of the bells, I felt an absurd excitement. Soon after my ring, a woman's voice came over the entry phone, and it actually seemed possible to me that she might be the descendant of a woman who had stolen Byron's memoirs.

'Good morning, signora.'

'What do you want? I warn you, you'd better not be trying to sell me anything.'

'On the contrary. I'm buying.'

What followed was vintage Wooldridge, worthy of the best days of my youth, when I'd prided myself on being able to get my foot into any door. Signora Apuglia – I assumed she was married, since she sounded only a little younger than me – was suspicious, to say the least, and refused to let me into the building. I had my patter all worked out: I was an English antiques dealer looking for Italian pieces, prepared to pay good money for what she might consider junk. What passed for junk in Italy was often a valuable curio in England . . .

I must have leant against that wall, being politely persuasive, for almost five minutes. Slowly, the rasping electric voice, which seemed to echo around the street, became softer in tone, and eventually the door buzzed to let me in.

Upstairs, I found a thin, grey woman with a timid air. She showed me around her flat rather obsequiously, obviously hoping by now that she would make a quick few thousand lire out of me. In this she was no doubt encouraged by my sombre charcoal suit and silk tie, which had been chosen for precisely that purpose. The flat was small. It had been furnished in the sixties and barely changed since. There was nothing which could conceivably be called an antique. While I looked round, humming thoughtfully at the kitsch, I asked about her family and found out that they hailed from Sicily. This was not encouraging. It seemed unlikely that her ancestors had been living in Naples when the memoirs were stolen.

'It's a beautiful flat,' I said at last, 'but I'm really interested in older pieces. Do you have anything like that, signora – family heirlooms and such like – that you might be willing to part with?'

'Well, I do have a box of things my husband left when he died. It's just old rubbish, though, worth nothing to you. In any case, I couldn't possibly sell, because of the sentimental value.'

It was by no means the first time I'd heard that line in the course of my career. People seem to set a lot of store by sentimental value, until you get your cheque-book out, that is. Then it's surprising how unsentimental they suddenly become.

'Would you mind if I had a look, anyway? Just out of interest, you understand.'

'Of course not. Have a seat. I'll go and fetch it.'

Although I was by now almost certain that the flat didn't contain the memoirs, a little of my excitement returned as she left the room. It was the kind of excitement I hadn't felt since the distant days of my first deals, the thrill of knowing that the hunt has started, the hunger for the kill.

As a professional must, I masked my anticipation, remaining poker-faced while Signora Apuglia walked back into the room and placed a dusty cardboard box on my lap. Her own uneducated assessment had been quite correct: the box contained nothing but rubbish. There were a few old photographs, a bundle of letters in Italian, a reproduction duelling pistol, a silver fob-watch of inferior workmanship and a rusty hand-grenade, which I assumed was no longer live.

The signora hovered nervously while I rummaged around. When I put the box down on the floor and stood up, she looked disappointed.

'Don't you want any of it, then?'

'No, signora. Thank you, but I rather think not.'

'Not even the grenade? People collect things like that, don't they?'

'They do indeed,' I said, making for the door, 'but I wouldn't want to deprive you of yours. All I could offer you would be money, you see, and I understand the sentimental value that grenade must have. Thank you so very much.'

Striding back towards the car, I felt almost my old, sharp self.

★   ★   ★

For the rest of that day, and well into the evening, I continued my search. By the time it was too late to politely call on people, I had visited the flats of seven Apuglias. Two of them had been out. The others had happily shown me the oldest of their belongings, none of which had much more than sentimental value: five little collections of junk, pathetic and moving. These attempts to salvage something from the wreck are always self-defeating. Far from cheating time, they become themselves the most perfect symbols of sorrow and decay.

Needless to say, there was no sign of the memoirs. Nor were any of the Apuglias really able to trace their family histories back to Byron's day. Returning to the hotel, past ornate civic fountains and curving palm-trees, I did some serious thinking. Even assuming that the letters were genuine and that a woman called Apuglia really had the memoirs, the chances of their having survived looked pretty slim in a city where the entire population seemed to live in blocks of flats. It wasn't like England, where dusty attics and barns could remain undisturbed for centuries. If the manuscript had been lost there, the whole thing would have somehow looked more promising.

The name Apuglia itself was only a starting point, of course. Maria could easily have married, leaving any property to her children and thus in a different name. Then again, there was no reason for the family to have stayed in Naples. They might have left the city or even emigrated.

As I thought about it all, whilst simultaneously trying to hold my own in the anarchic traffic, a part of me wanted simply to give up and go home. Five years previously, I would have done so: the whole venture was obviously an uneconomical use of time. Now, however, time seemed to have no better use. There was nothing left for me to do. I decided to at least visit all the addresses we'd marked on the map before returning to England.

As soon as I got back to my hotel room, I rang home to

see how everyone was. Helen answered in her usual cheerful voice. The sound was like an aural photograph of the house and everything it symbolised, the life I'd temporarily left behind. At that time of night, Helen would be getting supper, moving around the kitchen with the phone held in a lopsided shrug. Everything was fine, she told me. Fran was upstairs getting on with her revision. Ross had said he might pop round after supper. Christopher was already there. Everyone was happy. Everything was fine.

When we'd finished speaking, I hung up and went out on to my little balcony. There I leaned against the railing and stared across the black water. I thought about my family in England. They were perfectly happy without me there. From their point of view, I probably caused far more problems than I solved. If I were to die out here like a latter-day Gilbert, nobody would really mind. My daughter, unlike his, wouldn't be throwing herself into any lakes. There would be grief, of course, but grief passes of its own accord. Nobody would really mind.

As I felt these things, I was suddenly struck by how alien everything was, from the roar of the traffic below me to the warm smell on the air. Occasionally a whisper from the waves would magically find its way through all the commotion like a sigh at a party. That gentle intrusion, like everything else, was foreign: I was a stranger in a stranger's world. Without knowing why, I turned to look up at the gloomy hills to the north of the bay and I was suddenly filled with a loneliness more piercing than I had ever known. For the first time in my life, I had a vague intimation of what it must be like. For the first time, I knew the bitterness of exile.

Turning from the hills, I stared out at the dark bay. One of the vast, wedding-cake white ferries had just put out for the islands, a citadel of lights on the void, flickering in the haze.

★　　★　　★

Over the course of the next six days, I managed to interview all the Apuglias save one. As my lonely search progressed, I began to get to know the city better. The visitor to Naples is initially struck by the boiling noise of the place, the graffiti on the crumbling stonework, the gigantic palms, the rat looking idly up from its busted rubbish-sack. Yet always hidden away, just behind the surface, is the splendour of the ancient empire. Even in the old town, the poorest quarter, you can look through some huge iron doorway coming off its hinges and find a fairy courtyard with a baroque fountain at the centre, shady, cool, and asleep in the roar. Add to this the towering outline of Vesuvius, the smudged sketch of Capri on the horizon and the empty, magic atmosphere of all cities by the sea, and it's difficult not to fall in love.

The more time I spent there, the more I expected to see my apparition again. It seemed that he was always very near but just out of sight. When I turned one corner, I felt that he immediately vanished around the next before I could catch a glimpse of him. If I had just been a fraction quicker, I would have seen him hurrying away with that gliding limp of his, smiling at the child's trick he'd played on me. At its strongest and most irrational, this feeling almost had me running off along the Neapolitan streets after the elusive phantom. Or I would long to somehow creep up on him, as one might creep up on a grazing unicorn, and get a good long look: the mythical creature in his travelling-cap of gold braid, leaning on his sword-stick, lingering long enough to give me a bored look before dissolving in the light of the *piazza*.

Just as the search for the memoirs fed my imagination, my imagination in turn fed my search. The magic of Naples fed both, so that the whole story of the letters no longer seemed as unlikely as it had at home. At the stage when I should have been most disconsolate, my hopes were reaching their peak. The memoirs were there, just like the spirit of the poet himself, but somehow eluding me. All I had to do was pounce at the right moment.

On the morning of the seventh day, I rang Vernon in the bookshop.

'Good morning, Claude. Any progress?'

'No,' I said, squinting at the glittering water outside my hotel room and imagining the gloom of the office. 'I've visited all the Apuglias save one, and none of them has got it.'

'I'm most sorry to hear that.' The words were as light and dry as the husks of insects on a sill. It seemed absurd to me now that I could ever have suspected such an empty man. 'However, I can't say that I'm surprised.'

'I'm sure it's here somewhere, Vernon. I know it is. Very close. I can feel it.'

'What are you going to do, then?'

'Start researching the history of the family, find out if Maria ever married, and try to track down her descendants that way. First, though, there's still that last Apuglia to interview. He's been out every time I've visited him so far. I'm going to have one last try this afternoon.'

The last Apuglia lived on the outskirts of Naples in Accerra, a desolate little village with dusty streets and tragic, crumbling buildings. It had no apparent structure or centre. It was just there, sprawling on either side of a minor road, as though its founders had been too laden with sorrow to care where they settled. Apuglia's was the top floor flat of an ancient tenement, against whose wall two small children were kicking a ball when I arrived that morning. The soft, sandy stone, which seemed to be favoured in the neighbourhood, was so dry and flaky that you felt you could have pulled the place down with your bare hands.

As soon as I got out of the car, I felt an unbearable anticipation. Perhaps it was only because this was the last address on my list, my last hope of an easy end to the search; or perhaps, after all those apartment blocks, it was the ancient sadness of the place itself which excited me. Whatever the reason, as I approached the building I felt the sense of Byron's proximity more strongly than I had since my arrival in Italy, and I was certain that his memoirs were up there in the top-floor flat.

The two boys stopped playing football and watched me solemnly as I rang on the bell. There was no answer, so I asked them if they knew where Signor Apuglia was. They shook their heads and ran away. Deciding to try again in an hour, I wandered aimlessly off.

On the main street, I stopped for a cappuccino then strolled on along the sun-blasted pavement, looking in the windows of the shops, all poor and forlorn. After a while, I came to a sort of working-men's club, and decided there would be no harm in making a few enquiries.

It was a large room, strangely bare, with a few cheap tables scattered around and a shuttered bar. The floor was of ancient lino. The paint was peeling. Against the back wall, almost entirely obscured by a grey shroud of dust, a fifties pinball machine stood like something from a phantom amusement arcade. There were about ten men in the room, all playing or watching the same game of cards. None of them were younger than forty, and most of them looked twice that age. When I walked in, they all stopped what they were doing and stared at me.

'Good morning, gentlemen. I'm looking for Signor Apuglia.'

This produced no reaction, unless the ancient tableau in front of me could be said to have become more motionless.

'I've tried to visit him a couple of times this week, but he hasn't been in. He lives at the end of the main road. Does anybody here know him, by any chance?'

Wood grated against lino as one figure, perhaps the most ancient there, got to feet. The rest of the tableau remained motionless as before, so that the little old man looked bizarrely like somebody stepping out of a painting. He seemed toughened but very light, like a shrunken conker. Before he spoke, he rattled phlegm into his mouth, juggled it for a moment from cheek to cheek, then swallowed.

'I'm Apuglia.'

'Ah, signore, a pleasure! I was wondering if I could have a word.'

'Go ahead. I'm listening.'

'A private word, if you don't mind. A little business matter.'

'Business, eh? Very well.'

He began to move towards me. His companions came to life as though at the wave of a wand and continued their game, ignoring the pair of us. Shuffling slowly, with the aid of a walking-stick, the old man led me out into the dusty sunshine. On the pavement outside the club was a line of chairs, their seats made of coloured plastic cord.

As soon as we'd sat down, I instinctively went into my patter about being an antiques dealer from England. Apuglia listened politely, motionless, his head on one side. From time to time, his body would be wracked by a cough. Beneath his liver-spotted baldness, his face in the brightness was scored and hatched like a butcher's board. There was a greyish tinge to his skin.

When I'd finished, he sat and stared at me for a moment.

'I've got a lot of antiques. My flat is stuffed with them. Our family is old and I have travelled a lot. I was in the merchant navy. I gave my life to the sea.'

'I see. Well, if we could just – '

I made a move to get up and lead the way, but the old man remained motionless, staring at me through sharp blue eyes.

'Would it be one thing in particular you're looking for, perhaps?'

'No,' I said, not wanting to put my cards on the table until I knew exactly what the score was. 'Just general antiques.'

Signor Apuglia, resting both hands on his walking-stick, turned away from me and stared across the street.

'Don't lie to me, my boy. That is not the way to get what you want. I am not an educated man, but you should know that I am by no means a stupid one. You have an English accent. You know my name. You have travelled a long way to find me, then called three times in a week. There's nothing "general" about all this.'

'You're quite right, signore.' I spoke smoothly, but I was furious with myself for making such an obvious blunder. His age and ill-health had led me to underestimate him. 'I'm looking for one thing in particular.'

'Would it be a book, by any chance?'

I kept my voice calm.

'It might be, signore.'

'Very well,' gasped the old man as he levered himself to his feet. 'Come back to my flat and we'll talk business.' I stood up as well, but before we set off Apuglia placed his hand on my arm. At first it was weightless and empty, like a bunch of twigs, then suddenly it gripped painfully. 'Do you believe in fate, signore?'

'Well, I – '

'A simple yes or no.'

'Yes.'

Apuglia gave a strange laugh, which made him look almost as mad as he was old.

'So do I! Fate! My name is Giuseppe, by the way.'

With that, he led me off down the sunny street. It took us at least ten minutes to complete the short walk to his house, during which neither of us attempted to start a conversation. Everything about Giuseppe had rekindled the suspicions which Naples had just begun to dispel. If he had something which purported to be the memoirs, his story would have to be pretty convincing.

The flat, when we reached it, did little to allay my fears. At the top of a rickety staircase, the old man showed me into a tiny kitchen–diner. The windows were thick with dirt. The wallpaper was ancient and lumpy, one strip hanging off in a leprous triangle. There was a pre-war armchair positioned in front of a huge television which didn't look much younger. Apart from this, though, the place was like a treasure-trove, crammed with art and artifacts from all over the world. There were African statuettes on the rusty cooker, prints from Thailand on the wall, erotic etchings from India, an Arabic coffee-pot. A huge Chinese vase, full of walking-sticks, stood in one corner. There was a Cossack knife on the TV and a set of bagpipes by the armchair.

'This is amazing.'

'We are hoarders in my family.' Without consulting me, he placed two small glasses on the plastic table-cloth and filled them with some evil-looking local liqueur. 'And, as I told you, I have travelled. Sit down. Drink.'

The liqueur turned out to taste even fouler than it looked. Giuseppe drank his in a single swig and disappeared into what I took to be his bedroom. A few moments later, he shuffled back in, stopped over an inlaid mahogany box. My knowledge of the Italian stuff is not all it should be, but I would have guessed the thing was late eighteenth century.

Giuseppe couldn't have handled the box more gently and reverentially if it had contained the corpse of a baby. Having laid it on the table, he stood for a moment staring down at the pattern on the lid. Then, stiff and formal, he sat opposite me. There was a silence before he spoke.

'I have a feeling that this box contains what you are looking for.' He stopped for a cough which it seemed might finish him. Then he laughed weakly. 'I told you, I believe in fate!'

'Why? What's in the box?'

'A very old book.'

There was another silence while I waited for him to go on. Eventually I realised that he was prepared to sit there staring at the patterned wood all day.

'Tell me about it.'

'There is little to tell.' Giuseppe removed his eyes from the box and looked up at me. 'The thing has been in our family beyond the memory of my great-great-grandmother. Nobody ever told me how we came by it or when. Of course, there were always rumours that it was of great value, but nobody really believed them, least of all me. I am not a romantic man, signore. I do not believe in myths.'

'Only in fate.'

'Now that you have arrived, perhaps. The story went, you see, that somebody would come to claim the book in the last days of our line. Well, I am the last living Apuglia, signore, and you can see that I am not a well man. And here you are, just as prophesied! So, perhaps the story wasn't rubbish, after all. Perhaps this old book of ours really has some value.'

'There's only one way to find that out. What language is the book in, by the way?'

'I do not know. Not Italian. But I have only looked at it a couple of times. The writing is difficult to understand.'

'It's a handwritten book?' I took a deep breath. 'Right. Let's have a look at it, then.'

Guiseppe returned his eyes to the box and stared at it solemnly for a few moments, as though a great secret were to be read in its pattern if he only concentrated hard enough.

'The price for opening the box is two million lire.'

'Oh, I get it!' I said, quickly working out the figures and seeing that he was asking the best part of a thousand pounds.

'You don't think the thing is really of any value, so you're trying to fleece me before I've even seen it.'

'I am a poor man,' Guiseppe told the box with a slight shrug, 'and not a well one.'

'Heartbreaking,' I said, getting to my feet, getting tough and getting vernacular. 'You can't piss me around like this, mate. I've been in this game all my life and, believe me, this isn't the way it's done. Two million lire just to look inside some poxy little box is ridiculous. Good day.'

'Very well, signore,' he said as I moved towards the door. 'Your visit has been useful, in any case. Perhaps I shall try to sell the book elsewhere.'

'Do what you like with it,' I replied, and left.

Of course, I was only bluffing. There was a sort of low cunning about Apuglia which told me the best policy with him was to be brutal. The more weakness I showed, the more money he would try to cream out of me. In any case, I needed a little time to think. When I left Accerra, I drove straight to a bank in the centre of town, where I'd already made arrangements, and took out the two million lire. Then I went back to my hotel room, drew the curtains, lay flat on my back and forced myself to be still for two whole hours, collecting my thoughts. It was slightly discouraging that Giuseppe kept referring to the contents of his beloved box as a book rather than a bundle of old papers. I'd been expecting to find a loose folio manuscript of the kind burnt in Murray's fireplace. Yet I knew that during his Italina period Byron had used little black notebooks for his journal and observations. It was conceivable that the early draft of the memoirs which Maria Apuglia had escaped with was contained in one of those. The only way to find out, of course, was to cough up and have a look at the thing.

When I'd rested, I got out of bed and spent the rest of the day on the balcony, studying the samples of Byron's writing, trying to know it as well as my own, to internalise it. If Giuseppe had the genuine memoirs, it was little wonder he'd never bothered to try and read them: the poet's hand was jerky and florid, the letters at times crammed so powerfully together that the eye could barely jemmy them apart.

Evening was falling by the time I arrived back in

Accerra. Light was gleaming weakly through the grime of Giuseppe's high window. There is an air of expectation about these Italian evenings, something huge and warm, like the charge generated by a waiting crowd. The gloom seethes with it. As I got out of my car and approached the house, I was acutely aware that this was the most important moment of my professional life: the biggest find, the biggest deal, the crowning glory or humiliation.

It took Giuseppe a fairly long time to get to the door. When at last he did, he looked bored to tears, a real pro.

'This is a surprise, signore,' he said flatly, standing aside to let me in. 'You are the last person I expected to see.'

'Indeed. You still have the box?'

'Yes.'

'I am prepared to pay your price for the privilege of looking inside. Cash.'

'Come upstairs, then. I think I should warn you that I have company.'

The company turned out to be a couple of young toughs with oily hair and Latin sneers, sprawled in front of Giuseppe's table. The box was still there, just as we had left it that morning.

'My friends, Luigi and Salvatore,' he explained. 'Wait outside on the landing, could you, boys? Don't go too far, though.'

The pair edged past me with insolent stares and left the room.

'You fear violence, signore?' I said, placing my briefcase on the table by the box. 'Some men would consider that an insult.'

'At my age one can't afford to be too careful. Forgive me, signore. Nothing personal, you understand.'

Before we started, I insisted on seeing his passport. It was covered in faded entry stamps and at least proved that he was a genuine Italian, not some London mate of Vernon's, and that his name really was Giuseppe Apuglia.

'Nothing personal, you understand,' I said, handing

it back to him. 'I just like to know who I'm doing business with.'

We sat down as we had done that afternoon, facing each other across the box. I opened my briefcase and slid an impressive-looking bundle of notes to him across the table. With a slight nod, Giuseppe produced a key from his pocket and slid it into the tiny lock. For a full minute afterwards, he fiddled unsuccessfully with it. I was beside myself, yet Giuseppe's face remained completely impassive. He was like a priest who finds he cannot open the tabernacle when the congregation are waiting to receive, yet knows that any sign of irritation on his part will destroy the ritual. The old man's solemnity, as he no doubt intended, communicated itself to me: I forced myself to remain motionless while he fiddled with the lock. At last it clicked. Still without speaking, Giuseppe slowly opened the lid and turned the box towards me.

The interior was lined with red velvet, dark and shiny in places. There was only one thing inside. It was a plain notebook, bound in black leather. After all the anticipation, the thing was somehow so small and ordinary that, as soon as I saw it, I felt sure it was nothing more than some old family diary. All the same, I picked it up reverentially and examined the binding. Though slightly frayed in places, it looked suspiciously new, but then I supposed that, if it had been locked away in the dark for all those years, it probably would. The flyleaf had a brown mottle on it which, to me at least, looked convincing. I turned it. The next page was filled with the handwriting I'd examined so carefully that afternoon.

For a few moments I could do nothing but stare at it in awe. Then I glanced up at Giuseppe to see if he would give anything away, but he seemed to have forgotten my presence. He was gazing at the lid of the box. The life had so entirely gone from his eyes, and the movement from his body, that he was like an ancient, shut-down robot. Trying to silence my breathing, I began to read.

'The truth – particularly for a man like me – who feels deserted by his friends – is a burden. The time has come for me to unburden myself of it . . . What I shall write will be the whole truth, uninformed by fancy, unpolluted by any fear of the world. It may never be read – not, at least, for a very long time – but writing it will one day serve a purpose – my own vindication before an army of detractors and persecutors . . .

'The truth – I want to record the truth of my life in exile – my present, lonely life – but I am afraid I shall be forced to write a great deal about the Past – Marriage, Fame, Betrayal – it sometimes appears to me that there is nothing left but recollection – so much now is recollection . . .

'Writing, of course, is no more than a way of talking to oneself. That is what, a lonely man, I am reduced to – greatness must always carry loneliness in its train – To be great is to be adored by some, reviled by others, and misunderstood by all – greatness is an exile of itself – yet now it is more profound for me – here in Venice – an exile not only spiritual, but geographical as well – an unbearable loneliness at times . . . One's own company – sweet burden! – is at once the greatest pain of exile and its greatest consolation . . . Solitude is the exile's only luxury.'

At that point I forced myself to stop and take stock, though all I wanted to do was to go on, to read until I had devoured every word. There was little doubt in my mind after reading the opening that the memoirs were genuine. The words rang true. The poet was speaking to me directly through them. I felt sure that these pages had been touched by Byron; I could even see, from the sudden thickness of the ink, where he had stopped to recharge his quill. I was the first person ever to be admitted to his thoughts in those moments, and this made the little book in my hands different in kind from any object I had ever held. It seemed to stop the progress of my life. My emotions piled into it like cars into a wall, all of them at once. Only the presence of Signor Apuglia on the other side of the table prevented me from weeping.

Taking care not to show any emotion, I held the book

at an angle to the light to see if any giveaway impressions had been left in the paper. There was nothing. Then I took the samples of Byron's handwriting from my case and began to compare them with the memoirs, word by word, letter by letter. Twenty minutes later I had not found a single discrepancy.

Giuseppe had looked away from his box to watch all this with the silent respect of an amateur.

'Well?' he said, when I eventually replaced the samples in my briefcase. 'Is this the book you're looking for?'

'It may be. But I will have to read it all before making a decision. Do you mind?'

'Not at all, signore. I shall wait.'

He didn't have to wait that long because, to my profound disappointment, there were only twenty pages. As I read them, something very strange happened. First, I was transported to Venice. I left Giuseppe and his cluttered little flat far behind me, I forgot his friends, waiting threateningly outside the door. Instead I saw, as I had so many times before, the young poet writing at his desk. I heard him muttering. Above the lap of the canals outside, I could just distinguish the scratching of his pen. The light was thrown upwards from the water in a shimmering curtain. Yet I was not on the outside, as I usually was, watching him from across the room. I was inside his head, reading through his eyes, so that the words filled me with a terrible and claustrophobic sense of *déjà vu*. I could almost predict what the next word would be before I read it. It was as though I were not myself, but Byron, reading through his own work in the pale light of dawn.

As the introduction had promised, what I read was the poet's vindication. Much of it dwelt on his brief marriage, painting his wife as a bitter, petty and malicious woman who resented his greatness and was determined to humble him. There were also, as promised, long sections describing his life in exile. A conversation with Shelley on the subject of reincarnation was reported at some length, along with Byron's thoughts on Italy (very similar to my own), women, and the question of spirituality in animals. It was only towards the end that Augusta was mentioned:

'I have loved and lost — in this I am like all men — though few have lost so utterly as me! The pain of the loss comes from the lost thing being a part of ourselves — the more of ourselves we find in it, the more we love — that is why the so-called unnatural loves have always seemed to me most natural . . . Let me here confess it openly — as I have half-confessed it in so many other places before — I love Augusta not only as a sister, but also as a woman.

'As a woman! The world will raise its hands in horror and call me monster — but what could be more natural — more human — than that I should love the one being closer to me than any other? And love her so much that the knowledge that such a one can have existed — and still does exist — albeit so many empty miles away — that knowledge, I say, is in itself enough to somewhat ease my loneliness.

'Yet — alone I am . . . how I would love to see one of my English friends — to talk with any Englishman at all — even Polidori, by God, would do. But Shelley is gone away from Venice all this month and nobody from England has troubled to visit me for an age — I am to make do with my pets and a low-born Southern girl who exasperates me with her dramatics — surely the most tiresome weakness of her sex. Tonight I must escape to the Opera, where I shall be bored — intolerably bored — and stared at, as ever.'

That was the last paragraph and, as far as I was concerned, the last necessary proof. The 'low-born Southern girl' was Maria Apuglia, with whom Byron had obviously fought that day. Though he made light of it, the quarrel had probably seemed like the end of the world to her. Desperate for English company, he had gone to the opera, met Gilbert, and invited him to dinner. Meanwhile, Maria, furious at being walked out on in this way, had disappeared with the little book.

In the end, making an effort to master my emotions, I

put the memoirs down on the table in front of me. By this time it was completely dark outside. The young had taken control of the town, and were calling to one another across the cobbled streets. Signor Apuglia was watching me carefully, with predatory narrowness, trying to calculate his price.

'You were right, signore,' I said. 'This might be the book I am looking for. Then again, it might be a clever fake.'

'Nothing is certain in this world. All I can tell you is what I have: the book has been in our family for as long as I can remember. Do you want to buy it or not?'

I paused. Common sense told me that I ought at least to ring Vernon, or maybe even summon him to Naples and let him look at the book. However, I could already imagine his scepticism and I knew that, no matter how sceptical he was, I would have to buy the memoirs.

'What are you asking?'

After staring at me for a moment, Apuglia named his price, which was in the region of twenty thousand pounds. Although this was less than I had been prepared to pay – and a fraction of what the volume, if genuine, was worth – I threw up my hands in horror. Too easy an acceptance of his price would have been an invitation for him to increase it. Then we haggled for a good half hour, by the end of which I had managed to beat him down to fifteen thousand.

'I can have the money for you tomorrow,' I said, 'but under no circumstances will I bring it to this house.'

Apuglia looked hurt.

'Why not, signore?'

'I don't like your friends signore. Like you, I am not a fool. You will have to bring the book to a meeting place. Ring my hotel at midday tomorrow and I'll tell you where.'

'Very well.'

'And listen to me, you miserable old man,' I said, leaning towards him across the table. 'I am immensely powerful and wealthy. If you sell the book elsewhere between now and tomorrow, or if I find out that you have tricked me in any way, you're dead. Understand? I'll have you hunted down and killed and all the teenage toughs in the world won't be able to protect you.'

How I managed to keep a straight face while saying that, I'll never know. Apuglia, being Italian, swallowed it unquestioningly.

'Signore!' he spluttered. 'Please! I am a man of my word!'

'Very well, then. Until tomorrow.'

The following evening, I stood on the sea-front and watched night settle on the bay. The book was in my briefcase and I felt I had been touched by greatness. For ages I stood and stared, imagining the size of the sea. The hills around the city seemed to grow more silent as the daylight went, as though the falling darkness muffled things like snow.

The following afternoon, I flew back to London. The briefcase never left my lap during the flight. The Range Rover was in the long-term carpark at Heathrow. Whenever I had to stop on the drive back to Greenwich, I couldn't help reaching my hand towards the passenger seat to touch the case, as though for reassurance.

Evening was falling by the time I got back home. The trees in the park, black and swaying, seemed smaller than they had before my departure. The air smelt of England and home. It felt chilly to me now. Opening the front door, I heard riotous laughter from the kitchen. The smell of home was stronger inside. As I walked down the corridor, I found there was a lump in my throat.

All of them looked up as I opened the kitchen door. They hadn't been expecting me. The laughter froze on their faces. Helen, Ross and Fran were there: three relationships which had somehow gone cold. Stepping into the room like that, back from another world, I suddenly saw it far more clearly than before: a dead friendship, a marriage I was too tired to sustain, a daughter who had outgrown my jealous love. They must have seen it more clearly, too, in the moment of shock when I appeared.

Helen was the first to speak.

'Claude! You're back! Did you have any luck?'

'No.' What right had they to know, after all? I meant nothing to them any more. 'There were no memoirs. The whole thing was a con.'

Before leaving Naples, I had driven up into the hills on the north of the bay, searching for the palazzo I had seen on the evening of my arrival. It had not been difficult to find. It was one of the largest and oldest buildings in the area, a magnificent ruin, its gardens a haven of palm-trees, fountains and lizards. As I had sensed it would be, the building was unoccupied.

'ATTACK!'

As the two punts drew level, a broadside of waterbombs curved through the swaying light beneath the trees. A moment later the air seemed suddenly full of glittering water. The exams were over and the undergraduates of Oxford didn't care who knew.

'Don't get involved,' I advised prudently, propping myself up on my elbow and looking over the edge of our own punt. Though we had come down to Oxford to relive old times, I has no intension of getting wet. 'This could turn very nasty.'

Ross, feet astride in the back of the boat, let it idle towards the end of its glide, angling the pole in his broad hands to guide us towards the safety of the opposite bank.

'Helen's worried about you, Claude.'

I stared up at the gliding leaves, waiting for the gentle bump of the prow against the shore. I knew why Helen was worried. In the weeks since my return from Italy, I'd hardly left the house. As I'd sensed it would, finding the memoirs had marked the end of my career. The book had stayed hidden up in my study. Now that I had actually found the thing, I saw that a lot of its importance had been illusory; the search itself had been what mattered. Yet the continued presence of my find seemed to slightly alter everything which had gone before, like a question-mark at the end of a novel. It had also become a concrete symbol of the gulf which had opened between myself and my family. Only I knew that it was there.

'What's she been telling you?' I said at last.

'Not much. Just that you seem very depressed and spend all your time moping around the house.'

'Oh, I don't know. I get out every once in a while.'

There was a weight about the house which I sometimes felt it necessary to escape. One day, I had driven down to Brighton and walked alone along the sea-front, eating candy-floss and staring at the greenish waves. One afternoon, I had spent hours in the hot garden, carving designs into a stick as I had done as a child. One evening, Helen and I had gone to a party, a big black tie job full of friends. I had sneaked away early, gone down to the river, and walked its banks until dawn.

The prow gently bumped.

'Feel like telling me about it?'

His voice had been straining to sound casual. It was a long time since we'd talked to each other about our interior lives. Our friendship for years had been little more than a series of symbolic gestures and routines.

'There's nothing much to tell. If I haven't been out, it's just because I can't see much point. I don't need to work any more. I suppose you could say that I've retired.'

'Yes, but why?'

For a long time I lay in silence, thinking, listening to the shouting students and the sounds of water. The prow of the punt was lodged against the bank, and now the bows had begun to swing slowly, almost imperceptibly, downstream.

'Fran's got a lot to do with it,' I said at last. 'She's doing her last exam today, you know.'

'Yes, Helen told me. She also told me that you've shown hardly any interest in her for weeks.'

'Fran and I have had our problems, I suppose.' I stared up at the swinging leaves. It was easier to talk to Ross when I couldn't see him. 'It doesn't mean much now, of course. Our relationship was over years ago.'

'What the hell do you mean?'

'For a father and daughter, growing up means growing apart. It's like a messy divorce. Once it's over, you may maintain a civilised relationship, but the real warmth is gone. That all comes at the beginning.'

Only as I spoke did I realise how true it was. I was silent for a while. It seemed to me that the water-fight, now beginning to wind down, had noticeably cooled the summer air. The light swayed very slightly, no more than a swing when the child who last used it is already home and halfway through his tea.

'Helen thinks you've been depressed about not finding those memoirs.'

'That! That was just a way of distracting myself from everything. Perhaps it was symbolic of something wider, some desire for certainty or truth. I don't know. At any rate, all that was never the reason. Only the kids were, really, I think. Now they're gone, there's nothing.'

'Listen to me, Claude, damn it – '

The boat rocked. Lifting my head, squinting, I saw Ross get up and lower himself on to one of the little benches. Rather than have him talking down to me, I sat up myself, propping my back against the cushions in the prow. Ross stared at me intently, leaning forward in his most passionate way. He said nothing, but simply made a frustrated little gesture which meant that what he had to express was too big for words; it looked as though he were trying to shake coins from an invisible piggy-bank. Suddenly his arms flew apart.

'It's a wonderful world!'

For a moment he stayed like that, arms spread to show his statement should include it all: boats, trees, water, spires, the present and the past. Then, as though the emotional effort had exhausted him, he sagged. His back bent under the light, his face vanished into the darkness of his hands. At length, a more haggard Ross seemed to rise up from the wreckage, with a hollow voice and doleful eyes.

'Helen isn't happy, Claude.'

For the next few days, my life continued as it had done since my return from Naples. I stayed in the house. The phone would ring from time to time, but on the whole I was surprised at how smoothly my businesses seemed to run without any intervention from me whatsoever. The weather continued warm. There was little to do during the day. At times, I was tempted to get the memoirs down from their hiding-place in my study. I hadn't even looked at them since Naples. Something told me they were fake. Professional pride and the fear of deepening my mood prevented me from taking them up to the British Library.

After her exams, Fran went to France with some friends, leaving a sudden and shocking emptiness behind her: it was over. We were old. Once, I would have worried about who she had gone with and what she was getting up to, but there was no point in worrying any more. That relationship, like the others, was at an end. She had grown up and rid herself of those old emotions like a horse tossing its head to shake off the flies.

Each evening, Helen came home from the sandwich shop to find me alone in the empty house. There was an echo about the place. It seemed to refuse our voices in the way that derelict or unfurnished building do. However – perhaps because of this – we spoke little. Helen continued cheerful. It was her only answer to the world. In the evenings, she would often watch television in the living-room, as we had sometimes used to do, but I rarely joined her now. I fell into the habit of placing one of the pine kitchen chairs near the French windows and sitting there for hours, staring out into the garden as the summer night came down, allowing the weight to settle on me as it did on everything else. The darkness teemed from the sky, as quiet and velvety as blossom, burying the house.

At night, we never made love. Since my return from

Naples it had been accepted that this was something we didn't do any more. Both of us conscientiously avoided referring to the subject by word or deed. Yet it was always there, however carefully we trod around it. It hovered behind everything we said or did, just as all conversations with an aged relative are darkened by that one subject you feel you must avoid.

My stomach-aches grew worse, or perhaps they just seemed larger in the emptiness. Without the excuse of needing to run shops or look for memoirs, and prompted by Helen, I finally went to see the doctor. It was on the day before Fran got back from France. To my surprise, instead of being dismissive, he looked grave as I told him my symptoms. It sounded as if it was an ulcer, he said, but it would be as well to have some tests done in hospital, just to check. When he said that, I realised that he was thinking about cancer. I told myself I didn't care.

That was the night when Helen told me. I was sitting by the French windows in the kitchen when she got home. Evening was falling. Soon the night would open its invisible nets and release millions of black petals on to the world below, a vast and solemn sign. Lights would begin to wink throughout the hemisphere, returning the signal. When Helen said she wanted to talk to me, I refused to look at her, though she asked me four or five times, almost begging me. In the end she was forced to say it all to my left shoulder. She was in love with Ross. Since the year, desolate for her, when Christopher had gone to university, she had felt our marriage was dead. She had done everything she could to resuscitate it, but all to no avail. Neither of them had been able to deny their feelings. They had decided to wait until Fran had finished her exams before telling me. They were both desperately, unbearably sorry, more sorry than they could say. She begged me to try and understand.

There was a long silence. I stared out of the window. Death, even when the patient has been terminally ill for years, is always a blow. Yet I wasn't as shocked as I should have been. A part of me had known all along that there had been someone, and that it had been Ross, the man of passion whom it was difficult not to love.

'Claude, please speak to me.'

'Alright, then. Have you fucked him?'

'Don't use that word, love, please.'

'You make me sick. The word seems to bother you more than the action. Just tell me.'

'No. We never have.'

There was another silence. The trees on the horizon were already coated with the falling night. Shrunken by the height of the sky, they looked like cauliflowers dipped in ink. It reminded me of all the times I had sat on the front steps, smoking my last cigarette, looking at the park. That life was at an end.

'What's Fran going to say about all this? Or hasn't that crossed your mind?'

'Claude . . .' I heard Helen make a small movement behind me. 'Since that argument you had with her, when you found her smoking, she's been very upset. It's been hard for her, living with you – with us, perhaps – and sitting her exams and everything. She felt trapped. Try to understand.'

'Understand what?'

'I've had to tell her. She already knows.'

Now at last I turned from the window. Helen was sitting in her usual place at the table. Her face was covered in tears. She smiled, as though in a bleak attempt to cheer me up. When I saw that smile, I understood the essential fact about our relationship: Helen was a stranger. This knowledge sat like a physical change on her face. She was more of a stranger than any passer-by outside on the street, because at least there was a possibility of one day knowing them. Helen's smile told me that I would never know her. She was more of a stranger than the woman I had met all those years before.

Encouraged by my turning to face her, Helen crossed

the room and crouched down next to my chair, though she still didn't dare to touch me.

'You've told her,' I repeated in disbelief. 'My daughter knew you were going to leave me before I did.'

Helen started babbling on, asking me to forgive and understand, but my brain couldn't take any of it in. I cut across her.

'And what did Fran say to all this?'

'She was upset, of course, terribly upset, more upset than you could imagine. But in the end she agreed it was the only thing to do. Things just aren't working between us all. She's going to come and live with us for the moment. With me and Ross, I mean.'

Suddenly it seemed to me that until now I had been asleep. Since my return from Italy, I had accepted the death of our marriage with a strange numbness. Only this news about Fran really woke me up. I saw that this evening marked the beginning of a pain than would never end. Its sharpness made me gasp.

'All cooked up behind my back!'

At that, Helen started babbling again. I watched in fascination. Only a face so completely familiar could be suddenly so strange. I couldn't have been more astounded if some household object had come to life and started speaking to me.

'You're a stranger.'

'Never, Claude, never.' Now Helen did reach out a hand and place it on my knee. The tears were streaming down her face. 'Oh, my darling, never that. All I hope is that we can still all be close to each other and friends and – '

'Get out.'

'My poor love, I know it's going to be difficult for you to accept at first . . .'

She was still speaking when I hit her. The blow was a hard one, full on the side of the head, and it sent her sprawling. From the floor, she stared up at me with the hurt astonishment of a child or a pet which has never known malicious pain.

'Claude!'

'Get out.' My voice shook. I was staggered by what I'd done. 'Now. Or I'll do it again.'

'I'm not leaving you, love, not like this.'

I stood up and gave her a kick which made her scream.

'Get out. Go to him,' I said, and this time she went.

Alone, I sat back down, stared out at the garden, and thought. I thought: we are all alone. We inhabit a stranger's world. Everybody is a stranger. It's just that you have to live with them for a long time, at close quarters, to really understand that fact. Now I am alone. Nobody will care if I do have cancer now. This way of life is at an end. The past ends here. We don't forge friendships or relationships of love along the years. All that only has one end: to show that all of us are strangers in a stranger's world.

For a long time after she'd gone, I sat and smoked by the kitchen window. The doubt which had started during my search for the memoirs returned and consumed everything. I had been mad to accept Helen's assurances that she hadn't slept with Ross. Of course she had. After all, our marriage had been dead for years. Helen had known Ross almost as long as she had known me. Their affair could have started at any time since then.

In the end, my doubt stretched right back to the beginning. I saw that the children might not be my own. Then, as though this were the sign it had been waiting for, the past overwhelmed me. I saw Helen walking into my first antique shop on the day I met her, a slimmish woman then, very pretty, with a constant smile. Then there was the hospital on the day of Christopher's birth. Then there was the same hospital, this time with Christopher on my knee, thoughtful even then, waiting for Fran to be born. Ross, standing gravely by the font, looking like a sombre stranger in his suit, renouncing the Devil and all his works. Fran, running across the room after her first day at school, leaving Helen, forgetting her now that I was home, running to throw her arms around me and tell me she had missed me. Then giggling and shrieking as I whirled her round the room.

All of it was suspect now. In the doubt of the early hours, it all looked like a fake. Those were not my children, that was not my life. Somehow, it was someone else's life. Ross had never been a real friend, nor Helen a real wife. Perhaps only the guilt of a professional liar could have made me feel it so completely. The whole thing had been a charade. It had all been someone else's life.

In the end, though, I saw that, real or fake, the past was full of nothing but happiness. Then, perhaps out of sheer exhaustion, I began weakly to knock my head against the wood of the window. As soon as I stopped doing this, I fell asleep and had an achingly short dream. Fran and I were sitting at the breakfast table. Helen was charging out into the sunny garden to rescue the sparrow. Somehow I knew that if I followed her and arrived at the same time, the bird would live. To save it, all we had to do was touch it simultaneously, lift it in both our hands. I sped out into the garden. As I arrived, Helen turned towards me. To my despair, I saw that she was already cradling the sparrow against her nightie.

'It's dead,' she said flatly.

When she opened her hands, I saw that she was not holding the bird, after all, but a bloody piece of meat. It had been torn out of something alive and was still pulsing softly. Tubes protruded from it. It was covered in deformities and growths. Recognising the thing, I lifted my hand to my chest. It came away bathed in brown blood. The strength thundered from my limbs. Liquid began to fall in large drops on to the mangled lump in Helen's hands. Where the drops fell, the raw flesh hissed and steamed. Looking up, I saw that the woman was not Helen, after all, but Fran, and she was weeping.

When I awoke, the sun was shining on the garden outside, just as it had been in my dream. The grass was beaded with dew. Staring out at it, I realised that Fran's betrayal was the most painful of all. She was happy to go and live with Helen and Ross. Our love was genuinely at an end. Perhaps it had been the only real love. Then the doorbell rang, and I realised that its sound had woken me in the first place.

The pine chair had been a hard place to spend the night. Standing up sent pain shooting down my spine. My legs would hardly move. Wincing and rubbing my stubble, I walked stiffly to the door.

It was Ross. He was standing there, haggard and unsmiling, but somehow startlingly solid in the thin morning air. For a moment we stared at each other, me taking in his bald head, his beard, the sunken dark circles of his eyes, owlishly mournful. All I saw was the thief of my family.

'Can I come in?' he said at last.

'No.' My voice was a whispering croak. I tried to make it firmer. 'No. I've done enough for you. Too much.'

'We've got to find a way of sorting this out, Claude, if only for the children.'

'I don't care about them any more.'

'You know that isn't true. Now let me in.'

I shook my head and we fell silent again. Birds were singing all around us. I wondered what the time was. It was going to be a perfect summer's day. Where the sun fell across the drive the gravel was already glittering. At this evidence of warmth, my body began to shake as though I had just emerged from hours in a freezing bath.

'When did it start?'

'What?'

'You know what I mean. When did you first – '

'We never have.'

'I don't believe you. I can't believe anything either of you says any more.'

Ross began to move up the steps in my direction. There was a look of sympathy on his face which infuriated me. He reached out an arm.

'Claude – '

As soon as he was in range, I punched him. The power of it frightened me. He fell down the steps and went sprawling on the gravel. For a moment he lay still. Then he rubbed his jaw and shook his head.

'Shit!' He sat up and glowered at me. 'Feel better now, do you?'

'No. I'm sorry, Ross. I didn't mean to do that. I'm sorry.'

The stocky man stood, beating crossways at his trouser-legs. He straightened.

'You're just saying that to try and make me feel guilty.'

'No.' I sat down at the top of the steps. My body started to shake more violently. 'No. I'm not sure what's happening. None of this seems real.'

'I know. I feel the same way. So does Helen. It's like a nightmare.' He paused and pulled a funny face, pushing his tongue into his cheek. 'Jesus. I think you've loosened a tooth.'

Weakness suddenly overcame me, and I found myself seeing him not as a traitor, but as a friend.

'Help me, Ross. My life's falling apart. What am I going to do?'

Still trembling, I hid my face. A moment later, I felt his big hand on my shoulder, and suddenly was furious again.

'Get away from me!' I shouted, shrugging him off. 'You're the one who's done all this, you back-stabbing Brutus! I was your friend! Your friend, for God's sake!'

I stood up, waving my arms violently, shooing him away down the stairs like a trespasser.

'That's it! Clear off, you bastard!' With a slight shrug, he began to walk away, deliberately kicking his feet so that he left scuff-marks in the gravel. As he was about to reach the gate, I realised I couldn't bear to see him leave. 'Ross!'

'What do you want?' he said, turning at the gate. His hands were thrust deep into his pockets, so that he looked like a miserable little boy, or the student I had first seen looking glum at a party.

'Why did you do it, Ross?'

Ross looked more miserable than ever. My heart went out to him.

'Work it out for yourself,' he said grumpily, and left, stomping off down the road.

For the next hour, I sat in my seat by the window. In spite of everything, I wanted Ross to come back, as though there were some way of putting things right. Instead of that, it was Helen who came, opening the door with her key. I didn't look round when she arrived. No exile examines photographs of home. I just sat there, staring out of the window as I had the night before, but I was unable to stop myself from listening. The particular sounds of Helen entering the house and walking towards the kitchen were familiar to me at the deepest level, like the sounds of traffic or rain.

'Claude. We've got to talk.' I could hear from her voice that she was on the edge of tears. 'We've got to sort things out.'

'You're right. What sort of settlement will you want?'

She came and squatted next to me and started sobbing.

'Claude, please. I think I'm going mad.'

'Spare me the melodrama and just tell me what you want. You must have decided, if you've been planning this for so long.'

'I don't want to talk about it.'

'Look, Helen.' Her name seemed to burn my mouth. 'Just tell me that first, then we'll discuss everything else.'

'Alright, then. I only want the sandwich shop and the flat above it.'

'Are you sure that's all? You could easily get more.'

With an effort, I looked down at her and smiled. This trivial kindness seemed to break her; she threw herself across my lap, weeping piteously and begging for forgiveness. In spite of myself, I started running a hand slowly through her greying hair.

'I'm sorry I lied to you, Claude!' she wailed. 'That night when you asked me, up in the bedroom. I'm so sorry!'

'It's alright, Helen. It's alright. I understand why you've done what you've done. I know things haven't been easy all these years. Just tell me one thing: have you been unfaithful to me?'

'No.' Her voice was muffled. 'Of course I haven't.'

'It's over now, Helen. You don't need to lie any more. Just tell me the truth. How about last night, for example?'

There was silence except for the sound of her sobs. It was a relief, in a way. Knowledge brings a sharper but more simple pain.

'I'm not going to go through the usual stuff about how and when and why. What I can't guess I don't need to know. Only tell me, please, are the children mine?'

Helen stopped sobbing and lifted her head, staring at me through angry red eyes.

'Claude! How can you even say such a thing? Of course they're yours!'

'I'm sorry. But you see what you've reduced me to, with your betrayal and duplicity. I can't bring myself to believe a word you say any more.'

'What's the point in asking, then?'

'No point. I won't bother again.'

'Believe me, Claude.' Her voice was suddenly the voice of the young girl I had first met, low with tenderness and love. More than any sound, that voice was the sound of home. My mind over the years had slowly grown to be moulded around that aural shape, which now eased itself in like a cat into its favourite basket: 'Ross and I have only been – '

'I don't want to hear it!' I bellowed, jumping to my feet and moving away, leaving her crouching by the chair.

'None of it, you understand?' I took a deep breath. 'When does Fran get back from France?'

'Tonight. Around eight.'

'And she's going round to Ross's, is she?'

'Yes. I've spoken to her.'

For a moment I was silent, absorbing this fresh blow. Then I went on.

'Tomorrow you are both to come here and pick up your things. I shall be out. You will leave both your sets of keys on the kitchen table. After that, neither of you will have access to this house. Anything further you have to say will be said through lawyers.'

'What! I mean, I – '

'I'm a businessman, Helen, and this is just another kind of deal. I have to protect my interests. At the moment, my interest lies in being free to choose when I next see you all.'

Her big face looked so child-like and confused that I was suddenly filled with sympathy for her. I crossed the room and offered her my hand.

'Come on, love, hup! On your feet!'

'What's happening, Claude?'

Putting my arm around her shoulders, I began to guide her towards the door.

'You're leaving, that's what,' I said kindly. 'You're not to ring or try to contact me in any way. I need some time to myself before I can start being civilised. You understand that, don't you?'

'Yes, love.' Her voice was meek. 'I understand.'

'And then, when I've worked everything out, I'll get in touch and we can all be friends. Just leave me alone for a couple of weeks, alright?'

We had reached the front door. I opened it and we stood there, blinking in the bright morning sun. Everything looked somehow more familiar and more real. Silver and green, the leaves in the park were floating on the breeze, slowly, as though in the drag of sunny water, unwaveringly clear. Helen and I turned to face each other. She'd been crying so much it looked as if she had an allergy.

'To think that twenty-seven years should end like this!' I said. 'Still, perhaps it's as good a way as any to end.'

I bent to kiss her lightly on the cheek, but Helen threw her arms around my neck and wouldn't let go. The strength of her grip was painful, and I found myself grinning over her shoulder: it had been a joke with us since the early days that Helen would eventually choke me with a hug.

Helen liked her hugs to be long ones at the best of times. This one, since it was the last, went on for ages. We stood there on the bright doorstep, our bodies swaying as though anchored in a tide. The movement reminded me of the last couple at a fifth-form disco, shuffling through the streamers and paper cups, almost too tired to stand. I'd always felt a little guilty about finishing those hugs, though the fact was that one of us had to. But when I at last tried to wriggle free, Helen clung to me even tighter.

'That's typical of you!' she whispered fiercely in my ear. 'Typical! You always tried to get away from me, to escape into your study or one of your shops.'

With that, she released me and walked down the steps without a backward glance. Still swaying with the rhythm of the hug, I watched her leave. She was wearing one of her favourite floral dresses, a light cotton tent which billowed gently around her legs. As often before, I was struck by the fact that she seemed not to walk, but rather to glide, somehow moving with a delicacy that belied her size. By the time she reached the gate, this impression was so strong that she seemed barely physical at all, the mere image of a fat woman mysteriously projected on to the drive. Watching her walk the same way that Ross had recently gone, I realised that, while he was definitely something solid, of the earth, Helen could only be a creature of the air.

I watched closely, taking in the dimpled elbows, the strong calves. As she was about to vanish, I was filled with the impulse to call her back. Perhaps, as much as the sheer hopelessness, it was that sensation of watching an apparition which made me hold my tongue. When she floated from view, I had the feeling that she had not merely turned the corner, but physically dissolved and disappeared. If I ran out on to the street, I'd find that there was nothing there.

In any case, she was gone, and she never appeared to me again.

That house had always been too big for us, even when both the children had still lived at home. Now that I was alone there, it became a huge accusation whose very size and emptiness demonstrated how my time had been misspent. The memoirs had been the final grand illusion of my career, which, having captivated me for years like a master magician, had now vacated the stage. Released from its spell, I'd turned around to find myself alone.

It had, however, left me wealthy. The following day, although still unsure of my own intentions, I went out and had preliminary meetings with accountants, solicitors and estate agents. When I returned in the evening, I found that Helen had been as good as her word. There were two sets of keys on the kitchen table. Her things were gone from our room. Fran's room had been cleared.

The end of a relationship is a negative copy of its beginning. There is the same feeling of unreality as when you have just fallen in love, the same loss of appetite and sleep. The strange numbness, like the shock after an accident, is exactly the same. A relationship is like a holiday from loneliness, beginning and ending in the same airport. The most awful thing about the end is that it reminds you so clearly of the beginning, of the joy with which you set off. Everything is the same, yet everything has been inverted by grief.

For a full week, I stayed in the house. The long journey back into loneliness was beginning. Not for years had I been so reminded of my youthful love for Helen. I didn't shave. I hardly ate. What sleep I managed to get was taken in a bed made up on the sofa downstairs. Our bedroom was too empty to endure. At times it seemed to me that the whole thing had been the fault of Helen and Ross. Then fury filled me and I felt that I had been too forgiving with them. But sometimes it all seemed to have been my own fault. They had been driven to it in some way. This brought guilt and the feeling that I was the one who needed to be forgiven.

Helen broke her promise and rang me on the second day with tears in her voice. I put the phone down on her without a word, afraid of what I might say. She didn't try again. All of the others – Ross, Christopher and Fran – tried to ring me at some time during that week, but my son was the only one I spoke to. I told him that I didn't blame his mother or Ross for what had happened, but that for the moment I couldn't bear to see them, or even him.

As soon as I put the phone down, I realised why he had been the one I'd been prepared to talk to: I didn't love him as much as the others. It was something I hadn't been able to admit while the family was still together. Lack of love had made my relationship with him easy and pleasurable, just as too much love had soured my relationship with Fran.

For the first couple of days, I wasn't sure what I was going to do. It seemed to me that perhaps, as I had said to Helen, all I needed was a few weeks alone before I could start being civilised again. Slowly, however, it dawned on me that this couldn't be so. Forgiveness would be more difficult to find.

Only on the third day did I clearly see the course my future would take and, when I did, I was even more surprised at what I was going to do than I was at everything which had already happened. It took me a full day just to take in what it all would mean. When I had, I spent almost two solid days making phone calls.

On Friday, I was due at the hospital for my tests. Needless to say, when I awoke that morning, my stomach-ache

– which had become an almost permanent feature of my life during that week – had almost entirely disappeared. I went upstairs through the empty house and shaved my grey beard with a certain ceremony: I knew this was one of the biggest days of my life.

After I'd shaved I went, with great reluctance, into the bedroom. There I stood before the wardrobe mirror and put on a suit, just as I had done for work in the old days. I could almost smell the past on the air. I quickly packed a few things in an overnight bag and left.

Outside, it was another beautiful summer's day, full of warmth and distant sounds. Putting my briefcase and overnight bag on the doorstep, I carefully locked the house. When I'd opened the car, I was unable to resist pausing and turning round for one last look at the building. I squinted up at the windows, our bedroom on the right and my study on the left, two silent, expressionless signs. I would have liked to say goodbye to each memory in turn, but there was no time. I got into the car and drove away.

Rather than going direct to the hospital, I first made my way up to town, crawling with the rush-hour traffic. I had a little surprise for Vernon.

When I arrived at the bookshop, Freddie was rummaging around in the bin outside. He raised his head as I approached. Although I hadn't been up there for weeks, he didn't seem at all surprised to see me.

'Ah! Mr W!' he said, in a slightly reproachful voice, as though we'd had an appointment and I'd kept him waiting. 'There you are!'

Though we were by now well into June, Freddie still insisted on wearing two overcoats. In addition to these, he had now taken to wrapping his hands in oily rags. It occurred to me that perhaps a man who sleeps rough never quite evicts the chill of winter from his bones. Then I was suddenly struck by the extent to which, with his haggard face and enormously long beard, Freddie resembled a prophet or a sage. One day he would reach into that green plastic bin and take out a tablet which explained it all.

'Morning, Freddie. How's tricks?'

'Not too bad, Mr W, not too bad.' Freddie seemed contented. He stooped back down as though to read the gently semaphoring shadows of the leaves, then looked expectantly up again. 'Come to move me on, have you?'

'No, Freddie, I haven't. Not today.'

Freddie's face dropped. He knew that being moved on by me always meant a hand-out.

'Oh. I thought – '

He stopped when he saw me reaching into my pocket. I took out my wallet and handed him two notes.

'There you are, Frederick, my son. Have one on me.'

'What are these?' said Freddie, bending over the notes and examining them minutely. He looked up at me with innocent bewilderment 'Never seen these before, I ain't.'

I didn't know whether to laugh or cry.

'Those are fifties, Fred,' I said kindly, 'real ones. Accepted at all good stores.'

'Fifties! But there's two of them . . . that means – '

'Go on. Impress me.'

'No, no, Mr W. No, no. This ain't proper.'

'Nonsense, Fred.' The fact was that some of those phone calls I'd made had begun to reveal the exact extent of my own wealth, and I felt almost guilty about it. 'You just enjoy it. Take a few days off. Put your feet up.'

I began to move off towards the bookshop door, swinging my briefcase almost jauntily through the sunny air. After a week cooped up with my misery, I felt like a convalescent by the seaside. It was good to be out and about again.

'Why so much, Mr W?' said Freddie from behind me.

Glancing over my shoulder, I saw that he was standing just as I had left him, holding the money away from his body with exaggerated awe. I stopped and turned around, squinting across the brilliant street. I found to my astonishment that, for the first time since Helen had left me, there were tears in my eyes.

'Because it'll have to last you, Fred,' I said. 'We may not be seeing each other for a while.'

In the bookshop, I found Caroline polishing the glass of the display case which contained the most expensive volumes. Vernon was sitting primly at the desk, pricing up a pile of new stock. I knew exactly how he did it, his pencil sharp as a pin, his light hand almost invisible, the writing of a meticulous ghost.

I hadn't visited the shop since my return from Naples, and Caroline was obviously surprised to see me.

'Mr Wooldridge.' There was something subdued about her voice and I realised that, of course, she would have heard everything through Christopher. 'We weren't expecting you.'

'No. Nothing like a nice surprise, is there?'

If Vernon felt any emotion, he failed to show it. He was wearing a rather smart mustard-yellow waistcoat with a silk, leek-green bow-tie.

'Good morning, Claude,' he said, looking up gravely, pencil delicately poised. 'An unexpected pleasure, indeed.'

I'd forgotten how dry he was, how whispery his voice, the sound of a snake whipping over sand. I was suddenly filled with affection for him, perhaps only because he was so much a part of the recent past and, like it all, about to disappear.

'Don't start dancing on the table yet, Vernon. Come upstairs. I want a word with you.'

It took ages for him to reach the office on his arthritic legs. I helped him, supporting him by the elbow. For the first time, I noticed how his jaw trembled weakly with the strain, and this saddened me.

The office was just as it had always been. Golden dust wheeled through the buttress of light between the window and the desk. The books in their piles seemed more still and solemn than ever, their millions of silent words combining to create an aura which subdued the sound of traffic. They were like the pillars of a sacred site, loaded with hidden meanings. To break them up after all those years would be a minor tragedy, yet the time could not be long delayed. Only Vernon knew all their secrets, and he was an old man who would never have an heir. My intervention had secured the shop no more than a temporary reprieve.

I was pleased to find that there was still some Glenfiddich left in the strong-box beneath the picture of Shelley's cremation. Though it was still early in the morning, I poured us both a glass. Vernon, perhaps sensing that it was a special occasion, didn't complain. He just took a careful sip.

I placed my briefcase on the desk and sat down facing him across it, just as I had done on the day when we'd decoded the letters together.

'Vernon – ' I took a deep breath. 'It's difficult to know where to begin . . .'

Vernon said nothing, but made a small, understanding movement of his head, causing the light to sparkle across the frames of his glasses. Compared with his eyes, they seemed almost comically expressive.

'Well, you may have heard that I've been having a few domestic problems.'

'Yes, Claude.' He gave a soft cough which sounded like someone emptying a glass of dust. 'And I am most sorry, if I may say so.'

'Thanks. Anyway, the point is, there doesn't seem much point in going on with things, so I'm selling up. Everything, I mean: all my houses and shops, including this one.'

As I had known he would, Vernon showed no sign of emotion at all. He merely pushed his glasses gently up his nose and took another sip of whisky.

'I see.'

'I'm giving you advance warning of this for two reasons. The first is that it will obviously affect you. I'll do my best, but I can't guarantee you a job any more. I mean, for all I know, the new owner may want to change this place into a café.'

'Perhaps that would be for the best, in a way, Claude. I've been thinking of retiring now for some time. There are still a lot of books I'd like to read and . . .' He seemed to drift off, staring up at the bright blue square of the window. 'What's the other reason for your telling me?'

'My family are going to come looking for me.'

Vernon's eyes snapped into focus in a way which made me remember him polishing off *The Times* crossword.

'Are they indeed? And why is that?'

'Because, Vernon, my dear chap, I'm going to do a bunk. The general consensus seems to be that I should stick around and continue civilised relationships with everybody. Well, I'm bloody well not going to. My wife and my best friend have been selfish enough to run off together, so I don't see why I shouldn't do something selfish, too.'

'Much as I sympathise with you, Claude, that is not a course of which I can bring myself to approve. You have children to think of, remember.'

'Grown-ups, Vernon, not children, and they're quite happy with their stepfather. Who'll miss the spectre at the feast?'

'I'm sure that if you thought about it, you'd – '

'In any case, I'm not so sure any more that the children are even mine.'

Vernon shifted in his chair. He looked embarrassed.

'I don't know your wife, Claude, but I'm sure – ' He broke off, looking across the desk at me thoughtfully, gently swilling the whisky around his glass. 'Well, perhaps you're right, after all. Perhaps you do need a little time to yourself.'

'Exactly. Now, when they come looking, you're to tell them not to worry. Tell them I'm OK and there are no hard feelings. Report this conversation to them, that's all.'

'And where will you be?'

'Maybe a thousand miles away, maybe right under their very noses. There'll be no point looking for me.'

'You've decided where you're going, though?'

'I have the germ of an idea.'

'Very well, Claude. I'll do as you ask.'

For a while we were silent, avoiding each other's eye. I looked around the dusty room, feeling the quiet, thinking of the quiet ahead of me. Byron was still standing frozen on his beach as though nothing had happened. Suddenly, I smiled.

'Remember the day we decoded those letters, Vernon? With the thunder and the rain pelting down outside?'

'Indeed I do.'

'I was in a right old state. The last search!' I shook my head.

'And all along, I didn't see how things were coming to their end.'

Once again, Vernon looked embarrassed. He sipped his drink but said nothing.

'Ours has been an awkward relationship, Vernon, in many ways. Now that it's over, I hope you'll feel able to tell me the truth.'

'Of course, Claude.'

'You know I suspected you over the memoirs?'

Vernon gave a small smile and tugged at the bottom of his waistcoat.

'I did have that feeling, yes.'

'And was I right to suspect you?'

'No.'

Suddenly I leant over the desk towards him.

'Tell me the truth!' I hissed viciously. I would have liked to grab him by the collar, but instead I smashed my hand down on to my briefcase. 'Were you really my friend? Was I right to suspect you?'

'No.'

His voice had been as calm as before, and suddenly I

saw that there was no point in asking him. The strength went from my body and I sagged back in the chair.

'You don't believe me, Claude?'

'No, Vernon, but that's not your fault. I've lost a lot of my faith in people.'

To ease the tension, I stood up, crossed to the window and looked down into the sunny street. Freddie was gone.

'You live alone, don't you, Vernon?'

'Yes. I have done for about fifteen years.'

I turned back. Vernon was sitting completely motionless at the desk, like a painting of a refined old man. I wondered what he had felt when his last boyfriend had left, wondered if perhaps it is more difficult for them as they get older than it is for us. Then I saw that it is difficult for everyone. There are as many different forms of exile as there are people in the world.

'And does it worry you, being alone?'

'Sometimes. But human beings can adjust to anything, Claude.'

This seemed somehow the saddest thing that anyone had ever said to me, yet there had been no sadness in Vernon's voice. Perhaps, when you've been alone for fifteen years, even sadness is overcome by the silence.

For a long time, I stood there by the window, staring at him, thinking again of the silence ahead of me. Then I crossed to the desk and snapped open my briefcase. I withdrew the small black book and pushed it towards him.

'This is for you. As a kind of thank you for everything.'

'What is it?' said Vernon, picking it up and examining the leather cover with a professional's eye. If his indifference was feigned, it was perfectly done.

'I'll give you a clue: it cost me the best part of fifteen grand.'

For the first time since I'd known him, Vernon actually looked astounded. His jaw may not have dropped, but his lips certainly parted.

'I don't believe it!' he said, turning the book before his eyes with slow awe. 'It can't be true!'

'You surprise me, Vernon. You treat the thing like a holy relic, yet I didn't think Byron was one of your favourites.'

'He isn't,' said Vernon with soft awe. 'But all the same, a poet is a poet. The great are the great.'

'Indeed. Don't treat that particular relic with too much respect yet, though.' I picked up my case and began to move towards the door. 'I'm pretty sure that it's a fake.'

'You're not really giving it to me?'

'Why not? If you were trying to trick me, then it's worthless. If you weren't, and it turns out to be genuine, then it's a fair reward for your loyalty and help. In itself it means nothing to me now.'

'No!' It was the first time I'd ever heard him shout. 'I don't want it!'

PART TWO

NIGHT HAS FALLEN. Looking up from my work, I find that the boats have lit their lights out on the snoozing black sheet of the bay. A giant moth has somehow found its way through the mosquito net which surrounds the balcony, and now it is stuck here with me, lightly imprisoned in a cell of gauze. In impotent rage it hurls itself against the light by which I have been writing, distracting me from time to time with the frantic patter of its wings or the furry thud of its body. The other animals are all asleep. Sipping the cappuccino I had brought up some four hours ago, I am shocked by its coldness as one might be by that of marble or dead flesh. It seems unnatural for anything to be so cold on a night as hot as this. The warmth is a second gauze through which the lights below me shimmer hazily; all asleep. The moth's shadow, flickering and magnified like the product of a fever, might be the only life in the entire town.

This is the present: this high balcony, this typewriter clacking on the steady night air, these overflowing dog-ends, this bottle of pills. The past is not entirely done with yet, but it is dwindling. The story is making ground on the teller. Soon it will catch me up entirely and join me here, leaving this narrative to disintegrate into a diary. That moment can't be long delayed. Like the future, the past is running out.

Helen, Vernon and the rest are gone. The antique shops, the house by the park, everything I owned is now in strangers' hands. Life is not as solid as it seems.

All I took for granted came undone. The bookshop, the whole of London itself, exists for me as no more than the muddled setting of a dream. I have come, as it now seems inevitable that I would, to live in the house high up on the hill which I saw on my first visit to Naples. My family and friends still haunt me, of course, absences so concentrated that they acquire presence and fill the empty rooms. They seem magnified out of all proportion with the reality, yet less substantial, like the shadows of gigantic moths.

Having an amount of money which surprises even me, and a limited supply of time, I am allowing myself to realise my old Byronic dreams in all their shabby splendour. To begin with, the house is larger than I remembered it during those last few weeks in England, when it became my private symbol of escape. In truth, it is not a villa, or even a mansion, but a small *palazzo*. The place is so ancient and regal that the estate agent, who'd been trying to shift it for years, was able to claim that it once belonged to a Neapolitan prince. Like many others up here on the hill, it stands in a large garden surrounded by a high fence, ostentatiously parading its distinction from the cluttered town below. There are ornate fountains at front and rear to cool the air before it rises up towards the balcony where I have sat every day since my arrival, hammering out my memories of home. There's a lot of cracked, baroque stonework on the facade, leprous cherubs and bunches of grapes half-eaten by the salty breeze. The place really is quite exquisite in its own way (as Helen would have said!), in its own crumbling, pompous, Italian way.

Exiles develop a taste for luxury; my Ranger Rover has been replaced by a Morgan Plus 8, which contrasts with, yet perfectly compliments the house. To see it parked under all that crumbling stone, lounging long and white in the shade of the palms, is one of my only consolations.

The inside of the ruin is just as impressive: marble floors, absurdly decorative stucco ceilings, more space than I could ever find a use for. The main room at the front has three tall French windows leading to the high balcony where I'm sitting now. The house was unfurnished when I moved in, but I've bought a few things, including the four-poster with its white veils, where I shall only ever sleep alone.

This place, grand though it is, suffers from the drawbacks of all Italian houses, which are designed with the sole purpose of minimising the heat. There's no carpet or softness, no sense of comfort. Everything is hard. Everything grates and squeaks and shrieks. You can't move without making metal scream against marble or glass rattle against wood. This, combined with the size and emptiness of the rooms, creates an atmosphere well suited to the state of my soul.

The loneliness was hard at first. The evenings, in particular, were unbearable. It often seemed to me that putting all that distance between myself and the others had only made them even more immediate. The invisible presences in the house seemed almost physical at times. In desperation, I would find myself wandering around Naples, stopping in bars to strike up empty conversations with strangers. One night, I went down to the road on the south side of the bay, where the pale prostitutes sway like a row of ghosts in the flicker of their bonfires, and paid one of them just to talk to me for hours.

After a week of misery, I did what Byron would have done, and set off in search of a pet shop.

I found one in a tatty side street near the port, though it took me a moment to spot it. There was nothing to convey the idea of pets other than an aquarium of tropical fish, barely visible through the filthy glass.

The first thing that hit me as I stepped inside was the overpowering smell of animals and their food. As my eyes adjusted to the gloom, I realised that the walls were entirely covered by ancient iron cages, right up to the ceiling. Many of them were empty. Others contained cats, dogs, gerbils and the like.

The proprietor was an old man in a grubby shirt. There was something about him and his dungeon that reminded me of Vernon, hiding in the piled clutter of Dewson's before I took it over. Being Italian, this fellow was far less courteous than my former employee, but he certainly had a Vernonesque approach to presentation. When I asked him if he ever dealt in animals more exotic than those on display, he sneered.

'I can get you any animal you want, signore, if you've got the cash.'

Encouraged, I told him what I had in mind.

'Animals like that are a lot of trouble,' he grunted. 'Why don't you just settle for a cat?'

'Thank you for your advice. Can you get them for me?'

'Sure, but they won't be cheap.'

'Which is exactly why you should encourage me to buy them, I'd have thought.'

This seemed to annoy him, so I decided to make a preliminary purchase by way of mollification. After a moment's thought, I settled on a large British bulldog. Even before I'd got him out of the shop, I'd decided to call him Trelawny.

A week later, the surly bugger rang me up to tell me that Percy, my parrot, had arrived.

Percy was big and colourful and quite indescribably beautiful. His wings had been clipped when I got him, to stop him from flying away, so I didn't need to keep him in a cage. He half-hopped, half-flew across the endless marble floors of my house, occasionally stopping to test the echo of his screech against the ceiling. To see him perched on the railing of my balcony, with the glittering bay and the blue profile of Capri behind him, almost made me forget the past. I began trying to teach him to recite various phrases, most of them obscene, but without success. He seemed to become attached to me, though, as much as a bird could. I decided to let his wings grow back to see if he would fly away.

A mere two days after the arrival of Percy, my supplier

rang again and told me that he'd just had a shipment which had included Castlereagh. Castlereagh was a fully-grown chimpanzee.

We quickly became great friends. Wherever I went, he wanted to follow, loping along by my side and, preferably, holding my hand. When I was writing out on the balcony, he would sit and watch me loyally for hours. He drank out of a cup and ate from a plate, albeit with his fingers. When I turned in each night, he scrabbled up the side of the four-poster and curled himself up in the canopy.

The animals were a bit messy. Trelawny tended to slobber a lot, leaving a trail on the marble behind him. Percy produced a quite incredible amount of crap as he hopped around. Castlereagh, at least, was easy to house-train. The first day I had him, he unceremoniously squatted down to take a shit in my stately front hall.

'Castlereagh, you disgusting animal! Go down and do it in the garden!'

He stiffened and looked at me for a moment out of his sharp little eyes, obviously hurt. Then he scampered out to the balcony where I was sitting, climbed the railing and, without even looking, launched himself into space. I thought he'd kill himself, but he miraculously landed in the palm tree by the fountain, shot down and shat by its trunk, looking warily from side to side as he did so. When he'd finished, he belted back up the tree and started jumping up and down, shrieking and waving the branches at me. It was the first thing that had made me smile for days.

A mere two weeks after I'd first got them, I began to feel that my animals *knew*. One night, after a particularly upsetting event, I came home and drowned my sorrows in gin, which always makes me thoroughly miserable. One by one, the animals appeared from their various parts of the house to console me. It was a warm night, but not stifling. Naples was a shimmering crescent below us. Floating lights were all that remained of the hills across the bay.

My animals came and sat with me and I couldn't help

feeling that they knew. It was obvious from the way Percy sadly cocked his head at me, from Trelawny's desolate eyes, from the mournful, tender way Castlereagh climbed up to lay his head on my chest, that they knew exactly what I'd been through and what I must yet endure.

The shock of exile is the shock of total change. An entire world has been destroyed, and thus a personality. It's strange, you see, to undergo this amount of loneliness and change.

Music is a strange thing.

Apart from people I chatted to in bars, and that one prostitute, I had no real human contact at all for the first few weeks out here. High on the hill, alone with the elaborate decay of my *palazzo*, I began to feel like an ogre in a fairy tale, waiting without hope. Late at night, when everything had closed, I would come home and walk up the echoing marble staircase, imagining my wife. How she would have loved this house! Fran would have, as well . . . but it's pointless to imagine. None of them will ever see this place.

I knew that even then. All the same, as I climbed the staircase I would find myself picturing one or other of them stretched out on the couch in the huge front room, miraculously waiting for me, asleep, or staring blindly at the decorative ceiling. Instead, only my animals were waiting: Trelawny bounding, Castlereagh shrieking, Percy hopping awkwardly, the cripple of the group. Somehow their very affection seemed to make the emptiness much worse. I often didn't sleep all night. I thought the loneliness would drive me back to England. Then I met Paulo.

Paulo worked in a rather snooty bar just down the hill. He was only thirteen, so I imagined that at the end of the summer he'd go back to school. Perhaps because he looked younger than his age, he seemed to feel he had to play the adult. Seeing him at work, carrying five plates at once or whirling behind the bar as though making cappuccino were a sort of martial art, you'd have thought he'd been a waiter for years.

When I first tried to strike up a conversation with him, he was very distant, almost rude. On finding out that I was from London, he said that, yes, London had its points, but it would never be Naples. With that, he stalked off, quite the little man. At my age, and after all I'd achieved, I had been crushed by a child. He wasn't to know, of course. The lonely, whose habitat is silent, are easily bruised by words.

A few days later, I spoke to the manager. Rather than trudging all the way down there, why didn't I have Paulo bring things up to me for a small supplement? (Lots of bars provide this service in Naples.) The manager was agreeable, so I gave Paulo the address.

His first delivery was a momentous occasion for me. I'd been in Naples for almost three weeks, yet he was the first person to visit my house. Before he arrived, I arranged everything with the idea of luring him into my life. The house was an elaborate trap laid by a lonely man: gate and front door open, sports car gleaming, exotic animals to hand. All of it should have made me certain of charming him, yet a few weeks of real isolation had left me feeling like a monster and a freak. I worried that he would find me frighteningly eccentric, or absurdly affected, or that he would simply be put off by the aura of my age and solitude. When I saw the slim, dark figure walking along the road towards my gate as solemnly as a altar-boy, carrying a tray covered by a cloth, my palms began to sweat.

I immediately sat down and pretended to work. Over the reports of my typewriter and the mantra of the crickets, I heard the gate open and Paulo's footsteps approach down the drive.

'Signore!'

'Eh?' Without getting up, I leaned over and looked down at him through the ornate, peeling ironwork of the balcony. He was standing by the Morgan, squinting up into the molten light. 'Oh, it's you! Just bring it up, could you? The door's open. Turn right at the top of the stairs.'

'Sure.'

A moment later came the boom of the closing door, followed by the echo of his footsteps on the marble. When he'd placed the tray on my table, Paulo lingered for a moment. I just sat and stared at my typewriter. He coughed.

'Nice car you've got down there.'

'Thanks.'

'I'm going to be a racing-driver, you know. All the best drivers come from Naples.'

After that, it seemed that we would run out of things to say. The deafening pulse of the crickets only emphasised the silence. Paulo brushed at a fly that was bothering him. I noticed that he had a large, painful-looking spot on his chin. He shifted awkwardly, preparing to leave. Then, in the nick of time, Trelawny trotted through the house to say hello and started slobbering all ove his smart waiter's shoes.

'Doggie,' the lad observed. Since he was now looking in that direction, he saw Percy hiding under the table. 'Oh,' he said lightly. 'You have a parrot, too.'

His tone made me smile. Deciding to play my trump card, I leant back and lifted my head.

'Castlereagh!'

There was a screech and the chimp came flying down towards us – he'd been up on the roof – and landed on my table, where he stood staring at my visitor and bouncing up and down with excitement.

'Fuck me!' said Paulo, jumping out of his skin. The ice was broken at last. 'Jesus!'

'This is Castlereagh.'

'My god, it's a monkey! I don't believe it! You've got a monkey! Fantastic!'

Now that the dam had cracked, his excitement and enthusiasm about everything came flooding out and he was like a six-year-old child. What did the monkey eat? Where was he from? How fast could my car go? Did the parrot talk? What kind of ugly great dog *was* that, anyway? He went on for far longer than he should have done, and in the end I sent him packing. I was worried he'd lose his job.

When he'd gone, I took Castlereagh in my arms and danced a little jig around the huge front room, elated by my success.

About a week later, I rang up the bar for a late snack. I was working, the sound of my two-fingered labours cracking through the hot afternoon like somebody learning the maracas. When Paulo arrived he appeared unwilling to talk, probably not wanting to interrupt me, but he didn't go back down. Instead, he went into the big hall behind the balcony and started playing with the animals so that his laughter and their various noises echoed around the empty house. Though I was pleased for him to make himself at home, I found it impossible to concentrate. After a few moments, I called over my shoulder.

'You've finished for the day now, have you?'

'Yes, Cloud,' which was how he pronounced my name. 'I'm on my way home. I'll have to go and get the bus soon.'

I peered into the gloomy room. Paulo had found a little ball which I'd bought for Trelawny, and they were playing piggy-in-the-middle, Trelawny himself cast in the thankless role of pig, with Paulo and Castlereagh throwing the ball above his head. It was really an incongruous sight, especially as Paulo was still wearing his waiter's uniform with its miniature bow-tie. Smiling, I went inside.

'Come on,' I said. 'I'll give you a lift home.'

His little face lit up. A ride in that Morgan of mine was obviously what he'd been longing for.

'Oh,' he said casually. 'Alright, then.'

'Trelawny can come, too, but you, Castlereagh, are to

stay here and be a good primate. I don't want you causing trouble with the locals.'

I was by now so used to talking to my animals that I saw nothing strange or embarrassing in it. Though I had spoken in English, as I always did to them, Paulo must have got the gist.

'We are taking Cassyree, aren't we?'

'No, Paulo, we are not. If I let him come, he'll learn how to drive by watching me, and then who knows what trouble he'll cause?'

The truth was that my car attracted quite enough attention on its own, and I felt that putting Castlereagh in it would be going just a bit far.

'Oh, please,' said Paulo, forgetting himself. 'Please can we take him, *please?*'

I looked down at the chimp, who made his own silent appeal to come by widening his eyes and holding his hand out towards me. Then I realised that, for a kid like Paulo, to be driven home in a big white sports car was one thing, but to be driven home in one with Castlereagh was quite another.

'Oh, alright, then,' I said. Paulo grinned, Castlereagh held his arms above his head and began running round the room, and I went to get ready.

Five minutes later, I stepped out of the bedroom wearing a cream jacket, a red polka-dot tie, a panama and a pair of expensive shades. The clothes would have been absurdly ostentatious in England. Here, they were just a way of blending in with the crowd. Paulo barely gave me a second glance.

'Right!' he said, hopping with excitement. 'Let's go!'

We roared into Naples with the roof down. Castlereagh loved it. At first, he wouldn't keep still or quiet, but when we got to the main road around the bay and I put my foot down, he shut up as though the thrill had taken his breath away. I glanced round to see him standing on the bucket seat in the back and leaning forward to grip Paulo's shoulders. Trelawny sat next to him, trying to look noble. Paulo himself was smirking in all directions, no doubt in the hope of being spotted by someone who knew him.

As I say, the car always attracted attention – the Italians aren't ashamed of staring, and would often break off their conversations to gawp at it – but with the chimp on board we literally stopped traffic. Byron and his entire entourage could hardly have caused a greater stir. Under those endless pairs of Italian eyes, I felt all my old affinity with the poet, and wondered superstitiously about the book I'd left with Vernon.

It turned out that Paulo lived in the oldest and poorest part of Naples, in one of those narrow, cobbled alleys, festooned with washing and teeming with life. There were two football games, five scooter repairs and countless conversations going on, all of which stopped as we rumbled over the cobbles. Paulo grinned delightedly and began waving at people as we got closer to his house. When we arrived, he screamed,

'Mama! Mama! Come and see!'

A thin, unhealthy-looking woman of about thirty-five emerged on to a balcony and stood there for a moment just staring down at us. Then she turned to call her husband.

'Bruno! You're not going to believe this!'

A chunky man in a vest appeared, took one look, and burst out laughing.

'*Buona sera*!' I called up, mortified, for the entire street was watching by this time. 'I'm a friend of Paulo's. I've only come to drop him home.'

'Come up for coffee,' said Paulo.

'No, no, I couldn't.'

'Yes, yes,' Paulo's father called down, managing to contain his mirth. 'Come up for coffee, signore!'

Well, that was it, I had to go up. A crowd of shabby-looking children was already gathering around the car when we got out.

'Trelawny, you must stay in the car, because I won't have

you dribbling over people's furniture. Don't bite anybody unless they say something nasty about Keats.'

Trealawny looked up at me sadly.

'*Inglese!*' the children began saying in wonder. '*Inglese!*'

'You, Castlereagh, had better come with me. Come on.'

He jumped out, took my hand, and Paulo escorted us up the dingy staircase.

The flat was very small and tatty, yet immaculately clean. Above the table in the kitchen was a faded picture of the Virgin, an almost inevitable apparition in the midst of Neapolitan hardship. Paulo seemed to have a limitless supply of younger brothers and sisters, who, screaming with excitement, took Castlereagh to play in their bedroom. Paulo himself, as you might expect, stayed with us grown-ups. As soon as I got in, I took off my hat and glasses, for I had begun to feel like a pretentious twit.

Paulo's mother, whose name was Anna, kept on apologising for everything – the house, the heat, the flies, the biscuits – implying that I must be used to much more genteel conditions. She made me feel like a fraud. I kept on wanting to tell her that her poverty didn't bother me. I also kept on wanting to reach for my cheque-book and write her a big one, but I managed to restrain myself. In this I was aided by Bruno, who treated me throughout with good-humoured amusement and didn't look in need of help from anybody.

We chatted about this and that. After my weeks of solitude, the sudden excess of company was almost surreal. It turned out that Bruno was a mechanic. He asked me a lot of technical questions about my wonderful car, but he was stretching my Italian to its limits. All I could really tell him was that Morgans were built almost entirely by hand.

'Ah!' he said, nodding heavily. 'That is the best way.'

When they asked me what I did, Paulo butted in before I'd had a chance to answer.

'He's an English writer. He writes all day. It'll be a great book, I think.'

This, of course, only doubled his mother's embarrassing respect for me. I didn't contradict, feeling that everything about me was so fraudulent that it wasn't worth the trouble. After that, Bruno refused to call me anything other than *Scrittore* which he did with gentle mockery, as though he'd known me for years.

As soon as I politely could, I left, exhausted by it all. Meeting people, as it often does, had made me feel lonelier than before. I needed to get back home, back to my solitude, where I could quietly collect my thoughts.

Paulo came downstairs to see me off. The sun was retreating from the street, already driven away from all but the highest windows. In the gloom, the Morgan looked almost luminous. There was by now a sizable crowd of kids around it, leaning over to peer at the dashboard, yet being very careful not to touch anything. They all kept about six inches away, as though the car had come from outer space.

The crowd parted for me and my monkey. As I called goodbye to Paulo over the roar of the engine, they all looked at me so plaintively that there was only one thing I could say.

'Come on, then. Get in.'

A couple of seconds later, we had broken the world record for getting children in a Morgan. All of them – except Paulo, who obviously considered it beneath him to travel with the plebs when he knew me personally – had found a seat or a foothold. They were crammed in the back, standing on the front seat and holding the windscreen, sitting on the bonnet and lined up along the running boards. I had to have Castlereagh on my lap. Bruno was watching from his balcony, bellowing with laughter.

When we started, ever so gently, to move, they let out a huge cheer. Every window down the street had two or three faces peering out of it. They laughed, shouted, and waved to their friends. Near the end of the street, I checked that they were hanging on tight and gave them a quick burst of power and you could have heard the scream in Whitehall.

At the end of the cobbles, they all got off, thanking me profusely, asking me if I would ever come back, saying how fantastic it had been.

'No, you're fantastic,' I said, looking at their radiant little faces. They couldn't understand me, because I said it in English, and, because of my sunglasses, they couldn't see that my eyes had filled with tears. 'I love you. I love you all so very much.'

With that, I drove away, disgusted with myself. Yet a few minutes later I had to stop the car because I was weeping like an old woman at a wedding. I just couldn't understand what had come over me.

My animals knew.

When I got back to my huge, empty house on the hill, far up and away from all that teeming life, and sat out on the balcony with my bottle of gin, my animals gathered round me. Percy managed to hop up, via a chair, on to the table, where he cocked his head at me sadly. Trelawny followed me through the empty rooms to sit at my feet and stare mournfully into my eyes. Castlereagh climbed up and hugged me, laying his ugly little head against my chest. He did it tenderly and gently, because he knew, as they all knew, that I am dying.

12

IN NEXT TO no time, I became a star.

First, I became relatively well known in the area where Paulo lived, since I got into the habit of giving him a lift home each evening. On my arrival, the local kids would always stop what they were doing to pile themselves into and on to my car for their short ride down the street. They never seemed to get tired of it. As they converged, the grubby crowd would scream out '*Scrittore! Scrittore!*', for the nickname which Bruno gave me had not only stuck, but somehow spread. A few adult faces would appear behind the fly-blown windows to watch the children's fun. Paulo's parents often used to come out on to their balcony to invite me up for coffee, but I always refused, pleading pressure of work.

This would have been celebrity enough for me. But then, shortly after I'd first taken Paulo home, came a phone call from a young woman called Simonetta, who had seen me driving round town with Castlereagh (since that first outing he insisted on coming everywhere with me) and wanted to come up to the house. It turned out that she worked for a local paper.

At first I curtly refused to meet her, without really knowing why. Only when I'd put the phone down and stared at it for a few moments did I see in my reaction the perverse shyness of a lonely man. Now that I had my animals, and had made friends with a thirteen-year-old boy, I was starting to cocoon myself. When I'd realised this, I thought in turn how happy Paulo would be if I appeared in the press. About ten minutes later, I rang Simonetta back and agreed to be interviewed on condition that the paper printed a photograph of Paulo and me together.

We were both waiting up on the balcony when she arrived the following day, driving the inevitable Fiat. Even from that distance, we could see that she was a little shocked as she got out and approached the gate. There was good reason for her reaction; by that time my standards of housekeeping had already gone into decline.

First of all, there had been a couple of explosive thunder-storms, and the torrential water coupled with the heat, which was becoming extreme, had had a remarkable effect on my gardens. All sorts of exotic vegetation had sprouted up, some of it quite beautiful. This new growth was so high that my graceful palm-trees now looked as though they were struggling to keep their heads above the rising green tide and my low-slung Morgan was all but invisible from the road. The house itself now seemed to be not only crumbling, but actually sinking like some fantastic stone ship into the greenery. I was too lazy and listless to go and start hacking away at that jungle in the crackling heat, and I was the only one it affected, so it was simply left.

Then I found out that my two baroque fountains, splendid though they were, required a modest amount of maintenance and care to keep them going, so I switched them off and left them. In no time at all the water had gone a thick green colour and magically filled up with dead stag-beetles, water-boatmen, frogs, and the most astonishingly large lilies. Rising from this opaque pea-soup, the decorative fountain-heads looked rather mournful and neglected, yet somehow more noble, too. The stagnant water gave off a rich, still smell of decay which I did not find altogether unpleasant. It reminded me of the smell I sometimes used to catch off the Thames at Greenwich. In any case, it attracted dragonflies into my garden. They were larger than the ones in England and even more colourful, and I could watch for hours from my balcony while they darted, hovered, and darted again, until it seemed they must be dancing out messages for me in some exotic script.

The finishing touch had come from the pet shop a few days before: a pair of young peacocks, left to strut freely around the garden, their blue-green plumage adding a lush shimmer to its decline, their mournful cries a distillation of the emptiness inside the house.

Add to all this the gradual decomposition of the building itself, which had been underway for centuries before my arrival and manifested itself in cracked plaster, rusting balustrades, crumbling ornamentation and peeling green paint on the shutters, and you will have some conception of the splendid, insipid decay into which I had slipped. No wonder Simonetta was a bit taken aback.

She couldn't have been more than twenty, and, although she was short and dark, there was something about her than reminded me of Fran. Perhaps there would be something about any girl of that age which reminded me of Fran. As I opened the gate for her, it struck me that, for the first time since my own twenties, I was a bachelor, and free.

Slowly, at the pace of the promenading peacocks, I strolled towards the house, leading Castlereagh by the hand. My aloofness was inspired partly by the desire to create an impression, mainly by shyness and nerves. Paulo and Simonetta followed a little way behind. The girl's presence seemed to turn up the heat and amplify the electric pulsing of the crickets. The lizards basking on the bonnet of the Morgan watched as though in catatonia.

Inside, Simonetta demanded the full guided tour, so I took her round, answering her questions on the way. There was a note in her voice which I hadn't heard for a long time, especially from a girl so young. I wondered whether it was just the house which attracted her.

In the bedroom, she looked admiringly at my four-poster and asked, with the brazenness of her race, if I had it all to myself.

'Naturally,' I replied. With that I haughtily walked out, leaving them to trail behind me, but my breath was short and my heart was labouring like a fly in jam.

After the questions, Simonetta and Paulo rounded up the animals for a group photo on the balcony. I smiled obligingly at the lens.

'No, no,' she said. 'Don't smile. You're ruining the effect. Try to look more English.'

As she spoke, I remembered Byron's famous 'expression' which he used to affect whenever anyone did a portrait of him. So I lifted my chin, turned down my mouth at the corners and stared scornfully over Naples.

'Perfect!' cried Simonetta, and started clicking.

When she'd taken photos of us in various parts of the house, Paulo declared that he really ought to go back to work, and before I knew what was happening Simonetta and I were left alone on the balcony. For a moment she looked at me with a strange concern in her eyes.

'I hope you don't mind my asking,' she said kindly, 'but what's the matter with you, signore?'

'How do you mean?'

'All those pills in the bedroom . . .' I was silent, shamed by this evidence of mortality and age. 'Sorry. I shouldn't have asked.'

'Don't worry. It's nothing. Nothing serious.'

'Ah.' The concern was still there; she obviously wasn't convinced. 'I see.'

To cover my awkwardness, I went and got us mineral water, which we sipped out on the balcony, each smoking a cigarette. Simonetta smoked prettily, lifting her pointed chin to exhale.

'So, you're all alone here?'

'Yes. I recently separated from my wife.'

'Is that why you left England?'

I shrugged, trying to copy her calm.

'Partly.'

For a moment I stood watching her profile as she stared

out across the city. The blood seemed to be boiling in my veins, but Simonetta's face as she turned towards me was placid.

'You've chosen a beautiful house, *signore*.' She looked straight into my eyes. 'It suits you perfectly.'

As I leant forwards to kiss her, a light breeze from the bay lifted a strand of her hair. The kiss only lasted an instant. The cool point of her tongue flickered across mine faster than a lizard's, and I immediately withdrew.

'I'm sorry.' I stared at the floor to cough, then found myself unable to look back up again. 'I think you'd better go.'

'OK.' She was airy and composed as before. 'Whatever you say.'

In desolation, I watched her collect her things. Then I escorted her, awkwardly, silently, down to her car. Helen's presence was stronger than ever. Absurdly, I felt guilty about that brief kiss up on the balcony, as though I were still a married man, restrained by duty rather than fear.

Before she drove off, Simonetta wound down her window and smiled up at me.

'Don't worry. I think I'm going to write a very . . . sympathetic piece about you, *Scrittore*.'

Alone again, I went back out on to the balcony. It was a perfectly still day. The light crawled on a calm sea. The heat seemed to hum in my ears. For the first time I understood the extent to which the house with its lush, stagnant gardens, its tatty grandeur, its rather pompous air of emptiness and desolation, was a symbol of my soul.

The article duly appeared and made me a local character, the eccentric Englishman who lived on the hill. Suddenly everybody seemed to know me. I hadn't been expecting the article to have such an impact, but I suppose thousands of Neapolitans must have already made a mental note of me, driving round in my English car with a chimp in the passenger seat and a bulldog in the back. My house was soon a popular tourist spot. People in couples or small groups would drive up here to form a line in front of the building as though it were some crumbling continental Buckingham Palace. There were always a few of them watching, clinging to the rusty bars of the fence, gawping at the condition of the villa and its gardens. The adults would stand on tiptoe with the children on their shoulders, all straining to get a good view above the overgrowth in the hope of glimpsing a peacock, a chimpanzee, or, most fabulous creature of all, the reclusive millionaire. No doubt they all used the mysterious foreigner as the basis for their own private fairy tales, painting him as mad ogre or charming prince, according to the bias of their imaginary worlds. In truth, that silent figure, chain-smoking on his balcony, or gliding through the gloom behind the tall windows like a ghost from the building's more illustrious past, bore them no resentment. They weren't to know how they increased my sense of isolation and despair.

The next time I saw Paulo's parents, I took the plunge and invited them to supper. They looked pleased and called down from their balcony that they would love to come. I checked that the children who had been piling into the car while we spoke were all safely aboard and crawled off over the cobbles.

As soon as the step was taken, I regretted it. The idea of meeting people made me anxious and I certainly didn't feel like cooking. Though I used to love cooking in the old days, back in England, since my arrival in Italy I'd done nothing but eat out. This wasn't due to laziness, or even depression. In fact, I was afraid of cooking, because I knew how much it would remind me of standing in the kitchen at home at the end of a day's work, chopping things up and chatting to Helen while we waited for Ross to arrive.

The following day my guests turned up right on time in a rather decent-looking Alfa, which I suspected of belonging to one of Bruno's clients. He was probably meant to be under the car rather than in it. Castlereagh and I went down to open the gate for them. I was hoping that the chimp would help to break the ice, a process which I was dreading, and to this end I had dressed him up in a wing collar and bow tie.

The ploy was successful, and all my guests were laughing as I led them through the overgrowth. Before we started supper, Anna asked to be taken round the house, by which she was duly amazed, although she said it could do with a bit of attention. Paulo, to prove that he had seen it all before, said that you got used to it after a while and that I was very comfortable there. Bruno pronounced it perfect for a single man.

We ate in the front room, with the tall windows open to let the heady night air in through the mosquito nets. Anna and Paulo seemed a little tense, but Bruno really began to unwind after his first few glasses of wine. I asked him how work was going.

'Not too bad,' he said in his slow, heavy way. 'It's boring, but – ', here he gave a resigned shrug typical of southern Italy, full of peasant stoicism, 'but what can you do? A man has to work. Even you have to work, *Scrittore*, in your way.'

This wasn't strictly true, but I let it pass.

'Paulo, sit up straight!' said Anna shortly, for her son was letting the side down by slouching over his plate to listen.

'Oh, mama, please!'

'Leave him, signora!' I interjected, perhaps unwisely. 'There are no manners in this house. This is a slouching house. Why, look at Castlereagh! He's not even eating with his knife and fork!'

Castlereagh, hearing his name mentioned, began squawking and jumping up and down on his seat.

'Cassyree is a gibbon,' said Anna, rather rudely, I thought. 'Paulo must learn to be a man. Can't you do anything with your son, Bruno?'

Bruno looked serious for a moment, deliberating.

'If this is a slouching house, he must slouch. Traditions vary. He must learn to adapt. Slouch, Paulo! Just don't let your mother catch you doing it at home, that's all.'

'The wisdom of Solomon!' I said quickly, because I saw Anna preparing to snap back. Bruno accepted the compliment with a grave nod, while I leant forwards. 'More salad, Anna?'

For some time after that, Paulo sulked. I felt for him. The image of maturity which he'd carefully projected to me over the previous few weeks had been destroyed at one fell swoop. Mothers can be terrible.

I found myself beginning to dislike Anna as the evening wore on. Though she deferred to Bruno, I felt that this was only a matter of form, because they were in company. He was too easy-going to really master such a character in his own home.

The meal was lent a slightly surreal air by the fact that, while we ate, Percy kept making short circular flights above the table. His wings had by that time grown back quite nicely, though flying still seemed to tire him and he never stayed aloft for more than a minute or so. Besides being surreal, Percy was also preying on my mind, for I had nightmarish visions of him shitting on Anna's head while she was holding forth about something.

After dessert, she said it was time Paulo was in bed, which was the last straw for him, poor chap. Bruno and I protested, but she was adamant. In the end, I persuaded her to let Bruno stay and help me with a few bottles of wine I had left over. She could drive back with Paulo and I'd arrange a cab for her husband.

When they were gone, we sat out on the balcony in our shirt-sleeves, drinking and chatting. Outside the netting the warm gardens were alive with mosquitoes, bats and moths. At odd intervals, from the direction of one of the fountains, came the belching of a frog. Below it all the scythe of lights around the bay gently shimmered and seethed, humming like a giant generator.

I was far more at ease than I would have thought possible, almost luxuriously at ease. Bruno was honest and kind. He'd never had an affair, he confided solemnly, partly out of love for his wife, but, even more, out of love for his children. He lived for them.

'They'll let you down!' I said with the beginnings of drunken anger. 'Bound to. Children always do.'

'Not my Paulo!' said Bruno, taking umbrage. 'He'd die before he dishonoured me.'

'Would he, now? How very Italian.'

'You have a family, then, *Scrittore*?'

'Not any more I don't. My wife went off with my best friend.'

'Did you kill him?' asked Bruno in a matter-of-fact voice.

'Of course. With a potato-peeler. Here, look, why don't we go for a swim?'

'Because it's past midnight, for one thing. And, in any case, you can't swim in that bay. It's filthy.'

'Take me where we can swim, then. We'll go in my car. You can drive, if you like.'

That settled it. We left the animals sleeping in their various parts of the house, threw a couple of towels into the boot of the Morgan, and a few minutes later were roaring north along the coast road. Bruno took us to the northern end of the famous bay, rocked the car into a side-road and jerked to a halt near the sea.

'You really want to swim?'

'Of course,' I said, beginning to unbutton my shirt.

'I always knew the English were crazy.'

We got undressed, hobbled gingerly towards the edge of the rocks, and dived. As soon as the water closed over my head, I was completely sober again.

For a while we did the things which men must do on these occasions: had a race or two, did a few more dives, had an argument over who was the better diver, which we settled by splashing and ducking each other until I gave in.

'Let's float,' I panted, 'and recover.'

We lay on our backs and drifted in the long, broken path of the moon, gently waving our arms as though motioning imaginary fish away. The water was calm. To our right were the lights of Naples and, further off, the slumbering bulk of the volcano.

'This wasn't such a crazy idea after all,' said Bruno after a while. He did a few strokes on his back, windmilling his arms with the laziness of a natural athlete. 'It's nice to swim at night.'

'Yes, it's been fun. Thanks for coming.'

'I've enjoyed it . . . Hey, have you ever been diving?'

'No, never.'

'Would you like to? I could teach you. I've got a spare aqualung.'

'That would be lovely. Have you got a boat, as well?'

'No. I used to have, just a dinghy, but when the babies started arriving I couldn't afford it any more. I just dive from the beach.'

'That'll do. I'm not fussy.'

Bruno laughed.

'I've noticed! You seem very easy-going for a wealthy man.' He dived like a dolphin and vanished for what seemed an eternity. Just as I was beginning to think he'd drowned, he surfaced right next to me, spluttering and glittering in the moonlight. 'We'll go on Saturday, then.'

It's a strange thing how one's mood can change. (Music is a strange thing!) Those were the first carefree moments I'd known since leaving England, yet as soon as I parted company with Bruno, they gave way to the deepest despair.

I didn't sleep at all that night. I sat out on my balcony and stared across the sleeping city, smoking and sipping gin. Friendship with Bruno would never be enough. The emptiness which had swallowed everything at home would easily devour such trivial relationships.

About twenty minutes after the sun had risen, as though

emerging from a trance, I noticed the world around me. The air was still cool, but somehow already tense with the threat of the heat to come. I stood up stiffly, stretching, slightly drunk, and raised the mosquito nets which surrounded the balcony. Leaning against the railing, I took in the seething sea, the solemn, hazy hills.

As I was standing there, I heard a sudden noise, so close behind my ear that it caused me to duck. A dark shape shot past my shoulder. Straightening, I realised that it was Percy. He flew past me and out over the town. Flying was obviously still strange for him, because he soon stopped to have a rest on an aerial.

When I realised what was happening, I was seized by an unbearable anguish. I started jumping up and down on the spot, shouting out his name, waving my arms like a lunatic, hoping he was just practising his flying and would come back to me, but he paid no attention. He took off again and flew away from me, dipping at first, but then gaining height and strength, flying south over the clutter of Naples, down towards Africa.

I watched until he was no more than a dot floating against the blue veil of the hills. As he reached the limit of my vision, I began to lose sight of him and think he was gone, only to make him out again. This happened two or three times before he vanished entirely, lost in the layered haze. This time I knew it was for good, but for ages afterwards I stood and stared at the last point where he had been. Here for once was an easy sign to understand.

13

NAPLES WAS DESERTED. The streets and bars were empty, many of the shops were shuttered up. It was August and most of the city had gone away on holiday. As I was driving Paulo home along the sea-front, I saw one of the last ferry-loads leave, a humming white castle so huge that it looked immobile on the water. But there were cries from the quay, and giant ropes, as thick as an arm, splashed and snaked across the calm surface; the leviathan was already underway. As though to emphasise the emptiness it was leaving behind, the ship gave a long, baleful blast on its horn, which washed across all other sound, echoed three times around the bay, and disappeared.

Only the very poor stayed in the city that month. Paulo's family was still there. Although trade would be slack in the garage, Bruno couldn't afford to go away. A few foreign tourists wandered the streets, but there weren't enough of them to restore the atmosphere. Up against stiff competition from Venice, Florence and Rome, Naples is little visited these days.

Up here in my huge ruin on the hillside, even my animals seemed quieter than before. Perhaps this was because they had caught the canker of desolation rising from the town below, or perhaps, more likely, it was due to the heat, which had become insufferable. I had taken to working into the small hours and sleeping through the worst of the day. Trelawny had barely moved for some weeks, except in darkness. He would stretch himself out on the cool marble, head on paws, and stare for hours into nothing. My lavish indulgence had left him so overweight that I feared the heat might bring on a heart attack. From time to time, he would rouse himself and go outside to wallow, despite all my admonitions, in the filthy green water of the fountains, which seemed to be rotting more quickly now. Even Castlereagh, who was used to the heat, was unusually insipid, moping around the house or disappearing to sleep all afternoon in the jungle which now surrounded it.

There had been no sign of Percy. Each afternoon, on waking up, I would go to stand out on the balcony and scan the seething blue sky for him, hoping against hope to see him dipping towards me above the aerials, in from the south. Something told me that, one day, he would come back, before the end.

Now, as the time approached, I began to be gripped by a desperate illusion: my family would somehow track me down. Even now they might be searching, following the clues of my former life. At any moment, one of them might ring the bell at the gates of my *palazzo*. I clung to this idea as though such a visit would somehow save me, but I knew it was just the hypnosis of despair.

Naples was deserted. There was that same hot desolation of a school in the summer holidays. You couldn't imagine the place ever filling up with life again. It was as though the air of my own exile had put an enchantment on the entire town. The source of that strange atmosphere was up here, perched in the hills above the bay, where everything seemed to sleep in the afternoons: Trelawny sprawled on the marble, Castlereagh curled under a palm, the bats which hung from the stucco of the crumbling dining-room downstairs. Hiding in the ruins, protected from the outside world by their overgrown gardens, I was beginning at last to know myself; and I slept, too, dozing through the afternoons like an ogre under a soporific spell.

*   *   *

After our midnight swim, Bruno proved as good as his word, and taught me to dive. We loaded the gear into the Morgan, and he directed me to a relatively secluded bay to the south of the city. On the way, he ran through some of the dangers for me – equipment failure, the bends, panic, claustrophobia, inexplicable euphoria at certain depths which could cause you cheerfully to drown yourself – and taught me the sign-language by which one communicates underwater.

The experience brought me a strange joy. As soon as I was under, I felt immediately at home. Lolling in the shallows, in the steady shafts of sunlight from the surface, with no sound other than the thunder of my breath and the rumble of bubbles, I began to forget my problems. All I knew was the weeds waving, the clumsy lobsters, the shoals of fish flashing all at once, as though at the jerk of an unseen magnet. After a while I lost the sense of responsibility and time, and found myself with an irresistible compulsion to go deeper. I signalled this to Bruno and set off.

At about fifty metres, the wildlife became more sparse, the rocks larger, and I felt perfectly removed from everything at last. As I was floating there, lost in the euphoria of depth, I felt something touch my shoulder and turned slowly around. Bruno had followed me and was signalling that we should return to the surface. We went up slowly, pausing and clinging to the rocks at certain depths while Bruno stared at his watch.

When our heads finally exploded back out into the noise and light, I removed my mouthpiece and asked him what the problem had been.

'You went to fifty metres, *Scrittore*! You must be mad!'
'How come?'
'Nobody goes to fifty metres on their first dive. People of your age shouldn't really go that deep at all.'
'Well, we're alright, aren't we?'
'So far. But I didn't have my decompression tables with me, so I had to do the whole thing by guesswork. We may

have the bends.' He shook his head at me. 'I was planning on a shallow dive, you English idiot.'

'Sorry.'

We waded out and sat on the beach with our equipment, waiting for the tell-tale pins and needles. Bruno wasn't angry with me, although he had every right to be. He just made light of the whole thing. It took me a while to realise that he had risked his life to come and fish me out.

'I didn't really understand what I was doing, Bruno. I do apologise.'

'Oh, it's nothing. You can't dive without danger. All the same, there's no point in taking unnecessary risks.'

That was all he had to say on the subject, although, unlike me, he had plenty of reasons to go on living. Thank God, we were all right, and we drove home closer friends than before, exhilarated by our escape.

After that, I thought nothing could unsettle him.

A few days later, I called for him at his house in the late afternoon, sitting in my Morgan and sounding the horn. Only one or two kids appeared in the hope of a ride. Most of them were away. After a few moments Bruno emerged on to the balcony, dressed in a vest and shorts, running a hand through his rumpled hair. He'd obviously been sleeping through the heat.

'*Scrittore!*' he called down. 'What is it?'

'I'm taking you up to my place! I've got a surprise for you!'

'Oh God,' I heard him mutter. 'It better not be an expensive present.'

'Only one way to find that out!'

Shaking his head, Bruno went in to get dressed.

An expensive present, of course, is exactly what it was. I'd had the men who delivered it leave it outside the house on its trailer, sunk in the blooming vegetation. As soon as Bruno saw it, he said, 'You got this for me?'

'That's right.'

'How ridiculous! I can't accept it, of course.'

'Yes, you can. You saved my life the other day, and I got this to say thank you. It wasn't that dear, in any case.'

We were standing next to it, and as we spoke he was scowling at the flashy dashboard and the sharp white lines and the outboard, which was the biggest on the market.

'You can't fool me,' said Bruno. 'I know how much a boat like this costs. I won't have anything to do with it.'

'You will. Think how much pleasure it will give to Paulo.'

This made him pause momentarily before refusing again. Only by giving way on the question of ownership, and suggesting that he should simply be my captain, taking me out whenever I fancied a trip, did I get him to accept my gift.

When we took it out the following day, the boat astonished me. It was one of those ones that screams along at breakneck speed, bucking and bouncing over the water. Everyone's seen them, but it's impossible to imagine what riding in one is like until you've done it. You have to hang on tight to avoid being thrown straight back over the engine. Then there's the wind, the roar, the smell of salt, the constant cool spray. When the boat turns, it throws up a curtain of water about twenty feet high and pushes your stomach into your shoes. I christened it the *Ariel*.

It changed our lives. Paulo spent every free moment with it, polishing it and trying out the controls. Bruno and I took him with us whenever we could on our diving expeditions. We would thunder across to Capri in under an hour and be the envy of the holidaymakers on the beach. Even Anna enjoyed coming out for the occasional sedate cruise when she could get away from the kids. She would sit primly in the passenger seat under a broad straw hat, looking like nothing so much as an English governess being rowed around the Serpentine. She was starting to relax a little in my company, with the result that she was now much shorter with her husband, admonishing him if our speed rose above a crawl, warning him of every potential hazard well in advance, and generally leaving no doubt as to who wore the trousers.

I also issued a standing invitation to Bruno's colleagues in the garage whenever they felt like a dip. They were a young, rowdy lot, who enjoyed impressing girls in the *Ariel*. I liked them well enough. They were good fun and they took my mind off things. Yet they depressed me, too, because I knew that Bruno really had more in common with them than with me.

For a while, everyone seemed happy. I enjoyed riding in the boat, having picnics, diving. It was always good to get out of the house, where I could never stop listening for the sound of the bell. Bruno, although he tried to deny it, was delighted, and Paulo could hardly talk about anything else.

When he came up one evening to bring me my last cappuccino, I was expecting the usual conversation about the boat. When were we next going out? Should he go and polish the chromework first? Could his friend from next door come with us? Instead of this, however, he just handed me my coffee, leant on the railings of the balcony and stared out across the gloomy bay.

Pushing my typewriter away like an unfinished meal, I sat and looked at him for a moment. Though darkness was falling, it was still hot, the shirt clinging damply to my back where it had touched the chair. The nets had already been lowered for some time, the garden given over to mosquitoes, frogs and moths. The bats would soon be out.

'What's the matter, Paulo?'

'Nothing,' he replied, in a small voice and without looking at me. As soon as he'd done so, he turned quickly around and sat down at my table. Even Castlereagh seemed to sense that there was something wrong, looking at him with a thoughtful concentration which was like a caricature of my own expression. Trelawny woke up and moved from under the table to slobber on my shoes.

'Don't you want to tell me about it?'

'I told you, it's nothing!' said Paulo, suddenly flaring up. 'Who are you to ask, anyway? We don't owe you anything just because you're rich, you know.'

'No, I know.'

For a while he sat there glowering at me. Then he turned and looked out towards the black shapes of the hills across the bay.

'My mum's got cancer.'

'Nonsense,' I said promptly. 'What gives you that idea? She's far too young.'

Even as I said it, though, I remembered how ill Anna had looked, tense and pale under her hat as she directed operations in the boat.

'It's true. She's been to the doctor. Dad told me last night. Cancer of the breast. He says it may be very serious.'

'Not necessarily,' I said lamely. 'The majority of women recover, you know. That's a fact.'

Paulo turned and smiled at me grimly, playing the man. Castlereagh, showing more sensitivity than me, jumped off the table and patted the boy's knee with a gentleness you wouldn't have expected from a chimp, looking up at him with a comical expression of sympathy and sorrow. Paulo laughed and stroked his head. Then he began to cry.

I sat and waited for it to pass, feeling useless, as I had always felt before Helen's tears. Eventually, Paulo sniffed.

'Do you hate your mother, Cloud?'

I smiled.

'My mother's dead a long time now, Paulo. But I do remember hating her at times, yes.'

'Sometimes I hate mine, but I don't want her to die.'

'She's not going to. Bruno and I are going to sort it out, I promise you. There's no need to worry.' He went on looking at me and said nothing. 'Don't you believe me?'

'Yes.' Paulo wiped some of the snot and tears from his face. 'I suppose so.'

'Good. Hang on.' I reached into my jacket, which was hung over the back of my chair, and produced a handkerchief. When I handed it to him, Paulo blew his nose noisily. At that moment, far below us, one of the huge ferries blew its horn as though in mournful mockery.

'Go home now,' I said. 'Tell your father to come and see me.'

When he was gone, I sat there motionless, thinking not of Anna's tragedy, but of my own approaching end, for which no one else would really mourn.

Bruno arrived about two hours later. I could never have imagined him showing such open signs of agitation and fatigue. His face was dark and drawn; he seemed unable to keep still. We went upstairs in silence and he sat down at my table, nervously bouncing his foot against the floor. My cheque-book was there waiting.

'Now, Bruno, at last you're going to have to accept some of my money. This is one present you can't refuse.'

Bruno shrugged and said nothing. I began to write the cheque.

'I want you to stop work to be with her. I want her to go to the best hospital, even if it's in America or Switzerland. All right?'

I handed him the cheque.

'This is too much,' said Bruno. 'We don't need so bloody much.'

'Spend what you need and return the rest when she's better.'

'Right.' Bruno sat in silence for a few moments, struggling to produce the word he obviously hated to say. 'Thanks, then.'

* * *

Anna went, as a preliminary step, to a specialist here in Naples. When I visited her, she was far more gushing in her gratitude than Bruno had been, which I found rather unpleasant. Mainly for the sake of her husband and son, I hoped she would recover.

Both of them still came to visit me after Anna went into hospital, but we no longer went out in the boat. They brought up to my house on the hill a heavy, infectious grief. All of us sensed she was going to die. In a way, I felt jealous of her. She was lucky to be going surrounded by so much sorrow. For myself, I was coming to accept that my own family had already got used to life without me.

More than anything, Anna's illness underlined the fact that I, unlike all the others, was alone. A lonely man has his special rights. Even if he causes suffering in enjoying them, he must have his compensations, his little luxuries.

On top of all our private grief, there was the mourning of the city itself. Naples was deserted. Everyone had gone away. My animals sweltered in the heat. In my gardens, the vegetation silently grew thicker and higher, the fountains crumbled, the dragonflies flickered and danced. The burning days were insufferable to me, I tried only to come out at night. High up in the ruin on the hill, everything slept in the afternoons, spreading a kind of enchantment over the town. Each evening, I would stand at my balcony and search the sunset for a sign of Percy, always in vain.

The sun sat and seethed on the empty piazzas. As I drove around those abandoned streets, with only my animals for company, I found that the desolation struck a chord with me, its taste far sharper, I think, than it would be for another man. Perhaps I knew something of what Byron must have felt. Sometimes I would just drive around for hours, feeling that the town was hushed by the deepening quiet of my own soul. The place was perfectly in tune with me, it had fallen under my soporific spell, and I would simply drive for hours, thinking of all those I would leave behind, savouring the luxury of exile.

14

TOWARDS THE END of summer, it was as though nature, like the entire country, bowed down before the calendar: the first day of September not only ended the holidays but also brought a marked change in the weather. The heat began to shrink, the blue sky seemed shallower, a cool wind blew in from the bay as darkness fell. The droves of holidaymakers poured off the glimmering ferries, quieter than when they left. August had been sad for those of us who remained in the city, but somehow this mass return to work was even worse. High up on my balcony, which was suddenly bearable again even at the height of the afternoon, I watched the ferries coming back and felt that the world was moving on without me.

The spell which spread over Naples in August now retained its power only here. The palm-trees out in the garden looked more relaxed, hanging their heads towards the green fountains. The lamenting peacocks strutted through a jungle which was in its last and lushest bloom. At night, the bay was already chilly, so that I had to wear a sweater for my last cigarette out on the balcony. The seasons change so rapidly.

The coolness rejuvenated my animals. Castlereagh jumped and scampered around with all his former zest. Trelawny was energetic enough to go for ponderous walks in the garden. Both of them adored me, following me wherever I went, Castlereagh holding my hand and Trelawny trotting by my side, leaving a treacherous trail of slobber on the marble.

In their new lease of life, I found I pitied them. They couldn't know that beyond these walls the great world was getting underway. They had no sense that all the desolation of Naples in August had been pushed out of the city and settled on my house, my gardens and my mind. They didn't know what all this meant. For them, the cool wind which blew up from the bay held no threat of winter.

About two weeks after the holidays were over, there came good news from the hospital: it seemed the cancer had been caught in time. Anna was responding well to treatment and was almost certain to get better. Paulo held me personally responsible for saving her life and adored me for it, almost like one of my animals. He had by that time stopped working in the bar and gone back to school, so I didn't see as much of him as before. I could tell that his mother's illness had aged him, though. At last he was beginning to acquire the maturity he'd always wanted.

Now that Anna was getting better, we started taking the boat out again, but the end of summer made our outings less exuberant than before. We knew that there were not many trips left for us this year.

A couple of weeks ago (how the past gains ground!) Bruno and Paulo came round for dinner. After the meal, we drank Scotch – at least, Bruno and I did, for Paulo is not so grown-up yet, whatever he may have suffered – and talked about Anna's recovery, and joked as we had before she got ill.

'So, *Scrittore*,' said Bruno, smoothing his eyebrows with a heavy finger, a mannerism of his which I rather like, 'when are we going diving again?'

'Whenever you like. Tomorrow?'

'Yes, I think I can spare a few hours in the afternoon before I go to the hospital.'

At about one in the morning, Paulo, who is only young,

after all, curled up on a *chaise-longue* in the front room and fell asleep. Bruno and I went out on to the balcony to enjoy the view, speaking in low voices so as not to wake him. From below, our murmured conversation would have been inaudible above the din of frogs and crickets. Far off, the lights of a few boats out on the black water rose and fell sleepily, in a dream. They seemed to be signalling to us from the void, but tiredly, like castaways who had grown old on their islands and long since abandoned hope of rescue.

Suddenly I sensed that the time was almost at hand. It was too much to bear alone. Lighting a cigarette, I leant against the railings next to Bruno, so that we were standing side by side, staring out across the quiet town.

'You know that I'm ill, don't you, Bruno?'

'Yes. I've seen the pills . . . I can tell that sometimes you're in pain.'

'Yet you've never asked me why.'

Bruno shrugged.

'I knew you'd tell me when you were ready.'

'It's nothing terribly serious, just a stomach ulcer. At the beginning, they thought it might have been cancer.' I paused for a moment, smiling: even my body couldn't help faking things. 'In any case, I might live till I'm a hundred. So I've been doing a lot of thinking recently about my future.'

'And I hope you've decided to go back to England.'

'No. There's nothing for me there.'

'Your family is there, whatever may have happened. A man's place is with his family.'

Smiling at this last comment, so typical of my friend, I turned towards him.

'They don't need me, Bruno.'

'Rubbish!' he whispered fiercely. If it hadn't been for Paulo sleeping behind us, he would have shouted it. 'That's just an excuse, an easy thing for you to believe, because

245

you don't want to face your duty. You've got to go back and start again.'

'It's too late.'

'In any case, you need them as much as they need you.'

'Not at all, in other words.'

He looked at me for a moment as though I were mad then turned and stared across the bay. After a moment's silence, he sighed.

'It's not for me to lecture you, *Scrittore*. There are lots of differences between us. It's hard for me to understand what you must feel.'

'Good. I hope you won't stand in the way of my decision, Bruno, whatever it may be.'

'No, I won't stand in your way.' Again, he fell silent for a while, and I wondered if he understood what I had meant. 'If there's ever anything you need, don't hesitate to ask.'

'Thank you, Bruno. I really appreciate that.'

The next time he spoke, I could hear that he was straining to keep his voice low, and I knew he'd understood.

'I'll be sorry to see you leave.'

I smiled.

'The holiday can't go on forever.'

As I said that, he put his arms around me and, in true Mediterranean fashion, kissed me on the cheek. Then, without saying anything, he went inside, woke up his son, and left. A few moments later the engine roared below me and a cone of light swung across the garden. At the end of the overgrown drive, they paused a minute while Paulo got out and fumbled sleepily with the gate, then they were gone. I watched the lights move down the hill until they had been absorbed into the shimmering carpet below.

When the house was silent again, I stayed out on the balcony, leaning on the railing and smoking my last few cigarettes. It was pleasant to smoke without worrying about my health, and this was another of my little luxuries. That cool breeze was back, chilling my bones. Even the lights below me were beginning to look hard and cold. The summer haze had gone from the air.

Then, as I was leaning there and staring into the night sky, at the stars coming out above the black cut-out of Vesuvius, I saw a dark shape skimming the aerials. It dipped, then rose again, gaining strength, climbing up towards the house. At first I didn't dare to hope, but as the shape grew there could be no doubt. It flew straight past me and into the room behind, where it circled once, then settled on the back of the *chaise-longue*, cocking its head quizzically on one side.

Percy was back.

'Percy! Where have you been?' I cried, running into the room.

The parrot shuffled edgeways, sinking his claws into the wood, and staring at me all the while from one beady black eye.

'Fuck off,' he said.

I was too delighted to even laugh.

'You can speak! All those weeks I tried to teach you, and you never said a word, then you come back and you can do it! It's fantastic!'

'Fuck off.'

'Yes, that's it, Percy, that's it, that's the cornerstone! All the rest is plain sailing from now on!'

Percy shuffled a little further and cocked his head on the other side.

'Fuck off.'

'All right, all right,' I said, already beginning to wonder whether a talking parrot was such a good idea, after all. 'I think I've got the message.'

'Fuck off.'

Then Percy did something else he'd never done before. He flew towards me and settled on my shoulder, just as a parrot should, and for the next ten minutes I was hopping round the room doing Long John Silver impersonations, laughing, but crying a little as well, because nothing can be more moving for a lonely man than an act of loyalty. He had come back to me after all those weeks, found his way back from Africa, or wherever he'd been, just to stay with me. I knew that he would never leave me now.

At the same time, I began to feel his arrival was symbolic, a signal that things were coming to an end. Eventually I flopped down on the sofa and began to weep in earnest.

'Oh, Percy, I won't be able to play with you much longer. My time's up. There's no point in waiting any more. They've all forgotten me, which is fair enough, you know. And how can I go on, Percy, how? It's too late to start again.'

Disturbed by my sobs, Percy hopped from my shoulder to my knee.

'I'm dying, Percy, dying just like my father did. There's nothing I can do about it. It's a kind of disease, my father's terminal disease. He passed it on to me. I'm dying, Percy. Despair must be an illness of the blood.'

I felt that Bruno, if he'd been there, would have applauded the bird's reply.

15

ON OUR LAST diving expedition I ran out of air.

We were deep, at almost fifty metres, just off Capri. I breathed out, then found when I tried to breathe in again that I was sucking on nothing. Bruno was some way off, searching for a cave which he'd heard was in the area but had never been able to find. It took me about ten seconds of hard swimming to reach him. This would normally have left me panting. When I touched his shoulder, he floated around, lips white in their bloodless pout, eyes strangely inhuman and removed behind his mask. I made the SOS signal, cutting across my neck with my hand. Bruno's arm drifted towards me, offering his own mouthpiece. The routine in these emergencies is that both divers return to the surface sharing the same aqualung.

With the perfect calm of someone close to panic, I took the mouthpiece from him and sucked on it, but my desperation was such that I'd forgotten what I was supposed to do. Before breathing in, of course, you must expel the water from the mouthpiece by pressing the button on the front, which causes a small explosion of air. Having failed to do this, I ended up sucking water into my mouth.

Bruno took the thing back to have his two-breath turn without noticing, while I choked on the utter silence. There was a sharp taste of vomit. For the life of me, I couldn't understand what I had done wrong. I knew there was some procedure to get the water out of the mouthpiece, but my mind was blank, I couldn't remember it, and I saw that I was going to die.

The knowledge filled me with an unexpected peace. As the choking stopped, I tilted my head back. The surface was invisible, there was nothing but a blue haze with no particular source of light. After a few moments, my body started floating backwards, slowly tipping, and I felt myself being gently tugged out into the colour, beginning to become part of it. It was a perfect euphoria, without fear or thought. My body tipped further round, making me giddy as I felt it fall away below me.

Suddenly I was called back. Bruno had his big hand around my neck, lifting my face. He inserted the mouthpiece and pressed the button. Air burst into my lungs and we began to float upwards.

Back on the outside it was almost winter. There were no other divers out that day. The *Ariel* tipped and rocked nearby. The only sound was the hollow slap of water against her sides. A short distance away was the deserted coast of Capri, grey rocks with the white sea sliding slowly down their fronts.

In silence, we trod water, helping each other out of our aqualungs, shrugging through the awkward harnesses. Only when we were actually on the boat did Bruno speak.

'That was close, *Scrittore*,' he said, undoing his weight-belt and lowering it with a clunk to the deck.

'Yes.' Having taken my own belt and flippers off, I stretched myself out on one of the cushioned benches in the bow and stared up into the miles of air. Two ghostly winter clouds hung high above me, floating beneath the domed surface of the sky like a pair of divers come to peer through our own blue element. With a sigh, I unzipped my wetsuit to let the winter sun at my skin. 'Why do you think it happened?'

'I don't know,' said Bruno, crouching to examine the yellow cylinder. 'Probably a faulty pressure-gauge. I'll have the diving centre check it when we get back.'

'Well, Bruno, you really did save my life that time.'

The big man sat down opposite me and tugged his flippers off, making the rubber squeal. His voice became grumpy.

'Perhaps you'd have been happier if I'd done nothing.'

It took me a while to understand what he was talking about, for months had passed since our conversation on the balcony, and there'd been no more discussion of my future.

'No, you did the right thing.' The sea rocked the boat like a cradle, and I felt a deep, sleepy peace. 'I'd just forgotten the procedure.'

'I've been a bad teacher, then.'

'No. I panicked, you see.' I lifted my head to look at him. 'What would you have thought of me if I'd refused the air?'

Bruno shrugged but said nothing.

In any case, the incident had served a purpose. I knew how I would do it now. When the time comes, I will take the boat out for the last dive, on my own. I shall plop silently over the side and swim down until the pressure affects my blood and euphoria overcomes me. Then I'll undo my aqualung.

Bruno looked at me for a long time, while I lay there, gazing up at the feathery winter clouds with the sensation that I was returning their stares. They weren't motionless, after all, but gliding very slowly southwards, drifting with the current. Eventually, I heard him get up and weigh anchor.

'Right. Let's see what this boat can really do.'

He fired the engine and opened the throttle so wide that I thought we would flip over. Of course, we didn't, because Bruno is a master of these things. The *Ariel* simply screamed and bucked, turned in a wall of spray, and scudded back towards the mainland.

Ever since Percy returned, I've known that my time has run

out, that I have no excuse for continuing. Yet I've lingered on, afraid. While I've procrastinated, winter has come to Naples. It's December now. This place loses everything in the cold. There's simply no reason to be here once the sun has gone. But London, London! London is everything in the winter, it comes into its own. The best of it is then: the red reflections of the buses in the black puddles, the misty aura of the theatres, the trailing breath. There's nothing to equal that atmosphere. Naples, on the other hand, just dies in the winter. It isn't even cold. It's a non-time, waiting for another spring.

In other words, I have begun to miss my native town most bitterly and to feel increasingly out of place here. The disillusionment seems to have worked both ways, for the Neapolitans greet me less enthusiastically than before and no longer make the effort to visit my house. All those who were interested must have already come and grown bored. My little fame is at an end; I was just a one-summer sensation. If I stayed on, it would be as no more than an oddity.

After that dive, when the practical problems of my departure were solved, I realised that the only way to do it was to firmly fix a day. Accordingly, I decided to give myself one last week (which ends, incidentally, the day after tomorrow). Perhaps the strain of having finally taken this decision was what finally unbalanced my mind.

That night it was difficult to get to sleep. The day was fixed, and for hours I lay there imagining it in terror: the one perfect loneliness, the final luxury. Long before dawn, I noticed a strange glow in the room, and lifted my head.

A pale young man with dark eyes and chestnut curls was standing in the corner. It was Byron. He was wearing the loose white shirt from the room in Venice. In one hand he held, raised above him with a touch of drama, a huge iron candlestick, which was almost entirely obscured by fantastic cascades of wax. The light from the flame bounced and danced around the room, throwing huge pantomime shadows across the walls.

'I've come to thank you for finding my memoirs,' he said. 'If you want proof that they are genuine, look inside the back cover. There's a symbol there which I think you'll recogise.'

Daylight filled the room.

As the week passed, my fear grew, but so did my determination to go through with it, and I found myself longing for another apparition. One afternoon I almost thought I saw him, complete with dandyish travelling-cap and sword-stick, lingering for long enough to give me a bored smile before dissolving into the thin winter sunlight of the garden. The following day, there was a crackling electric storm, and I half-conjured him, on horseback, clattering at full gallop down the road towards my house, a brace of pistols at his belt.

In truth, of course, there was no apparition, because that, like everything else, has been a fake.

Two days ago, Anna paid her final visit to the hospital. Last night, I held a little party here to celebrate her recovery, not telling them that it was also a party of farewell.

Things have changed since our last gathering, before she got ill. For one thing, winter has stolen the atmosphere of the house. With the windows closed and the curtains drawn, it is dark, echoing and solemn; even Bruno's laughter can't entirely fill these rooms. Anna has lost a lot of weight, young Paulo is more pensive than before.

All the same, we managed to make a cheerful enough evening of it. Dear Castlereagh sat at the table and shared our meal. Trelawny slobbered around us, his claws, which need clipping, clicking on the marble as he looked hungrily up for scraps. Percy sat in the corner practising his obscenities.

There have been changes in this family, who are all I

have left for friends. Anna is as stiff and erect as ever, but she seems gentler towards Paulo. He slouched at the table and even swore, but she let him get away with it. Perhaps she has finally come to accept, as I somehow never could with Fran, that he must grow up alone and work out his own way of doing things.

As for Bruno, his attention to his convalescent wife was quiet and unassuming, apparently full of love. I felt sure it was fake, because there is nothing vaguely attractive about Anna. She is just a thin, haggard woman, resentful and bossy. Yet perhaps a fake really is just as good as the genuine article, after all, if it makes people happy. There was no way I could help remembering the cooling of my passion for Helen and wondering whether I'd do things differently if I were able to go back.

After we'd eaten, I said I wanted to talk to Bruno alone. I opened the tall windows and we stepped out on to the balcony. It was cold out there, with a wind coming in off the sea, blowing a wintery hardness across the lights around the bay.

We leant against the railings, shivered and watched.

'I'm going diving in a couple of days, Bruno.'

Understanding, he nodded but said nothing.

'Apologise to Paulo for me, but tell him that I wasn't unhappy at the end. I know it sounds strange, but it's true. I've got to leave, that's all.'

'I'll tell him, *Scrittore*. I must say, I admire you in a way, for seeing things so . . . absolutely.'

I shook my head.

'Don't feel obliged to lie.'

He turned in that slow way of his.

'No, I'm serious. It's been a privilege to know you. I've never met anybody quite like you, so extravagant, so much larger than life.'

'Fuck off!'

We looked down and found that Percy had joined us on the balcony.

'Quite right, Percy, you tell him. I think he's gone barmy, actually.' This was in English, since my animals are all too snobbish to learn Italian. 'In any case,' I went on, switching languages, 'I've left you some money and the house.'

'Don't want it.'

'Look, I'm too tired to argue now, honestly. Argue with my lawyer or give the cash to charity or something. The only thing I ask is that you see my animals are looked after. Will you do that?'

'Of course.'

We stood there for a moment in silence. I was enormously grateful to him for not trying to dissuade me at the last minute. It made everything much easier. As we watched, one of the huge white ferries, almost empty at this time of year, put out into the bay. To us, it was just a tiny smudge of light inching across infinite blackness, a point of warmth on the void. It sounded its horn and, as though this had been a signal, Bruno squeezed my shoulder.

'Bruno – ' When I turned to look at him, I found I had nothing to say.

'It's all right, *Scrittore*. I understand.' He held out his hand and I shook it. 'Goodbye and good luck.'

'Goodbye, Bruno.'

And you who are listening, goodbye to you. Goodbye to you, my dear audience, assuming I shall ever have one. The tale has caught me up and I have shown all that I can bear. The last scene would be too desolate to witness or recount.

Even now I could go on writing, describing the horror and despair I feel, but what would be the point? There have already been too many words. The last character, with a rather melancholy bow, is stepping backwards into the shadows and this, which after all has been no more than a lengthy suicide note, is finally at an end. I have shown all that I can bear. Has it been fine or tawdry, risible or sad? I really don't know. I am too tired now to care.

Helen, Ross, Fran, even Byron, all of them are gone, finished and done with, and now I can feel myself beginning to dissolve, to move back into their gloomy half-world. Like them, I shall soon remain only as a character in a story. There is nothing more to say. My typewriter is clacking towards its end. Silence is approaching this cold balcony as swiftly as Percy once did, spreading and raising its wings, preparing to settle on my shoulder. The silence is upon me! I am stunned by the speed at which my last few days and weeks have gone. It's the same as when you get really involved in a book, look up, and find that night has fallen as you read. Even at its very worst, life has always engaged me like that, and its end seems to have crept up on me as suddenly.

You must leave me now, whoever you are. The last episode is too much to witness or recount.

I have to say goodbye to my animals.

16

SURPRISE, SURPRISE.

When I wrote my final words of farewell, I really thought it was the end. I pulled the last sheet from my typewriter in the belief that it had fallen silent for good. Life, however, had something up its sleeve. The story hasn't finished with me yet. It has dragged me back to relate one last episode. I have been granted a reprieve, or perhaps a final chance at redemption.

On the eve of my departure, feeling that going to bed would be not only pointless, but somehow a waste, I sat out on the balcony. Despite the cold and my own predicament, I dropped off to sleep at about five o'clock. Four hours later, I awoke stiff and numb in my chair and stared at the glittering sea.

As though to prove to myself that I wasn't afraid, I had a shave and a light breakfast. The knowledge that it would be the last time I did either of these things made the experience peculiarly intense and thus slightly unreal. Then I dressed in fresh clothes and said goodbye to my animals in the huge front room, patting Trelawny on the head and shaking Castlereagh by the hand. I did it as though I were just popping out to the shops, and they didn't guess that anything was wrong.

When I looked around for Percy, I found that he was nowhere in the house, and guessed he must have gone off for his morning flight. This is something that he often does, because he likes his freedom and I trust him enough now to leave one of the kitchen windows permanently open for him. Secretly grateful to have an excuse for delaying my departure, I sat down to wait.

Now that I had nothing else to do, I began to go through the whole thing in my mind: starting the engine, edging the boat from its berth as I had seen Bruno do so many times, then scudding out across the bay. I had decided to stop at a point midway between the mainland and Capri, where the sea was empty and deep. There, staggering around in the swell, sickened by the smell of salt, I would struggle to put my gear on. It would be a strangely lonely process, since Bruno had been there on all my previous dives. I could almost feel the chilly wind and the silence around me already. With the mouthpiece in, my breathing would become unnaturally loud and slow, as meditative as the breathing of a patient under gas. When I rolled backwards into the water and began to swim down, the iron cylinder on my back and the soft bellows of my lungs would be hissing and sighing together with the rhythm of the sea, two halves of the same machine. How would I ever find the courage to separate them?

After ten minutes, I was shivering. Although the house was chilly, sweat had begun to trickle down my back and to drip from under my arms. There was a knot in my stomach which reminded me vividly of having exam nerves at school.

With a jerk, I stood up and began to walk rapidly around the room. As soon as I did so, at last scenting my death in the air, Trelawny threw back his head and howled. I'd never seen him do it before, and the empty, mournful echoes of it made me feel suddenly nauseous. His grief communicated itself to Castlereagh, who began shrieking and slapping the marble with the flat of his hand. Then the peacocks out in the garden joined in, throwing up to the house their desolate, inhuman lament. This cacophony would have been almost comical if I hadn't been so shivery and sick. Instead I felt harrowed by it. The time had come to set off, whether Percy was back or not.

As I left the room, my mind was so full of the final and absolute loneliness which awaited me that I didn't notice I was being followed. Only at the top of the broad staircase did I realise that my dog and monkey, still making a frightful din, were trailing behind me. When I stopped and told them sternly to stay, they howled so piteously that I was almost tempted to stay myself. I looked down at them for a moment, then, partly in anguish, partly just to block out their noise, I threw back my own head and wailed. As soon as the echoes had vanished into the empty house, the doorbell rang.

Absolute silence followed the sound. My panting breath seemed to fill the entire hall. All three of us stood motionless at the top of the stairs, and perhaps the animals felt, just as much as I did, the insane hope of a reprieve. After a few seconds, the bell sounded again, an extraordinarily still, calm sound, intrusive in its normality. I went down to answer like a murderer or a pervert interrupted by the ordinary world, my body moving numbly, my mind racing.

I opened the front door and squinted out into the diluted winter sunlight of the garden. On the other side of the gates, a tall blonde was standing by a taxi. She was wearing a well-tailored blue jacket and matching skirt. When she saw me she gave a big white smile.

'Dad!' she called. 'I've found you at last!'

It would not be entirely correct to say that I recognised my daughter Fran. Recognition is a calm, cerebral thing compared to the jolt which leapt through me. She might as well have been a dead relative, materialised from some other world.

Unable to speak, I simply slammed the door. The bell immediately started ringing again. I turned away, meaning to go back upstairs and hide, but my legs suddenly went weak and I slumped against the wood of the door, shuddering. After so many months of secretly longing for a meeting like this, and hating myself for it, I had been caught at my weakest moment. Of course, it didn't occur to me to be suspicious about this piece of perfect timing. I simply put it down to fate.

For about a minute I stood there, trying to collect myself, while the bell went on and on, sane and emotionless, remorselessly invading the empty house. In the end I saw that I would have to let her in.

I felt an absurd shame as I walked towards the gate. The old ruin had never looked worse. The drive was now so overrun with weeds and grass that it was barely more than an undulation in the garden, while the palm-trees and the fountain rose from masses of scrubby winter vegetation. There was a vague smell of excrement and decay. When she saw me coming, Fran stooped down to pay the taxi driver. By the time I arrived at the gate, he had already set off down the road.

'That was a mistake,' I said to her through the bars. 'You'll have to leave now. Today isn't a good day for me.'

'Welcoming as ever, Dad,' said Fran briskly. 'Come on, open up and let me in. I haven't come all this way to be turned away at the door.'

At any other time I would have been angry, argued, driven her off. As it was, I could barely manage to repeat myself.

'This isn't a good day. Please come back tomorrow.'

'Nonsense.' Fran didn't seem to notice how close I was to breaking down. 'Come on, let me in. I want to talk to you.'

For a moment we stared at each other through the bars, and I saw that all my recollections of her had been wrong. There was nothing of the child in her at all. Instead, I sensed an air of relaxed power, and I saw that, though not yet even twenty, my daughter was already well-accustomed to the servitude of men. This realisation conjured a shadow of the rage she used to make me feel.

'Come on,' she said again. 'Open up.'

'Oh, go away. Why don't you just go away and leave me alone?'

'You know what you remind me of, Dad? A big sulking kid who refuses to come down from his room, that's what.'

It was almost like old times. Before letting her in, I even gave her a bit of a glower through the gate. As we walked towards the house, I tried to see it as it must appear to her: the Morgan black with dust, the cracked ornamentation, the peeling shutters. When I showed her inside, into the main hall with its stately staircase, she stood still and just stared. Her voice bounced off the crumbling stucco.

'What an amazing place.'

'I don't use the downstairs.'

'I should hope not. It's virtually falling to pieces. And you haven't made much of an effort with the garden, have you?'

She made for the staircase, swaying in her skirt, and began to glide up. To me, after so long away from my real life, her appearance had a sort of fantastic, accentuated normality. She was like a make-up girl who'd wandered on to the set of a period film, incongruously ordinary, instantly destroying the illusion. I just stood and watched her, feeling too many things to be sure of what I felt. Halfway up the stairs, Fran let out a little screech, because Trelawny and Castlereagh were still sitting exactly where I had left them.

'My God! Brilliant!'

She began running up the stairs in delight, suddenly ungainly, and I thought that perhaps there might be just a grain of the child left in her, after all.

'Say hello to the pretty lady, boys.'

Trelawny stood on his hind legs, wagging his tail and slobbering, while Castlereagh turned somersaults by way of greeting. I made my way up the stairs, slowly enough, for I was ready to drop with strain, and showed Fran into the front room. She took Castlereagh's hand and followed me in.

'What lovely pets! Tell me their names!'

'The dog is Trelawny. The chimp is Castlereagh. The parrot you will see flying towards the house, if you look out of that window there, is Percy.'

Fran turned to the window to watch as Percy flew straight through it at high, silent speed and glided to rest on my shoulder.

'Amazing! Incredible! Fantastic!'

'Tell her, Percy.'

'Fuck off.'

'It's like a fairy castle!' cried Fran. 'Oh, Dad, it's brilliant!'

I felt suddenly bleaker than before.

'This is normality to me now. You're the only fabulous creature here. I can't believe it's you. Not today, of all days.'

With a huge smile, Fran crouched to put one arm round Castlereagh and pat Trelawny on the head. It was really her. It was my daughter.

When she next spoke, there was a catch in her voice.

'You know what it reminds me of? Those stories you used to read to me when I was a kid, when you came to tuck me up in bed. It's just like one of those fantastic stories.'

As soon as she said it, I knew what she was thinking. She saw herself as the child come to play in the mysterious garden, bringing a breath of innocence and the ordinary world outside, so that the ogre awakes in his lonely palace and repents. But this sophisticated young woman was far from being a child any more, and my life in Italy, despite appearances, has been no fairy-tale.

'No, Fran. This isn't one of those fantastic stories, I'm afraid.'

Once again, I was reminded of how unlike Christopher she had been as a child, crazy for stories about princes and magic, demanding that I read certain of them over and over again. How I loved her then. She would hug me each night with the greedy selfishness of children, who are unaware of any happiness they give. Even now, I could remember those things, but only as scenes from someone else's life. The woman in front of me bore no resemblance to that child. I was no longer that young father. Somewhere along the line I had said goodbye to him.

That was why the sight of her had caused me to feel such desolation. Only a memory was left, flat and threadbare, of how I loved her then.

When she'd finished making friends with the animals, Fran insisted that we sit out on the balcony. I told her it was too cold, but she said no, it was like a spring day, I'd forgotten what real cold was. So I opened the French windows for her, then went to my bedroom to put on some warmer clothes.

Going back out to join her, I felt there was a deep emptiness about the house, worse even than it had been on the night of my arrival. On the balcony, it seemed to me that this emptiness had settled on the entire scene: the great bay, the cluttered city crushed around its rim, old Vesuvius itself, all seemed unusually huge and bleak. Like a stage-set between acts, the place had lost its charm.

We talked awkwardly at first, avoiding the subjects on both our minds. A school-friend of hers, passing through Naples on a trip round Europe, had spotted me in my car and tipped Fran off. Once she'd arrived in the city, finding me had been easy. Everybody seemed to know me.

'What is it they call you?'

'*Scrittore.*'

'Which means?'

'Writer. Just a little thing I've been doing. A sort of memoir, I suppose.'

My voice sounded strange and hollow, too much my own, as though played back on a cheap tape recorder. Fran's, too, had an empty ring. We talked on, lurching clumsily round the central issues, until Fran, overcome by the awkwardness of a long pause, reached into her bag and took out a pack of English cigarettes. Moving with an odd deliberation, she lit one, then sat and stared at me expectantly, as though I'd missed my cue. It took me a moment to realise that she was waiting for me to tell her off. She hadn't understood that the old anger could no more function here than a match could flare in a vacuum.

'You don't mind my smoking, then?' she said at last.

'No, why should I? You go ahead.'

'Oh.' Fran looked a little hurt. 'I still smoke dope as well, you know.'

I stared at her, baffled as to why she felt it necessary to make this declaration. She had the freedom she'd always craved, and here she was, now that I had gone from her life, trying to provoke me back into my old repressive role.

'That's fine,' I said lightly. 'You smoke what you like.'

We lapsed into a silence which was even more awkward than before. Eventually, I saw that the moment could no longer be delayed. The knot in my stomach tightened again. My pulse was racing. As though sheer space could calm me down, I turned away from Fran and looked out to sea. The emptiness seemed to come at me in waves.

'So,' I said quietly, 'how's Helen?'

'She's not with Ross any more, if that's what you mean.'

It was a strange moment. Fran had leaned forward across the table as she spoke, openly studying my face. The animals, scattered around the balcony, all happened to be watching me, too, as though they realised the importance of what had been said. I stared back out to sea, losing my awareness of them all. The shock was one of the worst I could remember. It was the shock of nothingness.

Any normal husband would have felt something, some flicker of emotion, however faint, at the news. I felt nothing. As the moments passed this became horrific to me. I was like a blind man waking up and groping around

264

only to find that all the furniture had been removed from his bedroom. In despair, I waited. Then it slowly dawned on me that not only the furniture, but the walls themselves had been demolished. The whole structure of life had vanished into nothing. At last I understood the extent to which I had made myself an exile.

Fran was still staring at me.

'Why?' I said, without turning.

'They got on terribly. Ross has got too used to living on his own, I think. Mum put him off his work. He used to get in these terrible moods, far worse than you, and she just couldn't stand it in the end.'

'I see. And how's young Christopher?'

There was a pause.

'Fine.' I could hear that she was disconcerted at my changing the subject so quickly. 'He's gone back to university to do some postgraduate thing in philosophy. And he's engaged to Caroline. You know, who used to work in the bookshop.'

'Good,' I said without inflection. 'They suit each other.'

For a while I forced her to chat on like that, telling me the news, taking me on a brief tour of my former existence. I asked after old acquaintances and places. Each answer made me feel nothing at all, but I pressed on, investigating the extent of the emptiness. All the while I could sense that Fran wanted to move back to the subject of Helen and myself. In the end, I decided to get it over and done with.

'So,' I said, turning towards her, 'why have you come all the way out here?'

Fran drew a deep breath.

'To ask you to come back to England.' I said nothing. After a moment she went on. 'Look, what Mum and Ross did to you was pretty rough, but I know for a fact that they both regret it now. That was the real reason they couldn't live together. They just felt too guilty about everything, I think.'

Fran had misunderstood it all. She saw me as a victim, a man who had been betrayed by his wife and best friend, driven to leave his country and his home. She had no way of knowing how my own interior emptiness had drained both friendship and marriage many years before.

'They shouldn't,' I said tiredly. 'They've no reason to reproach themselves.'

'If you really think that,' pressed Fran, and I had never seen her look so sincere or grown-up, 'come back and try again. Mum hasn't actually said it in so many words, but I know she'd be overjoyed to have you back. You should have seen her face when she heard I'd tracked you down! It was as if – '

'I'm not going back. I'm never going back to England.'

The flatness of my voice shut her up for a moment. Then she went on, more quietly.

'If you won't do if for Mum, then do it for me.'

'What do you mean?'

'I miss you, Dad. Things aren't the same without you there.'

For the first time since her arrival I felt a glimmer of what a human being, a father, ought to feel, something which gave momentary shape to the darkness. A strand of blonde hair fell across Fran's face as she spoke, and I was struck by her beauty. I found myself imagining what it would be like for a young man to hear a girl like that say she loved him. It would seem a miracle, a wonderful impossibility. Any young man hearing those words from her would think himself in heaven.

The shape vanished back into the darkness. The moment was past.

'I'm sorry Fran, but you're a grown-up now. You'll just have to learn to do without me. Life's like that, I'm afraid.'

Her blue eyes widened, and it was obvious that, for her at least, life wasn't like that at all. Men didn't say no to her. Imagining this scene in her mind, she'd probably seen me agreeing to her plan not only without argument, but with gratitude.

'You really won't come back?' she said, unable to hide her astonishment.

'No, Fran. I'm sorry. I'm never coming back.'

That was when she lost her temper. She stood up so aggressively that her chair clattered to the tiles behind her, frightening the animals. Then she started shouting down at me, far more like the Fran that I remembered.

'You just don't care about the pain you cause, do you? Or maybe you don't realise what you put us through, disappearing like that, you selfish bastard. We looked everywhere. Mum and Ross put adverts in the personal columns asking you to get in touch. It was terrible. All of us thought you might – ' Her voice broke. 'It's stupid, but after what your father did and everything – '

I said quietly 'Perhaps my father had an outlook on the world.'

Fran looked at me blankly, too wound up in her own emotions to take in what I'd said. She was busy switching from anger to pathos, changing gear.

'And now that I've found you and come all the way out here you haven't even thought to ask me.'

'Ask you what?'

'Whether I passed my 'A' levels.'

For a moment I stared at her, astounded by the extent to which we inhabit different worlds. She was on the edge of tears.

'All right, then. Did you pass your 'A' levels?'

'Yes, I did. You never thought I could do it, did you? You were always too busy putting me down and worrying about my love life to imagine that I might have a brain. Go on, ask me what grades I got.'

'What grades did you get?'

'Straight As. Now I'm taking a year off, then I'm going to Cambridge.'

'What was wrong with Oxford?'

267

Fran picked up her bag and swung it across her shoulder. The animals looked up and watched her forlornly, thinking she was really going to leave.

'You went there.'

I would have thought she was joking if I hadn't heard the unsteadiness of her voice.

'Are you off now, then?'

'Yes,' said Fran, barely keeping control of herself. 'I've tried, I've done everything I can, but I'd forgotten just how impossible you are. If you're determined to stay out here and sulk, there's nothing I can do except forget you. I'll just have to pretend you're dead.'

She waited for me to answer, but I said nothing. After a moment, she backed towards the French windows, still looking down at me.

'I'm sorry, Dad.'

Her perfect chin crumpled and she swung her head away, raising a twirling skirt of blonde. Long, angry strides took her across the echoing front room. I watched her go, somehow knowing that her departure wasn't real. Sure enough, when she reached the door, Fran stopped dead.

'Shit!' Brushing fiercely at her eyes, she clicked back out to the balcony. When she arrived, she stood by the table, rummaged for a moment through her bag, and produced a small buff envelope. She held it out to me with angry defiance, as though to prove it was the only reason she'd returned. 'I almost forgot. When he heard I was coming out here, Vernon was very eager for you to have this.'

'What is it?'

'Search me.'

I took it from her with a lump in my throat and ripped it open. Sure enough, the Byron memoir was inside. Leaving it there, I pulled out the accompanying letter. As I read it, I felt the kind of sickening excitement no letter had made me feel since I'd received my own exam results so many years before.

'Well?' said Fran. 'What's it all about?'

'Byron's memoirs.'

'I thought you never found the stupid things.'

'It's a long story,' I said. For some time I was silent, reading the letter, which turned out to be largely one of apology. When I'd finished, I folded it and put it back in the envelope with the book. 'A long story which doesn't matter now. Vernon took me for a ride.'

'Eh?'

'It was all as I suspected. The whole thing was a fake.'

Vernon's letter explained it all not only with contrition, but also with a quiet pride. The memoris had been a Victorian fake which he'd bought as a curiosity shortly after the war. A few years later, he'd gone as a weekend visitor to Millbank House, where the story of Gilbert's mysterious death and Amelia's suicide had fired his imagination. It seemed remarkable that Millbank had gone to Venice at precisely the time when Byron was there, then suddenly fled to the south of the country and never returned. An amusing fantasy had slowly grown in Vernon's mind. He had forged the letters mainly as a way of filling his long, empty days in the shop, inventing the code himself and inserting the name of an Italian lover of his who came to London from time to time: Apuglia.

In other words, the trap had been laid many years before I took over the shop. Vernon had never actually intended to use the letters, seeing them as a kind of insurance policy to fall back on if times ever got really hard. When I arrived and started lording it over him, he was immediately tempted, but he resisted. Even when I disclosed my obsession with Byron and erected the marble bust, Vernon refused to act. Then, one Wednesday about two months after the takeover, Dubious Dave arrived with a box of books which turned out to be from none other than Millbank House. If this wasn't fate, it was certainly an irresistible temptation. Nothing could be simpler than to drop the letters into the box. Yet still Vernon gave me a chance, hiding the letters in the spine of one of the books, where I would probably never find them. He privately vowed that, if I didn't, he would forget the whole thing.

Again, fate seemed to take a hand: I found the letters. After that, the con acquired its own momentum. Trying to stall me in London, Vernon tracked down his old friend, sent him the memoirs, and briefed him on what to say and do. Paradoxically, my discovery brought a certain warmth into our relationship, and Vernon slowly began to regret the whole thing. When he gave the letters to the British Library, it was in the belief that they would be revealed as fakes. But Vernon's own work, as he modestly admitted, had simply been too good. After that he had never had the guts to tell me the truth. All he'd been able to do was warn me, again and again, against believing the preposterous story. Eventually, when I proved my friendship by actually giving him the memories, he had been overcome by guilt. By then, of course, it had been far too late. Now he understood that he'd misjudged me. All he wanted was to return as much of my money as he could. He would do everything in his power to make amends.

Dropping the envelope on the table, I stood and walked giddily to the railings. There I stood and stared, seeing nothing. My mind reeled.

'I can hardly believe it.' My voice shook. 'The whole thing was a fake.'

'Dad – '

Fran came and laid a hand on my shoulder. It was the first time she'd touched me since her arrival, the first time any woman had touched me in months.

'All a fake,' I said slowly, shaking my head. 'The whole thing was a fake.'

Out on the bay, one of the huge white ferries, almost empty at this time of year, was putting out for the islands, drawing a broad, smooth scar across the sea. Gulls circled fretfully over its stern, like sleepless souls, fettered to the world. As I watched, a vast moan of emptiness rose from the ship, reverberated around the hills, and vanished.

'Dad!' Fran was shaking my shoulder now. 'Look at me!'

I turned and stared at her blankly. Everything was unreal and dead.

'I thought you were leaving,' I said. 'You can leave if you want. There isn't any need to stay.'

'I can't leave.' She was distracted, almost in a frenzy, perhaps from proximity to my own bottomless grief. 'Oh, don't you see, I can't!'

'Why?'

'I was lying when I said a friend of mine told me you were here.'

I felt confused. I wasn't sure what was going on.

'Who told you then?'

'A friend of yours.'

'Bruno!'

Fran, who still hadn't taken her hand from my shoulder, nodded.

'He tracked us down last week. He sounds such a lovely man. He'd been trying to find us for ages. Between my little bit of Italian and his English, he managed to make me understand. He kept on saying you were depressed. He told me I had to hurry because he thought you might – ' Her face crumpled. 'And then I come out here and find you like, I don't know, like some sort of zombie, and – '

She lost control at last, burst into tears and threw her arms around me.

'Oh Dad!'

I stood and swayed, not knowing how to respond. The easy thing would have been to take her in my arms, but I wanted no more fakes and no more lies, so I just stood. Of course, I knew how my suicide would make her feel. I had been in that position, after all. I know what it is to see that you are incapable of giving or receiving love. It's a terrible thing. Better for her, better by far, if I developed cancer and died in agony before her eyes. At least she wouldn't have to face the fact that she was meaningless, a scrap of nothing in an empty world, a stranger in a stranger's world.

For some time we stood there on the sunny balcony, Fran with her arms around me, sobbing heavily. Over her heaving shoulder, I watched the white ferry slide sedately away, smoothing the wrinkled sea. Somehow I lost the sense of where I was. I felt nothing. Through her sobs, Fran was mumbling all the time, asking me to go back with her. Then she suddenly fell silent and did a surprising thing.

First, she released me and took a step away. There was something melodramatic about the way she moved, something almost ritualistic. Staring fiercely into my eyes, she knelt down in front of me. With her red, wet face, she reminded me of a woman at a funeral. There was real desperation in her voice.

'There,' she said. 'I'm on my knees to ask you one last time. Please come back to England with me. Come back and try again.'

I just stood and swayed, feeling nothing but an emptiness which was sharper than before. Refusing to give up, Fran took my hand, laid her wet cheek against the back of my fingers, and said what few daughters ever find the guts to say.

'I love you.'

That was the moment when a real father would have broken down in tears. Even I, exile that I am, felt the stirrings of a remote pity for her. It was distant, more distant than the last echo of the ship's horn, and as faint, but it was genuine.

'All right,' I said, 'I'll come back to England with you.'

Fran stayed in Naples for a week. She met Bruno, who had betrayed me, yet against whom I find it impossible to bear a grudge. He was only acting in what he saw as my best interests, after all. As for young Paulo, Fran completely conquered him. To see the way he looked at her made me feel insufferably old.

It was the strangest week I've spent out here, perhaps the strangest of my entire life. We roared around Naples in the filthy Morgan with Castlereagh and Trelawny in the back, though all these Byronic pretensions seemed rather hollow to me now that I knew for certain that the memoir was a fake. There had never been anything special between Byron and myself, after all. The whole thing had been in my imagination, one of my many attempts to fill the endless emptiness. It was time to face the fact that the poet had been just an ordinary mortal and, like all of his contemporaries, from the Prince Regent to the humblest chimney-sweep, is dead.

All the same, I rather enjoyed taking my daughter and my animals around the sights. The approach of Christmas has given Naples a little of its magic back. The alleyways are roofed with coloured lights, like paths to some enormous funfair. Huge cribs, almost life-sized and with real straw, have appeared outside the churches in the old town. The days are short, and the shops, brighter and warmer than before, seem to stay open long into the night. Fran was delighted with it all. I constantly asked myself how she will remember our week in Naples.

On her last day, we took a ferry over to Capri. We could have gone in the *Ariel*, of course, but I thought Fran would find it too bumpy and cold for such a long journey. Speedboats are definitely a luxury for the summer months. In any case, I rather felt like taking the ferry, having spent so long watching them come and go from my balcony.

I didn't regret my decision. The huge white hulk was almost deserted. Only a few poor Neapolitans, perhaps off to see relatives for the season, sat in the lounges and stared out at the uninviting green of the sea. The dotted figures seemed rendered meaningless by the hundreds of empty seats around them. It was impossible to get anything to eat or drink on the boat; the numerous bars and canteens were in hibernation behind steel grilles. Only the deep hum of the engine seemed alive, yet even that was an introspective, sleepy sound. Leaving Fran in the lounge, I went out on deck. In summer, this would be the most crowded place; you'd have to pick your way through an endless confusion of bodies and luggage. Now I was entirely alone, apart from a few gulls floating on the wind, eyeing the white-churned water. I had reached the very heart of that desolation which has haunted me since my arrival here.

That night was Fran's last. She had to go back to get on with her life. We had arranged that I would stay for a week or so after her departure, to sort out the animals and the house, then follow her on to England. After supper, as she had done every night, she insisted on having her coffee outside on the balcony.

'Thanks for a lovely week,' she said, lighting a cigarette and puffing elegantly.

'You're welcome.'

Her large eyes cast a sweeping look over the railing.

'It's a beautiful town. Have you been happy here?'

I smiled.

'I've enjoyed my time, I suppose. But all good things come to an end.'

'The future will be better, you'll see. I'm so glad you're coming back, Dad.' She reached across the table and took my hand. 'So glad.'

'You've changed a lot, haven't you, Fran?' I said, trying to keep the sorrow from my voice.

'How do you mean?'

'You're less wild than before. I remember you as always fighting, lashing out against things, always full of life. You seem calmer now.'

'Yes, perhaps I am.'

'Do you think it's to do with us living separately?'

Fran, still holding my hand, smiled softly.

'Perhaps.'

I laughed.

'God, but you were mad, though! You did such crazy things. Do you remember that time you lifted your skirt up in front of us all?'

As I spoke, the image of it flooded my mind. My throat was suddenly constricted. I could barely move. Indeed, I was afraid of moving, as though that would reveal something best left hidden. Then, when Fran spoke, I suddenly understood what would never have occurred to me before: she felt the same.

'Yes,' she said thickly, 'I remember.'

Her hand was still on mine. Both of us wanted to withdraw, yet neither of us could find it in us, so we sat like two figures under an enchantment. Images passed before my eyes. I saw Fran kneeling down and saying that she loved me. I saw her leaving the bathroom, naked, on that morning long ago, and realised that it had been no accident. She had planned for me to see her like that, desired it. That night, with a leap of intuition, I'd guessed that Gilbert was Amelia's father . . .

'Dad,' said Fran hoarsely, 'if – '

'My God!' I cried, leaping to my feet. 'And I didn't even think to look!'

Fran stared at me in astonishment.

'What's happened?'

'Nothing.' I turned and ran off into the the empty house. 'Just something somebody said to me!'

By my bed, I found the memoirs lying as I had left them. I snatched the book up and pulled it from its envelope. In that mad moment, it seemed possible to me that Vernon's letter had itself been some fantastic hoax, or that he'd somehow managed to pass on a genuine book under the impression that it was a fake. If the symbol which my vision of Byron had spoken of was there, then surely this would have to be the genuine article, after all. Breathless, fumbling, I opened the memoirs and looked at the inside back page.

It was blank.

★　　★　　★

I didn't go with Fran to the airport the following day. Airports are too public and impersonal, and, in any case, they have no style. The humblest railway station in the world is a better place to say goodbye than an airport. So, instead, we rang for a taxi, and I waved goodbye to her from my balcony, surrounded by my animals. It was how I wanted her to remember me. Now that she was gone at last, I could stop pretending, and I allowed myself to shed a few tears as I waved.

'I'm sorry.'

Fran waved back, innocently beaming her big white smile at me, happy in the belief that she would see me the following week. How could she think otherwise? I had played the last deception like the master faker that I am. Still smiling, she got into the taxi and disappeared, but I know that she will never be able to erase that final image from her mind: the grey-haired man in a white shirt, standing at the balcony of a crumbling foreign house, surrounded by exotic animals, waving from his exile. It will stay with her forever, just as the last image of my own father has stayed with me: the dead weight hanging from the cord of its dressing-gown, head on one side, sticking its fat tongue out at the world. At least I have left poor Fran with a little beauty, a little romance, a sort of style.

Of course, I knew almost as soon as she arrived here that her visit meant the end. There was never any possibility of going back to England and trying again. Seeing her that one last time helped me to understand, at last, what my father understood. None of it is real. Only the emptiness is real. He left at Christmas, too. I remember the tinsel which had somehow fallen from the banisters and draped itself around his shoulders. At last, I find it in me to forgive him, because at last I fully understand.

All the time, whether I was dealing with antiques, books or people, I was looking out for fakes. First I suspected Vernon, then Helen, even the children, but I never saw the real fake in the midst of them all, because it was myself.

It took a while in exile to make me understand. None of that former life was real. I was never a real father, or a husband, or a friend. All of it was empty, or else how could it have disappeared so fast? I forced myself to put on all those things, and believe in them, because the only other alternative was to accept that my father had been right.

Some of us have the casing of a human being, but are all hollowness inside. We're afraid of the emptiness within ourselves and try to be like the others. We fabricate our lives. In my case, I feel I have been slightly redeemed only by my love for Fran when she was a little girl. The magic innocence of a child can sometimes humanise an ogre, which is why I fought with all my might against her growing up. She transformed me for a while, but she is much too knowing and sophisticated now. As an adult, far from redeeming me, she brings out the most ogreish traits of all. Perhaps the most awful part is that she's implicated in the corruption of our love.

Despair must be an illness of the blood. We pass it on to our children through heredity and example. My father passed it down to me. Christopher is probably safe, but I fear that I have passed it down to Fran. My death will rock her world. As I did at her age, she will start to run, throwing herself into the business of fabricating a career and family life. Perhaps, as it did with me, the very desperation will make her rich and successful. Then, one summer thirty years from now, it will all fall to pieces in her hands. By the following Christmas she will have come to understand.

It's a strange thing, ending. (Music is a strange thing!) Words throng through my head, yet I know there's nothing else to say.

Fran left yesterday. Tomorrow I will take the boat out. Now, as I write these last words, it is evening. The ferries still come and go, just as they will tomorrow when there's no one watching from this balcony. Even now, one is setting out for the islands. I have just heard its horn, lonely and echoing around the hills. I turn to look: a huge white wedding-cake decked with lights, a perfect image of glamour and beauty and peace. Because of our outing a couple of days ago, I can imagine the utter emptiness inside, although it must be even worse at night.

The bleeding bird at my wife's breast opens its little beak and produces the sound of a ship's horn, that echoing, empty sound.

I will keep going until the *Ariel* is out of fuel. By that time I should be well away from land, right out in the silence of the sea. At last, after all those years of trying to be something that I'm not, I will be able to express my real self. My final action will cause pain, but it will at least be genuine. If my courage should fail me, I have only to think of that face, pop-eyed and poking out its bloated tongue at myself and my mother, at the tinsel of human love. My father's face will be there as I choke and thrash about, the perfect expression of exile.